--------------------- ★ ---------------------

The minister looked out over the crowd. "Let's begin this blessed day with a prayer." Cassidy lowered her head slightly. "Holy Father, I give in to Your keeping Max and Claire. May they live always in the light of Your—"

Max's head jerked wildly. Blood flew in all directions, drenching Claire's delicate cream-colored dress. The crack of a gunshot. Screams. Zach pushed Cassidy to the ground, covering her with his body. Peering through his arms, she saw Claire down on all fours, her mother and sister crowding in next to her, the best man hovering nearby. Molly tugged at Claire's bloody dress and wailed.

--------------------- ---------------------

"This book not only has a complicated plot, but it successfully explores different relationships. The characters are extremely interesting, and quite varied, and their interactions with each other add depth.... There is plenty of tension, and the plot moves along swiftly to its conclusion."

—*Mystery News*

Previously published Worldwide Mystery title by
ALEX MATTHEWS

DEATH'S DOMAIN

ALEX MATTHEWS

WEDDING'S WIDOW

W RLDWIDE.

TORONTO • NEW YORK • LONDON
AMSTERDAM • PARIS • SYDNEY • HAMBURG
STOCKHOLM • ATHENS • TOKYO • MILAN
MADRID • WARSAW • BUDAPEST • AUCKLAND

WEDDING'S WIDOW

A Worldwide Mystery/September 2005

First published by Intrigue Press.

ISBN 0-373-26540-9

Printed in U.S.A.

Acknowledgments

**For my husband Allen,
who makes all things possible.**

Many thanks to all the people who helped in the birthing of this book: my husband, Allen Matthews, whose fourth career has become book promotion; my editor, Chris Roerden, who would not accept less than my best; my fellow critique group members, Nancy Carleton, Cecelia Comito, Carol Hauswald, and Ginny Skweres, who faithfully refused to let me get away with anything; my publicist, Barbara Young, who applied her vast energy and enthusiasm to book promotion; Chicago Police Detective Anne Chambers and Oak Park Police Commander Robert Scianna, who educated me on police procedure; and fellow DorothyL member, Robert Avery, who provided the words, *Wedding's Widow,* when my brain refused to generate the right title.

Everyone gave freely of their time and expertise. Where errors exist, they are mine.

ONE

ALARM BELLS

CLAIRE LINDEN EXTENDED a shapely hand to show her large pear-shaped diamond ring to her therapist.

"It's gorgeous!" Cassidy McCabe exclaimed.

"It cost a fortune," Claire said in an uneasy voice, catching her lip between her small white teeth.

"You don't sound happy about it." Cassidy sat across from Claire in the office at the rear of Cassidy's house.

"It makes me nervous. I mean, what if Max wakes up one morning and decides he didn't get his money's worth?" Claire let out a small laugh. She was in her early thirties, slender and sprightly, with a sweet, childlike face.

If Max ever dares think such a thing, then he's a pig and doesn't deserve you, Cassidy thought. *Which in fact might be the case.*

"Are you afraid he might stop loving you?"

"I don't know, I don't know. He really hasn't done anything to make me doubt him." Claire ran her fingers through her long chestnut hair. "The other thing is, I can't imagine how he could afford it. I mean, the new job's going well, but twelve grand for a ring?"

There are some things about Max and money that don't add up.

"The problem really isn't Max, it's me. I mean, how can you feel lovable after being married to someone who told you on a daily basis how worthless you were?"

Right. And then he stalked you when you tried to leave.

"You know, the worst of it wasn't what Hank did to me. It was having Molly see me act like such a doormat. I hate to think of the effect it may've had on her—watching her mother be terrorized like that."

"Have you told Hank about the wedding?"

She shivered slightly. "I'm going to next week."

"You still afraid of him?"

"Just of what he'll say. When I'm right there in front of him, he can still make me feel like a slut for even thinking about another man. But then I'll walk out the door and remember the things you and I talked about and I'll be fine. Hank is all hot air. He'd never *do* anything."

"SO TELL ME ABOUT the couple we're driving way the hell out into the boonies to see get married," Zach Moran said from behind the wheel of his new red Subaru.

They were headed south along a four-lane highway an hour's distance from Oak Park. On either side lay wooded areas with bright green, newly minted leaves, interspersed with expensive new developments and freshly plowed, earthy-smelling fields.

"Claire's a real sweetheart," Cassidy replied. "Mother of a six-year-old. Married before to an abusive guy. Also had a couple of abusive boyfriends. She's been working in therapy to break the pattern." *And here's hoping she did.* "The guy she's marrying is a chef at some hot new restaurant in Naperville. Actually, not just a chef—he's part owner."

"What is this? You actually tossed me a few crumbs of information."

"If you didn't expect an answer, why ask?"

"I must like hearing you tell me in that cranky voice of yours that I should know better than to ask about clients."

Confidentiality is never getting to tell fun stories.

"Claire's pretty open about her problems. She said as long as you were coming, it'd be okay to fill you in on a little background.'' Cassidy glanced at her husband. Smooth dark hair above a bronze-skinned face. Although he lived most of his life in tee shirts and jeans, he'd considered the wedding a sufficient occasion to warrant a dress code upgrade: a designer jacket over a collarless black shirt.

Cassidy wore a new short-skirted dress, purple silk splattered with pink flowers, a prize she'd found at her local resale store. Frowning, she touched a snagged thread, picked off cat hairs. It had looked pristine when she'd donned it earlier that day, but because she was never able to resist her cat's wiles, it now resembled all the other items in her closet.

"I was surprised you agreed to come with me," Cassidy said. "I thought you wouldn't be interested."

"I like weddings. Reminds me of ours." He smiled fondly. "Used to be, I'd sit in the back pew and wonder how long the marriage would last. Now I get all misty-eyed." He furrowed his brow. "Look what you've done to me. Ruined my cynicism. How will I keep my edge?"

Cassidy screwed up her mouth at him.

"You know, I was meaning to ask. I'm not sure why we're even attending this shindig. I thought you never socialized with clients."

"Weddings are an exception. When I've worked with someone over a long period of time, I like to celebrate their triumphs. Especially if they invite me, which they don't always do."

Just wish I didn't have these teensy alarm bells going off in my head.

So what's the problem? Claire's crazy about Max. Max says he's crazy about Claire. No reason to think this won't be a happy-ever-after, stuff-dreams-are-made-of kind of marriage.

Except for those few small courtship irregularities committed by Max. Which you pointed out to Claire but she didn't want to hear.

They drove through Dorrity, population 4,300, and a rived at a vast green park, a dozen or so cars at the curb

Zach stopped behind a green Jaguar. As Cassidy reache for the door, he said, "Let me get that for you."

She sat back and smiled, remembering how snarly sl used to be whenever he tried to get away with any courte little gestures. *What a relief not to have my guard up a the time against the possibility that Zach might want to a something nice.*

Opening the door, he said, "Doesn't look like much a crowd."

"The wedding got thrown together at the last minut They only invited a handful of people."

"And you're one of them? She must really think she g her money's worth."

"Not everyone is such a therapy-heretic as you."

"So, what do you say when people ask how you kno Claire?"

"I lie, of course."

Cassidy raised a hand to shield her eyes from the brig May sun. The sky overhead was a deep cloudless blue. front of her stretched a lush expanse of rolling green par land, a round concrete-bordered pool in the middle, curve flower beds ablaze with red and yellow tulips on either sid Beyond the pool a white gazebo stood in a stand of flov ering trees, about twenty men and women in wedding fine clustered around it. In the distance a wooded ridge extend across the north end of the park.

They strolled in the direction of the wedding party. / they reached the fringe of the crowd, Claire, standing ne to a tall blond man, spotted Cassidy.

"Cass, you're here!" Dragging the man along with he Claire rushed over to hug her therapist. "I couldn't ha done it without you," she whispered in Cassidy's ear.

A small glow rose in Cassidy's chest. "Sure you could

Gesturing toward the man, her voice filled with prid Claire announced, "This is Max."

And isn't he something. Cassidy gazed into sky-blue eyes that were fastened warmly on her face. A thatch of corn tassel hair fell across his forehead. A wide slap-happy grin plastered on his mouth. *Looks shell-shocked. Just how he ought to look on his wedding day. Maybe it'll be all right after all.* Studying him, she noted the custom-made suit, the Rolex on his wrist. *The new restaurant must be raking it in.*

"She talks about you all the time," Max said to Cassidy. "Guess you're the one I have to thank for getting her to the point where she's ready to take the leap again."

"You just make sure she doesn't regret it," Cassidy said sternly.

"You can count on it." Max planted a lingering kiss on Claire's mouth. The bride, in a filmy, cream-colored dress that floated around her like a cloud, was just as stunning as the groom. A baby's breath wreath encircled her brow, and her glossy dark hair was pulled into a thick braid that hung halfway down her back.

She always seems so innocent. Hard to believe she's a high-level exec, probably earning twice what you and Zach do together.

They chatted another minute, then Claire and Max moved on.

Scanning the crowd, Cassidy tried to identify the players. Claire was deep in conversation with a matronly looking woman Cassidy assumed to be her mother. Next to Claire was a thirtysomething woman holding the bridal bouquet.

The sister, Erin. The older sister who swings back and forth between mothering Claire and picking fights. Claire had talked quite a bit about Erin in therapy. She was tall and thickset, with a square face and blunt-cut hair. She had, however, made the most of her plus-size frame by attiring herself in a long flowing dress. Erin glanced around at the guests, her mouth frozen in a camera-ready smile.

Cassidy suspected that the never-married Erin was less than thrilled at serving as maid of honor. *Can't be easy*

*seeing your younger, prettier sister sought after by a das.
ing Max when nobody—not even an undashing dork—h
ever sought after you.*

Cassidy could sympathize. After her ex dumped he
she'd gone through a period herself when weddings ha
felt like salt in her wounds.

Zach draped his arm across her shoulders. "Claire a
Max look so happy, they remind me of us."

Cassidy stood on tip-toes to kiss her nearly six-foot hu
band. Solidly built, with wide shoulders and a thick che
that narrowed to a not-exactly-slender waist. *Not half tl
dazzler Max is. But you wouldn't trade him for the han
somest guy in Hollywood.* She rubbed her garnet weddii
ring, worth pennies compared to Claire's big rock. Zac
had wanted to adorn Cassidy's finger with a pricey stor
but she'd insisted on the garnet, claiming not to be an ex
pensive-jewelry kind of girl.

A young, strawberry-blond woman drifted over to ta
to them. "Hey, I'm Julie, Max's sister." In a loose dre
and headband, she looked like a flower child from the si
ties.

After introductions, Julie tilted her head to gaze at then
Dreamy red-brown eyes in an elfin face surrounded b
curly tendrils of hair. "I'm an astrologer. At least, that
what I do to earn money. In my innermost soul, I'm a poe
but nobody pays you for that." She offered a wispy smil
"But I like astrology too." To Cassidy she said, "I'd lov
to cast your chart sometime."

*Your belief in astrology runs neck and neck with yo
belief in the National Enquirer.*

"Thanks, but—"

"That's okay. I run into a lot of skeptics. But I kno
the charts never lie." She turned to face the bride an
groom. "Isn't Max spectacular? And Claire—she's just s
beautiful. After today, I'll get to be an official aunt 1
Molly." She gazed into Cassidy's eyes. "But I'm not s
sure they ought to get married."

"Why not? Don't their charts fit together?" *Or whatever the hell it is charts do.*

"No," Julie said somberly. "Something else." She started to wander away.

"Wait," Cassidy called after her. "Why shouldn't they get married?"

Julie threw her another vague smile and kept moving.

Cassidy heard the sound of whistling and turned to see a broad-shouldered man approaching from the street. Thrusting out his hand to Zach, he said in a booming voice, "Nicky Andrews. Used to be Maxie's boss till he cut out on me."

"Zach Moran. And my wife, Cassidy McCabe."

"Name sounds familiar. Haven't I met you before?" The newcomer had a long snow-white ponytail that contrasted strongly with his tanned youthful face.

"I'm a reporter at the *Post*. Maybe I interviewed you sometime."

"Oh yeah, now I remember. We talked on the phone about that girl who disappeared from Le Barre." Nicky punched his right fist into his left hand. "Couldn't answer any of your questions, though."

"Nobody else could either."

"Real tragedy. So, what are you doing here?"

"My wife knows Claire."

"Well, glad to meet you." Raising his hand to someone in the crowd, he bellowed, "Yeah baby!" and took off.

Cassidy asked, "What story was that?"

"A girl in her twenties went to a bar one night, got a little drunk, talked to a lot of people, then just disappeared. Somebody thinks he saw her on the street later but no one knows for sure. This all happened a couple of months ago, and I wrote several column inches about it at the time."

"Of course. I don't know how I could have forgotten." Cassidy shivered slightly. "God, it's eerie to think of someone just vanishing like that."

"People, people." The minister addressed the guests

from the top step of the white gazebo. "It's time for th
nuptials to begin. Please gather around the steps whil
Claire's friend plays Bach's 'Sheep May Safely Graze'."

Standing to the left of the gazebo, a willowy woman wit
straight blond hair lifted a flute to her mouth, releasing
string of haunting, crystalline notes.

The guests shuffled into a semi-circle in front of the min
ister. As Cassidy moved into place, she noticed a stony
faced, fiftyish woman standing beside an elegant man ol
to the side. *Looks like somebody who got dragged by wil*
horses.

Claire went to stand on the left-hand side of the ministe
her sister next to her. At the same time Max took up
stance on the minister's right, his best man beside him,
darkly handsome fellow whose brooding aspect was as dil
ferent as possible from Max's sunny aura. The bride'
mother propelled Molly, a basket of rose petals over he
arm, into position next to Erin. Giggling, the child twiste
around to stare at the guests.

Warm sun bathed Cassidy's face; the fragrance of sprin;
filled her nostrils. A flock of small brown birds landed o:
the gazebo roof and commenced to make raucous conver
sation. Molly wandered away from her post, threw ros
petals at another young girl, then scurried back to stan
beside Erin.

Cassidy smiled to herself. *How silly of you to go mother*
henning Claire. Compared to all the grief Zach gave yo
at the beginning, Max's infractions hardly even count.

As the music ended, the minister looked out over th
crowd. "Let's begin this blessed day with a prayer." Cas
sidy lowered her head slightly. "Holy father, I give int
your keeping Max and Claire. May they live always in th
light of your—"

Max's head jerked wildly. Blood flew in all directions
drenching Claire's delicate cream-colored dress. The crac!
of a gunshot. Screams. Zach pushed Cassidy to the ground

overing her with his body. Peering through his arms, she
aw Claire down on all fours, her mother and sister crowd-
ng in next to her, the best man hovering nearby. Molly
ugged at Claire's bloody dress and wailed.

TWO

THIS BLESSED DAY

CASSIDY SQUEEZED her eyes closed briefly, then opened them and glanced around. Some guests were huddling on the ground, others running toward their cars or clustering around the fallen groom.

Zach got to his feet, then helped Cassidy up.

She took a step in Claire's direction, feeling a strong urge to be with her client. *Oh no you don't. You're not muscling your way in when she has her family beside her. That's who she needs now, not her therapist.*

Taking out his cell, Zach called 9-1-1 and reported the shooting, then said to Cassidy, "I need to go check on Max."

Shivering, Cassidy clutched her arms around her mid-section. "I'm coming too."

"This is not something you want to see."

"I have to be able to handle things like this."

You're nuts. You're a therapist, not a cop.

Zach scowled. "Okay, if you're determined to be a masochist, come along." He went over to the group around Max's body, Cassidy trailing behind. Some of the people were sobbing; others appeared numb. Taking one quick look, she saw that the back of Max's head was just a bloody hole. She fastened her eyes on Claire. Her client, sitting cross-legged on the ground, had picked up Max's hand and was stroking it. An overwhelming sadness filled Cassidy's chest.

As Zach led her away, she heard the first screech of sirens. "Could you tell anything from the body?"

"It was pretty much what I expected. A clean shot to the head. There was about one beat between seeing the body go down and hearing the gunshot. Maybe a thousand feet. The shooter must've been on that ridge over there." Zach looked toward the north end of the park.

The sirens grew louder. Cassidy saw two squads and an unmarked car jerk to a stop in the middle of the road. A couple of uniforms and a detective started across the field. Seconds later, a fire truck and an ambulance arrived, disgorging half a dozen more men.

The plainclothes cop mounted the gazebo and yelled at the crowd. "Move away from the body. C'mon, everybody, get moving." The beat officers herded them all in the direction of the highway. "You gotta wait in your cars till reinforcements arrive," the detective added. "The county sheriff's police'll be here in a few minutes to take you to headquarters. Please don't discuss the shooting amongst yourselves."

THE WEDDING GUESTS were transported to the Will County Sheriff's Headquarters, located in a town about twenty minutes west of Dorrity. Inside, the civilians clustered together in a small reception area in front of a wooden counter. Behind it a lumbering, red-faced detective, evidently the leader of the task force, was barking orders at his subordinates.

"Where the fuck you think you're going?" he yelled at a skinny officer heading toward the rear of the building.

"Just checking out that storage area in back. Thought maybe we could put some of 'em in there."

"We're not putting our guests in any storage areas. We're setting them up in interview rooms and offices. We'll just have to double up—stick more than one person in a room. Now get your heads out of your asses and start escorting the witnesses to the places we got."

So glad I live in a village with zero tolerance for rudeness from the guys who serve and protect.

AFTER CASSIDY AND Zach had waited a couple of hours in a windowless room with a scratched desk and two uncomfortable chairs, a plainclothes cop joined them. "I'm Detective Petry."

To Zach he said, "Would you mind stepping outside while I talk to your wife?"

Zach left and Petry settled behind the desk, a spiral notepad in hand.

Now what? Confidentiality won't allow me to even say how I know Claire.

Glancing at his notes, Petry remarked, "Miss Linden says you're her therapist."

Cassidy nodded. *Well, that's a relief. Now I won't have to pretend I accidentally stumbled on the wedding.*

"Do you know if Mr. O'Connell had any enemies?"

"I have no information other than what Claire told me in sessions, and that's privileged."

"Don't the interests of justice supersede confidentiality? Your client wants to see this killer caught. You'd be doing her a favor by giving us your perspective."

"There's nothing I could say that Claire can't tell you herself."

"Miss Linden is pretty upset. I'm sure you know things that might not even occur to her until she's had some time to calm down." He rubbed his elongated forehead.

Cassidy pressed her knuckles into her cheek. She really did want to help. And she suspected that Claire would approve of her giving out some pieces of information. But she didn't know which pieces and she didn't have a signed consent form. Once before she'd had to go in front of a review board for violating confidentiality. It was an experience she would vastly prefer not to repeat.

"I can tell you what I saw today but it would be a breach of ethics to reveal anything Claire disclosed in a counseling session."

He threw out a number of questions about the shooting, then asked, "Did you think Mr. O'Connell was a good choice for your client?"

You wanted to think he was a good choice. You tried to talk yourself into it. You hoped your alarm bells were wrong. She shook her head. "I can't discuss it."

He told her she could go.

ON THE DRIVE HOME, Cassidy stared out at a dramatic pearl-gray sky intersected with streaks of deep charcoal. A lump had formed in her stomach; heaviness weighed on her shoulders.

"What're you thinking?" Zach asked.

"Claire. What it'll be like for her."

"This'd be pretty awful for anybody."

"But worse for Claire." Cassidy sighed.

"Want to talk about it?"

"Yes, but I shouldn't." She felt tempted. Zach was a safe person. She knew he would keep her confidence, and it would be a relief to express her concerns out loud. But it wouldn't be right. "No, I can't."

He laid his hand on her knee.

What she wanted to tell him was that Claire had a particular vulnerability to loss. She had a history of plunging into depression whenever a relationship ended, which was the reason she'd stayed so long with men who mistreated her. It had taken antidepressants and a year in therapy to enable Claire to cut loose from her ex-husband, and even then she'd relapsed into a bout of depression afterward. *What happened today—so much worse than anything she's been through before. God knows how I'll ever get her past it.*

Zach said, "You given any thought to who might've done it? Or why?"

"Claire's ex had a pretty strong reaction when she told him she was getting married again. I believe he made some comment that could be construed as a threat. But she was convinced he wouldn't do anything."

"Didn't you say he was abusive?"

"Yeah, he was. Maybe Claire was deluding herself when she said he wasn't dangerous."

"So how bad is this guy?"

"The abuse was mostly verbal and emotional. Sometimes I think that's the worst kind because it's so hard to identify. He hit her on a couple of occasions but he never really beat her up. After she left him, she had to take out a restraining order to stop him from stalking her. So I guess Claire was being pretty naive when she said he wouldn't do anything."

Cassidy gazed out the side window at a plowed field with small green plants growing in neat rows.

"The other question is, why do it at a wedding?"

Cassidy shook her head. "I haven't a clue. I'm still pretty much in a daze about the whole thing."

"Any other possibilities besides the ex? People in the restaurant business have been known to pal around with some pretty rough types."

"There were a few things about Max that seemed kind of off, but I don't really know much about him."

They drove in silence for a while. Light broke through the clouds near the horizon, creating a starburst effect so intense Cassidy turned her eyes away.

Putting on wraparound sunglasses, Zach said, "What we've got here is either a skilled marksman or a professional killer. The cops'll be able to follow the trajectory of the bullet and locate its point of origin. If the guy's an amateur, they'll probably find some evidence at the scene. But if he's a professional, the cops won't find anything."

Not liking the sound of this, Cassidy clamped her lips together for a moment, then said, "Are you telling me, if it's a professional hit they won't be able to identify the killer? Or the person who hired him?''

"Cops almost never bust professionals. And as for the people who purchase their services, about the only way they get caught is if they shoot off their mouths, or if they've recently withdrawn a large sum of money they can't account for."

"So that means, if this turns out to be a murder for hire, the police may never solve it." She gritted her teeth. "But we don't know it was a professional. It could be some amateur rifleman with a grudge against Max."

The highway angled off to the right, putting the sunset behind them. Zach removed his glasses. "Was the ex-husband a gun nut? Or, more to the point, a really good shot?''

"I doubt it." *You would've known. Claire spent way more airtime on the jerk than he deserved.* Cassidy studied Zach's face: high forehead, thick straight brows, a hawkish nose. His expression was as unreadable as ever, but she detected a hint of tension in the set of his jaw.

"You think it's a murder for hire, don't you?"

"I just don't want you getting your hopes up that the police will break this case anytime soon."

Cassidy lowered her brow in frustration. "If there isn't an arrest, there won't be any closure. Which'll make it harder on everyone. Especially Claire." *And also hard on you. Deep down inside, you've got a part that wants to see people pay for what they do. An eye-for-an-eye, thirsting-for-vengeance part.*

THEY STOPPED for dinner, then returned to their house in Oak Park, standing tall on the corner of Hazel and Briar. Stashing the Subaru in the garage at the rear of the lot, they walked along the chain-link fence toward the back gate. Starshine, a petite calico cat, came running from the stoop to roll on the sidewalk and greet them.

Hunkering down, Cassidy offered a chin scratch. As soon

as she was done, Starshine jumped up, tail waving jauntily, and led them toward the door.

Zach took Cassidy's hand. "I need more alcohol."

Only one glass of wine at dinner. You thought for sure he'd be slurping down bourbons.

"So, it got to you too."

"I never said I was immune to seeing people shot in front of me."

"Well, I could stand another glass of wine myself."

"Let's take a bottle and go sit on the porch."

They settled on the enclosed porch that ran along the front of the house, a row of casement windows facing the street. Cassidy stared absently at the Victorian across from her. Fully leaved trees surrounded them: a row of elms on both sides of Hazel; a maple at the corner of their house; a lilac bush, heavily hung with perfumed blossoms, nestling against the south side of the porch.

In the background droned the constant traffic from Austin Boulevard a block to the east, the line that divided their middle-class, integrated suburb from an impoverished, solidly black Chicago ghetto, replete with gang-bangers and crack houses. The biggest problem Oak Parkers faced was the allure the reasonably affluent village held for the criminal population on the eastern side of the border.

They sipped wine, listened to the jangle of the wind chimes, and watched Starshine pounce on invisible insects. When the bottle was empty, Cassidy laid her head on Zach's shoulder. "I know it's only nine-thirty, but I can't wait for this day to be over."

"You mean you're not going to let me stay up all night and drink?"

Smiling to herself, she remembered how she used to worry about his drinking. *In the old days, he would've killed a bottle of bourbon after a day like this. Now, to keep you happy, he puts a lid on his indulgences.*

She wrapped her hand around his. "I keep thinking how

I'd feel if you were the one who'd been shot.'' She paused. ''What I'd like most is to climb into bed and just hang onto each other until we fall asleep.''

''You know, I think that's what I'd like, too.''

THREE

TYLENOL AND MUG SHOTS

AT TEN THE next morning, Cassidy sat up in the waterbed, both hands wrapped around her purple Laurel Burch cat mug, inhaling the steamy coffee aroma. Zach, in his blue robe, was reading the Sunday Post at his cherrywood desk, which stood in the far corner of the room. Her desk faced the wall a few feet from his. Zach had set up his computer equipment in one of the two rooms across the hall, but he'd kept his desk in the bedroom so they could work in the same room at least some of the time.

You should call Claire, see how she's doing.

You know how she's doing. Hanging on by her finger-nails. Talking about it might make her feel a little better, but it's going to make you feel a whole lot worse.

It was Cassidy's job to listen to people express their feelings of sadness, anger, and despair. To be open and responsive, but at the same time maintain enough distance so the feelings didn't swamp her. With Claire it would be harder than usual. Harder because Cassidy had let herself get too close, too invested in her client's happiness. And harder because she'd witnessed Max's death and had feelings of her own about it.

"Do you know why so many people attend a funeral, send a card, then run like hell?"

Zach looked up. His smooth dark hair fell in a jagged

line across his forehead; a morning stubble dappled his cheeks and jaw. "Because other people's tragedies remind us of our own."

"Denial really isn't such a bad thing after all. Without it, I don't know how we'd keep ourselves going."

"You wishing you could bail out too? Well, I don't blame you. I could never do what you do." He held her eyes, infusing her with some of his own steadiness. "But I know you better than that. You'll be there for Claire as much as she needs you to be."

Cassidy heard cat footsteps clomping up the stairs outside the bedroom.

"But not until I get my Starshine fix."

It was their morning ritual. Starshine ran downstairs first thing for breakfast, inhaled her food, then waited around a while as if hoping her bowl would magically refill itself. A short time later she reappeared in the bedroom. Both the calico and the human thoroughly enjoyed their initial cuddle of the day, although Starshine first had to establish her indifference to her two-legged cohorts before indulging in a warm, mooshy petting session.

She sauntered into the bedroom, jumped onto the nightstand, then stepped over to the radiator board beneath the west window. With her back to Cassidy, the calico stared out the window for nearly a minute.

There are two ways to learn patience. You can study Buddhism or live with a cat.

After a while, Starshine climbed onto Cassidy's chest, positioning herself so that her nose was a mere two inches beneath Cassidy's chin. Cassidy scratched behind the cat's ears and rubbed a fingernail along her jaw. The calico stretched her head back, squinted her eyes, and purred adoringly.

When Starshine was finished, Cassidy picked up the desk phone and called Claire.

A woman answered, probably Claire's mother or sister.

"This is Cassidy McCabe. I just called to see how Claire's doing."

"She's awake. I'll take the phone in to her."

"I don't think I'm going to make it this time, Cass." Claire's voice was thin and weak. Dry, as if it might crumble into dust.

"You will. We'll do it together." Cassidy paused. "Tell me what it's like."

"Everything's different. The colors have faded. The sounds are muffled. The only thing that's more vivid is the odors. I can still smell the tulips and the water and the blood. I can't get the stench of blood out of my nostrils."

"You said almost the same thing when you and Molly moved out of the apartment you shared with Hank." *Except that time there wasn't any blood.* Glancing at the window, Cassidy saw that the day was brighter than it had any right to be.

Claire said, "This is worse."

"Do you remember how you got through it before?"

"This is different. I can't get through this one."

"You took one tiny step at a time. The first step would be to get yourself into the shower." *A good strong dose of shampoo to wash away the smell of blood.*

"I can't do it. It's too hard."

"You just need to work yourself up to it. You need to lie there and focus all your attention on mustering the energy to get into the shower. How long do you think it will take?" Realizing that her hand was too tight on the receiver, Cassidy forced herself to loosen it.

"Who knows?" A short silence. "Maybe half an hour."

"Take your shower, then call me when you're done."

Replacing the phone in its cradle, she looked up to meet Zach's eyes. He was touching the scar that ran diagonally across his left cheek. "If I ever take a major fall, I want you to do that for me."

"Not if—when. Nobody makes it through life without taking a major fall now and then." *I'd do it for him. He'd do it for me. Together is better. Which is what Claire wanted for herself, but it got snatched away from her.*

IT WAS MONDAY NIGHT, three weeks after the shooting. Cassidy, on her way home from her mother's apartment, was driving east on Briar. Stopping at the intersection of Hazel, she glanced at her two-story frame house, noting that lights shone from every room Zach had inhabited during the course of the evening. Cassidy, raised in a penny-pinching, blue-collar household, had a deeply ingrained need to turn off switches. Zach, raised in an Oak Park mansion, did not.

She continued past the house toward the garage at the far end of the property, its driveway emptying onto Briar, its east side abutting the alley. Her eyes scanned the street and sidewalks, softly lit by street lamps and the mauve city aura. *Constant vigilance. The price you pay for living next to Austin Boulevard.* She noticed a white SUV traveling half a block behind her but didn't see any pedestrians. Punching the pad clipped to her sun visor, she watched the new garage door opener perform its electronic trick.

Mom did it to me again. Sang the why-don't-you-ever-have-time-for-me blues and guilted me into staying an extra hour. Cassidy drove into the garage and parked the Toyota beside the Subaru. Pulling her handbag over her shoulder and gripping the straps, she threaded her way past her battered bike and the tools on the wall, then pushed the button to start the overhead door creaking down again.

Emerging from the garage at the corner near the alley, she saw that the SUV had parked just before her driveway. A burly white guy climbed out of the driver's seat, then

stood looking her up and down in a manner she didn't lik
at all. There were two ways to get from the garage to he
house: she could walk down the sidewalk past the SU
driver to her back gate, or she could circle around behin
the garage and come in from the alley. *Why don't you n*
go past that fishy-eyed creep?

As she edged backward around the corner of the garag
she felt a hand yank at her purse straps. She clutched the
tighter. The hand pulled again, whipping her around an
bringing her face to face with her attacker. Black ski
shaved head, lips pulled back, large yellow teeth bared lik
a dog's. *Oh shit! Oh no!* His arm rose. His fist slamme
into her left temple, knocking her head into the garage. Sh
felt a flash of pain, then fell into nothingness.

FUNNY SMELLS. Antiseptic. Her head had become a recep
tacle for molten pain.

Zach's voice: "I think she's coming around."

The blackness was better. Nothing hurt in that deep blac
place. She squeezed her eyes tight and tried to retreat t
her warm fuzzy hole, but she couldn't find her way bac
to it.

She felt Zach lift her hand and stroke it. *He's waitin*
You have to get conscious. She made a great effort an
opened her eyes. The light was too bright. It penetrated he
pupils and set off a burning sensation in her brain. Sh
lowered her lids.

"It's all right. Take as long as you like."

She drifted off for a while, then thoughts began formin
in her mind, clear thoughts she couldn't push away. *Nee*
to tell the police, see if they can catch the bastard. Nee
to tell Zach.

She forced her eyes to stay open even though the ligl
still burned. Focused on Zach. He didn't look right. Fac
seamed with lines, worry in his eyes, mouth too tight.

"You're going to be fine."

If that were true, why was Zach so upset? She wanted to ask but moving her tongue to make words was too much for her.

She glanced around. A curtained room. Monitors, tubes, medical equipment. *Hospital, of course.*

She squeaked out some words. "Don't they have any painkillers in this place?"

Zach got a nurse to provide pills, then asked if she felt up to giving her statement to the cop who was waiting outside the room.

Statement? It happened so fast, it's not much more than a sound byte. She nodded and Zach waved the cop in. After listening to her story, he was gone in a matter of minutes.

"Not that it's going to do any good," she croaked to Zach, who was holding her hand again. "The creep undoubtedly disappeared into Chicago before the ambulance even arrived."

A tired-looking doctor asked her some questions, shone a light in her eyes, got her up and made her walk, then trundled her off for a CAT scan. When he returned, he pronounced her concussion-free. Instructing Zach to wake her several times during the night, the doctor sent them home.

As they climbed the stairs to their bedroom, Zach said, "First thing tomorrow I'm going to cancel your Tuesday clients."

For one instant she considered fighting him on it. Then she flashed an image of the dark face, the bared teeth, the hand slamming into the side of her head. *Even if you were able to sit in your chair and nod and smile, you wouldn't be there emotionally.* She started writing out client names and numbers.

WHEN SHE AWOKE in the morning, Zach was nowhere to be seen, so she wobbled into the bathroom, threw water on her face, sloshed down a couple of Tylenol, then returned to collapse on the bed.

Zach came through the doorway two minutes later. "Thought I heard you rattling around up here." He rolled his desk chair over to the bed. "Your clients are taken care of, your credit card's canceled, and I called Gran to let her know what happened. She offered to keep your mother out of your hair until tomorrow, but she wants to see you herself sometime today."

Cassidy smiled. *When it comes to comfort, Gran's even better than a bag of Reese's.*

Dragging herself upright, Cassidy shoved pillows behind her back. "I wish I knew how to handle Mom—or anybody else, for that matter—half as well as Gran does."

Raising Cassidy's hand, Zach kissed the back of her fingers. "What can I get you? Coffee? Breakfast? Peanut butter cups?"

"Nothing until the Tylenol kicks in." Remembering how anxious her usually unflappable husband had appeared the night before, she said, "You seemed so worried at the hospital. I thought I must be dying for you to look like that."

"It was the shock of finding you."

"How *did* you find me, anyway?"

The tension lines reappeared in his face. "I heard sirens go roaring past the house, and when I looked there were a couple of squads and an ambulance pulled up beside the garage. I went running outside and there you were sprawled out on the pavement. Fortunately, there was a witness who called it in."

"A witness?"

"Some guy who'd just gotten out of his car. He saw you backing into the alley and heard scuffling."

Boy, did you ever make the wrong choice when you decided not to go past the fishy-eyed creep.

"Anyway, when I went out and saw you not moving or anything.... Well, I don't when I've been so scared."

She reached for his hand. "I'm going to be fine. Just as soon as I get a new head. Do you suppose you could order me one on the Internet? Maybe a head with mysterious, almond-shaped eyes and silky blond hair?"

"How 'bout a brain with more of an urge to accommodate her husband?"

"You wouldn't like that model. You'd get bored if I didn't stir things up on occasion."

Half an hour later the front doorbell rang. "It's Bryce," Zach said, coming into the bedroom. "He wants to see how you're doing."

Bryce was Zach's college-age son, the product of a brief affair. Zach hadn't known of the boy's existence until Bryce's mother sent him to stay with Zach and Cassidy shortly before the mother was murdered.

"Bryce heard about the mugging already? How'd he find out?"

Zach explained that their neighbors to the south, Paul and Dorothy Stein and their brood of children, had all come out to see what the sirens were about. Since Bryce was attending a bereavement group with the Stein's older daughter, Melissa, he'd become a part of the neighborhood loop.

Zach said, "By now half of Oak Park probably knows."

The downside of living in a village that works so hard to promote a sense of community. Sometimes I almost wish we could move to an anonymous city condo. Except I'd never leave Oak Park.

"Bryce wants to see me?" Cassidy said, picturing the bruised, swollen, tangle-haired image the bathroom mirror had revealed. "Why don't we just tell him to come back later—after I get that new head with the blond hair."

"Do you realize what you'd say to me if I were tryin to avoid Bryce?"

"Um…unfortunately, I do." Cassidy had consistent pressured Zach to work on building a relationship with h son. "Okay, he can come see me in all my purple glory.

A minute later a lanky nineteen-year-old walked throug the door. Bryce sported a dark crewcut above a craggy fac his features bearing no resemblance to his father's smooth round countenance. It was only the deep bronze comple ion of both faces that had convinced Cassidy that Zach wa Bryce's father.

Zach settled in his desk chair while Bryce stood next the bed, feet planted wide, hands resting on his bel "Jeeze, Cass, you look awful."

"So glad you came by to cheer me up."

"I don't know anybody who gets herself beaten up ha as often as you do."

When Bryce had first entered their lives, he'd carried chip on his shoulder the size of Alaska toward his unknow father, and by extension to Cassidy, his father's girlfrien For a long time he'd appeared perpetually angry, but th bereavement group seemed to be mellowing him out.

Cassidy pulled herself straighter. "You're making sound like this is my fault."

He shrugged. "I just thought maybe you weren't bein careful enough."

Zach said from behind him, "Are you familiar with th concept of blaming the victim?"

Bryce shifted his weight. "Okay, so it's not your fau What happened, anyway?"

She was halfway through her story when the doorbe rang again. Zach went downstairs, returning with Cassidy grandmother, a tiny woman wearing a long black wig th dwarfed her gnarly face.

"Hey, Bryce," she said, throwing her arms wide. "I haven't seen you in a dog's age."

The teenager bent down from his six-two height to hug the under-five-foot senior. "Hey, yourself!"

Gran emerged from the embrace with long curls pushed sideways over her left eye. "You messed up my Cher hair." Straightening the wig, she added, "You think I should get thigh-high boots to go with it?"

Bryce grinned. "Sounds pretty hot to me. You can wear them the next time you invite me over for dinner."

"You're fishing, aren't you?" Gran said gleefully.

"Sure I am. You're the only person who ever feeds me pot roast."

"How 'bout we order in pizza at Cass's house? We can all crowd together on the bed and drop crumbs on the sheets."

"That's a great idea," Cassidy said. "I could have everybody I love most right here on the bed with me. And pizza to boot."

Zach stood. "Sorry to be a wet blanket but Cass and I have a few things we need to do today."

"Well, I gotta go." Bryce raised an outspread hand and left the room.

Gran leaned over to kiss her cheek. "You sound just as bright and perky as ever. I know you'll be back on your feet in no time."

"I'm amazed you were able to keep Mom from flying to my bedside. How'd you do it, anyway?"

"I told her the doctor wasn't allowing any visits or phone calls but I'd smuggle out some news from Zach."

AFTER SEEING Gran out, Zach stood beside the bed. "You up to running some errands?"

"What?"

"You need to look at mug shots."

She grimaced. "I never remember faces." Her eyes narrowing, she pictured the shaved head and fierce mouth. "Although the bared-tooth man might've engraved more of an image on my brain than most."

"The mug shots may not do any good but you still have to look at them."

"You said 'errands' plural." It suddenly hit her. "Oh shit! I have to replace everything! From the house locks to my driver's license to the handbag itself." Having your purse snatched was not as bad as your house burning or your marriage ending, but emotionally it ranked right up there with a nonfatal car crash. She'd had a couple of clients who'd spent an entire session processing the trauma of a lost purse.

"There are even a few things I'll never be able to replace," she added wistfully. "That cute picture of Starshine when she was a kitten. The photo I took of you putting up the tree last Christmas."

"It's a shame about the pictures." A dark look came over Zach's face. "And even more of a shame that these goddamn street thugs almost never get caught. But we can take care of everything else. The locksmith's coming today. And we can deal with the rest as the spirit moves us."

FOUR

AN UNSOLVABLE CRIME

CASSIDY WENT THROUGH the mug shot book but none of the faces resembled her attacker. When they returned to the house late that afternoon, she was ready for more Tylenol and a nap.

She laid her head on the pillow and minutes later was sound asleep.

Her eyes were glued to the white SUV as she hunkered down behind a foul-smelling garbage can, trying to make herself invisible. The large-toothed black man sat behind the wheel, the burly white guy in the passenger seat. For several minutes now they'd been cruising the alley in search of her.

"I know she's in here," the black guy said. "It's just a matter of time."

"You can have the purse," the white guy said. "I just wanna do her."

The SUV veered in her direction, the headlights bearing down on her garbage can. She gazed up at her house, focusing on Zach's silhouette in the window. He would save her if he could, but he didn't know she was out there.

The vehicle came to an abrupt halt in front of her. She tried to run but her legs were too weak. The black man jumped out of the car and began beating her head and shoulders with his fists.

She woke up screaming.

Coming into the room, Zach sat on his side of the bed and gathered her in his arms. She cried a long time, then tapered off into small hiccupping sounds. Finally she was able to tell him about her dream.

"I guess my unconscious still doesn't believe that the white guy wasn't a creep."

"You have every right to be afraid. It's not a weakness."

"Yes it is. V.I. Warshawsky would be out hunting him down instead of cowering behind a garbage can while he hunts her."

"V.I. is not a real person and you're not allowed to compare yourself with her. Why don't you let me do the driving for a while. Just till you get over the initial shock."

She started to shake her head but it hurt. "I can't be driven around like a modern-day Miss Daisy. I have to get back on the horse. I have to not let myself be afraid."

"What would you say to a client?"

"Shut up. I'm not a client so I don't have to think about it."

"However you choose to handle this is fine with me. Just let me know what you want."

"I want to get over this as fast as I can. The same thing you'd want."

"Well, you're right about that."

HEADING DOWN to the kitchen, Cassidy pulled a half-empty bag of peanut butter cups out of a cabinet, leaned against the sink, and slowly devoured them. The large old room, with its curling linoleum floor, worn-out linoleum counter, and scuffed wooden cabinets, was decades overdue for refurbishing.

Having bolstered her courage with chocolate, she trudged around the kitchen's oak room divider, passed through the client waiting room, and went out the rear door.

Time to face up to your fears. Which means, go stand in the place you got mugged.

Sun-dappled leaves canopied the street. Birds squawked

from every tree, like the tune-up of a screechy orchestra. The light was golden, the sun's rays slanting from the west, long shadows extending across the yard and street.

Her chest tight, Cassidy forced herself to walk around the corner of the garage into the alley. A woman and her children were digging dandelions in the yard across from hers. Three teens leaned against a beater car halfway down the block. Nobody paid any attention to her.

Nothing to be afraid of, she told herself. *The mugging was a fluke. No reason to think it'd ever happen again.* But the tightness in her chest did not go away.

IT WAS NEARLY nine when Zach left his computer and came into the bedroom where Cassidy had plunked herself down to read.

"Let's go sit on the porch."

Something in his tone set off a mild churning in her stomach. "This isn't just a random get together, is it?"

"Matter of fact, I do have something on my mind."

Not going to be a pleasant little surprise. Not just some fluffy happy talk to lift your spirits.

"I'm going to get a bourbon. You want anything?"

"Not on top of all these Tylenol."

They sat together on the threadbare cushions of an old wicker couch that had stood on the porch for more years than she could count. One casement window remained permanently open, a doorway onto the porch for Starshine, who also had her own personal cat flap for entering and exiting the house.

As soon as they were settled, Starshine plummeted through the window and began harassing them. She pranced along the rim of the couch, biting Cassidy's hair and swiping at Zach's ear. He hauled her down and held her in his lap, where she squirmed mightily, then nipped his finger and ran away.

"I've been curious about Max's murder investigation," Zach said. "The *Post* did that initial piece about the shooting, but I think an in-depth story'd be a real grabber. Although I suppose you wouldn't want me writing it.''

''You *can't* write it. It would completely compromise my relationship with Claire.''

Zach took a long swig from his drink. A convertible stuffed with rowdy teens cruised past their house. An elderly couple walked hand in hand on the opposite side of Hazel.

''Max's shooting—that isn't what you brought me down here to talk about, is it?''

''Cass, I think we should move.''

''Move?'' She blinked in surprise. ''You mean, go live someplace else?''

''This neighborhood isn't safe.''

She felt her spine stiffen. ''What do you mean it isn't safe? We've got all these families with little children on the block. They wouldn't be living here if it wasn't safe, would they?''

''Everybody's playing the odds. And we just lost.'' He paused. ''I don't want to live in a place where I have to worry about you getting home in one piece.''

''Where do you want to go? The Australian Outback? Crime happens everywhere. There isn't any place that's safe. And at least here in Oak Park we have terrific police coverage.''

Zach looked her in the eye. ''I knew you wouldn't like the idea. Yes, crime occurs everywhere, but it's not an equal opportunity phenomenon. Certain neighborhoods have more than their share, and ours is on the high side.''

She drew in a breath, suddenly realizing that a part of her secretly agreed with him, a part that never wanted to go back into that alley again.

We've paid our dues. Had our house broken into more than once. Now I've been mugged and Zach's gone through hell finding me out in the alley. What would be so wrong with not living right here on the border?

''Move where?'' A breeze rippled through the window,

bringing with it the scent of lilacs. The trees swooshed overhead.

Twisting to face her, Zach balanced his glass on his knee. "I was thinking maybe River Forest." River Forest was the more traditional, more affluent suburb directly to the west.

"River Forest?" She said indignantly. "There's nothing happening in River Forest. No factions or protests or controversies."

"I don't see you out there lobbying for social justice."

You don't want to actually get involved—you just like living in a place where other people do.

"At least I care about social justice. The only thing River Foresters care about is their tennis game and their stock portfolios."

"I thought you disapproved of stereotyping."

"I thought you wanted nothing to do with your family's privileged lifestyle." Zach had gone all out to be as opposite from his blue-blood family as possible.

"River Forest is full of rich people," Cassidy added. "I wouldn't feel at home there."

"I was just looking for a low-crime area that wasn't too far from the city. River Forest does have some affordable housing, you know."

"But it doesn't have integration or diversity."

"So how 'bout west Oak Park?"

"But where would I see clients? We'd have to find someplace with a waiting room and a home office like I have here."

You're setting up obstacles. Trying to get out of it.

No wait, a scared little voice responded, *I do want to move. I want to get as far away from that alley as possible.*

Zach laid his hand on her knee. "We could pick a place with a floor plan we like and remodel."

"You really want out of this house?"

"I really do. The safety issue is my biggest concern, but besides that, this is the place you and Kevin picked. I never had any say in it. And then there's the amount of work that needs to be done. Instead of pouring a hundred grand into this house, I'd rather start over with a place that's really ours—not just leftovers from Kevin.''

''I never knew you felt that way.'' A small part of her was hurt that he didn't love her house as much as she did. However, she had to admit that Zach deserved to have a say in where they lived, considering she'd added his name to the title and he'd been paying the mortgage since he first moved in.

''It's not like I've been brooding about it or anything. I've been happy here. But seeing you knocked out last night brought it all to a head. I suddenly realized I don't want to live here anymore.''

What if it was Zach who'd been mugged in the alley. Would you want to move? She didn't have an answer to that one.

''We don't have to decide right away, do we?''

''You can take as long as you need.''

How 'bout ten years?

WEDNESDAY EVENING Cassidy was at her desk in the bedroom waiting for Claire, who was due to arrive at six. Wednesday had been a big improvement over Tuesday. Cassidy had awakened without a headache, shooed Zach off to work, endured a couple of hours of her mother's fussing over her, and seen the day's regularly scheduled clients.

The back doorbell rang, indicating that Claire had just come into the waiting room. Cassidy left her air-conditioned bedroom and stepped out into the June heat and humidity, which had started rising earlier that day. The muggy air weighed her down, blanketed her, made her feel as if she were breathing through a wet sponge. By the time she rounded the kitchen room divider, she was already soggy and damp.

''My God, what happened to your face?'' Claire rose

abruptly from one of the two fan-backed chairs that stood in front of a wide south window. The waiting room was light and airy, with a filmy raspberry-colored fabric draped around the window and white paper displaying a small raspberry-colored design on the walls.

Cassidy touched her bruised temple. "I got mugged."

"How awful! Where'd it happen, anyway?"

Gazing through the back door window, she said, "In the alley on the other side of the garage."

You shouldn't have told her. It'll just make her nervous about coming here. Yeah, but spur-of-the-moment lies were never my best thing.

"That's terrible." Claire sighed. "Nobody's safe anymore."

Can't let her generalize into thinking everything's dangerous. "I got a small lump on my head and now I'm fine."

She led her client into the paneled office. Claire took her usual place on the sectional; Cassidy sat in her director's chair. Through the window behind Claire's head Cassidy could see the small tree in her back yard, a clear blue sky behind it.

"So, how you doing?"

Claire shrugged, her weary eyes underscored by dark circles, her long chestnut hair lackluster and unwashed. Although usually meticulous in her grooming, she wore a suit that looked as if it had been going back and forth to work for a week straight without benefit of an iron.

"I feel as if I'm floating somewhere out in space and nothing is real."

"Have you had any panic attacks? Or flashbacks?"

"I have a lot of anxiety but I'm not having any of those attacks I used to have. The main thing is the depression. Most days I can get myself to work, but I'm just going through the motions, certainly not earning that big salary they pay me. I'm not even taking very good care of

Molly—who knows if I ever will again. We eat takeout every night and I barely talk to her.''

"Of course you can't think about Molly yet. You're still in shock.'' Cassidy propped her toe on the edge of the low wicker table that stood between them. "Is Molly still having night terrors?''

Claire nodded. "I know you gave me a referral to a child psychologist and I haven't called yet, but I will.''

"Can you make sure to do that tomorrow?''

Claire nodded.

"Was Molly attached to Max? Is she grieving as well?''

"You remember, I told you that Max went out of his way to be nice to her but she never really liked him. I think she was jealous of my attention.'' Claire caught her lip between her teeth. "If only I'd concentrated more on Molly and stayed away from men.''

"You've got nothing to blame yourself for,'' Cassidy said. "Let's just work on getting you through this grieving period. Then you can be the kind of mom you were before.''

"Even though I feel hopeless sometimes, I really know that eventually I'll get back to my old self. But right now it isn't the depression that's bothering me so much as this other thing.''

"What thing is that?''

"It's this unfinished feeling about the murder. I mean, how can I ever stop obsessing if nobody's brought to justice?''

Good question. You've been feeling pretty unfinished yourself.

This was Claire's third session since the slaying. In the earlier sessions, she'd told Cassidy that her grandfather, a Dorrity resident, had a buddy in the sheriff's department, and that the buddy didn't have high hopes for solving the crime.

Sliding lower on her spine, Claire looked up at Cassidy from under her brows. "Everybody thinks it's my ex.''

"Yes, we've talked about that."

"My grandfather's buddy has been giving him a blow-by-blow of what the police are doing. They've driven into Chicago to go through Hank's garbage, they've checked all his phone calls, they've been over his financial records with a fine tooth comb. They can't come up with a shred of evidence but they're still convinced he's the one." Claire's darkly circled eyes filled with tears. "I just can't stand thinking Hank would do such a thing."

Grabbing a tissue box from the wicker table, Cassidy handed it to Claire. "What makes you feel so bad about that?"

"I don't know, I don't know." Squeezing her eyes closed, Claire wept quietly for a moment. "It means the guy I married is even more of a scumbag than I thought. It means I'm partly to blame for Max's death." She blew her nose. "The worst of it has to do with Molly. People are so thoughtless. Max's mother pronounced Hank guilty right in front of Molly and now she thinks her father's a murderer." Claire shook her head. "I hate the idea that my daughter might grow up believing such a thing."

"What about you? Do you think Hank's guilty?"

"My gut says no. I mean, there were only a couple of times he actually got violent and those were both when he'd been drinking. But who knows?" Claire rubbed her left hand slowly up and down her right arm, a gesture she used to comfort herself.

Cassidy watched a gang of birds alight in the tree outside her office. Children's high-pitched voices yelled back and forth on Briar. A blue minivan parked at the curb next to her office.

"But didn't Hank make some kind of threat?"

"I don't know." Claire bit her lip again. "When I told him about the wedding, he said that someday he'd find a way to get me back. That he wasn't going to let anybody come between us." She paused. "Not exactly what I'd call a death threat."

But not a Best-Wishes-on-Your-Marriage either.

"Claire, I can understand why it's so hard to think that the murder may go unsolved. Of course you want Max's killer to pay. And of course you *don't* want to think that your child's father might be guilty. But this is one of those situations you have no control over."

Claire fixed Cassidy with an intense look. "There's something I want you to do for me. I know this sounds crazy, but I have to ask."

Cassidy's eyes narrowed. *A crazy request from a desperate client. Not what you ever want to hear.*

Taking a deep breath, Claire continued. "I've read a couple of stories in the *Post* about you and Zach solving murders. You uncovered things the police completely missed. So what I'm asking is for you and Zach to take a look into Max's shooting. I realize this is a huge favor and I couldn't expect your husband to put time into an investigation unless he was able to use the material for a story afterward."

Cassidy reared back in surprise. *That's what you get for going around acting like you know what you're doing. Fooling everyone into thinking you're a competent person. If you just let the whole world know that deep down inside you're a flibbertigibbit, people wouldn't have these outrageous expectations.*

"I can't do that. I'm your therapist. But I'm sure Zach could give you the name of a good P.I."

"I don't want a private investigator." Claire pushed one side of her lifeless hair behind her shoulder. "I feel so raw—I can't imagine dealing with someone I don't know. I trust you, Cass. And I know Zach's done some amazing investigative work."

"But I couldn't see you as a therapist if I started digging around in Max's murder."

"You couldn't?" The color drained from Claire's face. "Why not?"

"It's complicated. Just trust me when I tell you that a therapist can't take on dual roles with a client."

"But I could see you again after the investigation was over, couldn't I?"

"That shouldn't be a problem." *Unless I do something to alienate her. Which could easily happen.*

"So I'd only have to go for a few weeks."

She shouldn't be without a therapist right now. Except that grief work is pretty generic and someone else probably could take my place temporarily. "If I were to agree to this"—*which I definitely shouldn't*—"would you see another therapist in the interim?"

Claire sucked in air through her mouth, then nodded.

"You told me you couldn't face seeing a strange P.I. But wouldn't an unfamiliar therapist be just as bad?" *Worse, I'd say.*

"I don't think so." Claire squeezed her eyes closed. "It's hard to explain."

"Just do the best you can."

"If I hired a P.I., I'd have to divulge a lot of personal information, and he wouldn't be kind and understanding the way you are. And no matter how good he was, I wouldn't have the same confidence in him I have in you." She stared at the side window, then looked at Cassidy again. "This is so important to me. It's just so important to find out who killed Max. And if I could temporarily see a therapist who was like you—someone you recommended—it wouldn't be that bad. Not as bad as seeing a strange P.I."

"But there may not be any evidence," Cassidy said in a gentle voice. "The police have much greater resources than we do. If they can't identify the person who hired the hit, there's no reason to think Zach and I would fare any better."

Twisting her hands together, Claire said, "I understand you probably won't be able to prove anything. But if you could just come up with an alternative scenario.... If you could find one other person who had a good motive... I think that would be enough for me to put this to rest."

Feeling uneasy, Cassidy asked, ''But what if we came to the same conclusion as the police? That Hank probably *was* behind it?''

Claire's face turned bleak. ''Then I'd just have to live with it. But at least I'd know that Hank wasn't under suspicion for the rest of his life just because the police were too lazy to look for anyone else.''

This is nuts. This woman is out of her mind with grief and you shouldn't let yourself get sucked into her delusional hope that you and Zach will be able to solve an unsolvable murder.

Yes, but you have broken difficult cases in the past. And if you did come up with some answers, it would help Claire to move on.

The odds of you outwitting the police one more time are about as great as the odds of the Chicago Bulls rising like a phoenix from the dust.

Cassidy stared at evening light that was just beginning to deepen. ''I'll see what Zach says.'' *Here's hoping he has enough sense to put his foot down. And if he doesn't, that I'll demonstrate an uncharacteristic streak of intelligence and nix it myself.*

FIVE

GLITCHES AND RED FLAGS

"SHE WANTS US to investigate?" Zach swiveled his desk chair to face Cassidy.

She monitored his voice closely, hoping to pick up a hint of incredulity or amusement. Unfortunately, the word that leapt to mind was intrigued.

"You're not taking this quite the way I'd hoped."

"Huh?"

Cassidy plopped down on the bed. "I was looking for a reaction more along the lines of—'This is ridiculous. How could she even think of such a thing?'"

Zach leaned back and laced his hands behind his head. "Well, but why not? I'd certainly like to look into it and I'm fairly sure my editor'd give me a thumbs-up, especially since we have an inside track with the bride. Although there isn't any reason for you to work with me. You could continue as Claire's therapist and I could go after the story. That'd keep everything cleaner."

He's right, you know. As her therapist, you ought to stay as far away from the investigation as you can.

Fat chance.

"Okay, what you say makes sense. But there's no way I'm going to let you do this without me."

"I do stories without you all the time."

"But Claire's my client. She came to me for help. I can't just sit on the sidelines."

"I thought you were hoping I'd consider the whole thing ridiculous."

"As her therapist I don't really think it's in her best interest. I'm afraid we'd just get her hopes up and then she'd crash again."

The furrows between his brows deepened. "Much as I'd like to do the story, she's your client and I won't try to overrule you. Not that I ever could."

Cassidy scowled. "I didn't expect you to give up so easily."

"I'm starting to get confused."

"Well, you should be. Everything I'm saying is confusing as hell." She stood, folded her arms across her chest, and paced back and forth beside the bed. "There's one part of me that really wants to investigate. I have all these questions about Max buzzing around in my head, and I'd love the chance to get some answers, even if we don't find out who killed him. But then there's this other part chanting in the background, 'Do no harm. The most important thing is to do no harm.'"

"How could it be harmful? She's begging you to take it on."

"What I said before. Setting up false hope."

"But if she's feeling so stuck, maybe another crash is what she needs to get her unstuck."

Cassidy stopped pacing and stared at Zach in amazement. She was used to his being the expert on real-world events but she never expected him to outdo her when it came to observations about people. "Psychological insight is my bailiwick," she said in an irritable voice. "You are not allowed to beat me at my own game."

Zach laughed. "So far all we've talked about is what's best for Claire. We also need to consider what's best for you and me. After watching the EMTs load you in the ambulance the other night, I'm not sure I could handle having you work with me on an investigation."

She sat her desk chair. "It doesn't seem like there'd be

any danger. If the police don't have enough evidence to arrest anybody, there's no reason to think we'd be perceived as a threat.''

"Some people get nervous when you start asking questions. And anybody who's capable of hiring a competent hitman has to be viewed as dangerous.''

She gazed at Zach's desk, almost as cluttered as her own: a stack of techie catalogues, a calculator, his briefcase, and a laptop. "You don't suppose the mugging could be connected to Max's murder?'' She paused. "No, of course not. That's just my imagination running wild.''

"Why, 'of course not'?''

"First, I doubt that anybody knew Claire was going to ask us to investigate. And second, the mugger didn't whisper in my ear or leave any notes in my pocket. What's the point of trying to warn somebody off if you don't tell them that's what you're doing?''

"Okay, so they're not connected. But that still leaves the problem I'm having with you getting anywhere near a killer.''

Standing behind his chair, she looped her arms around his neck and spoke into his ear. "Zach, I really want to do this. I'm not as obsessed as Claire, but I'm having my own problem with the case being so unfinished. I've worked for almost four years to get Claire to the point where she could start over with a new marriage and now some asshole's blown it all away. I'm really pissed that this's happened to her and I want to do everything I can to find out who did it.''

"If I let you work with me, will you promise not to go interviewing suspects behind my back?''

Stepping in front of him, she dropped a light kiss on his mouth. "I won't do a single thing without a go-ahead from you.''

He stood and rested his arms on her shoulders. "Well, once again you've talked me into doing things your way.''

Her brow knit nervously. "But you want to do the investigation as well, don't you? I mean, I'm not just being selfish, am I?''

"My first choice would be to do it on my own." He smiled. "You're like a little cat who keeps working away at me till you get what you want, and then you purr so seductively I forget I ever wanted anything different."

She remembered occasions in the past when she'd gotten around him: the time she'd made him include her in his investigation into the murder of Bryce's mother; the time she'd forced him to let her accompany him into a face-off with a rogue cop; the numerous times she'd coaxed him into talking when he didn't want to.

The truth is, when you really want something, you do get selfish. It's just that so far you've been able to get away with it.

Zach looked at the clock. "It's only seven-thirty. You finished for the evening?"

She nodded.

"Why don't you call Claire and see if we can get started tonight."

"Tonight?"

"The case is already more than three weeks cold. The sooner we get on it, the better."

"She may not be home yet but I can leave a message."

Cassidy pulled her dog-eared Rolodex to the front of her desk, the cards so old the alphabet tabs were starting to disintegrate. She flipped to Linden and dialed. When Claire's answering machine came on, Cassidy asked her client to please return the call.

Twenty minutes later, Claire obliged.

"We've decided to go ahead with the investigation," Cassidy said. "In fact, if you feel up to it, we'd like to sit down and talk to you tonight."

"Oh, that's great! And yes, let's start right away. That is, if you don't mind coming here. I just sent the nanny home and I have to get Molly ready for bed."

"We'll be there as soon as we can." Cassidy glanced at the address on the card. A lakeshore highrise.

"You ready to go?" Zach asked.

"A couple of things I need to do first. I want to call Maggie and make sure she can fill in for me with Claire, and I also think I better type up a special consent form." *Regardless of what she says now, you better have it in writing in case she changes her mind later.*

CLAIRE STOOD BACK to admit them into the entryway. "I'm so glad you agreed to do this, Cass. And Zach—I really appreciate your taking this on."

"I'd thought about writing a story earlier but Cass nixed it."

Claire wore knee-length overalls with a pink-striped tee and no shoes. *If you don't look at those big sad eyes, she could be the pretty perky girl next door.* The eyes, brown with short, thick lashes, bore a flat, glazed look that hadn't gone away since the shooting.

The three of them stood in a short hall, the living room to the left, the dining room to the right. The living room had a vaguely romantic look to it: a fuzzy afghan tossed across the corner of a low sofa, watercolors on the walls, a small table holding silver-framed photos. The dining room was sleeker: a white lacquered table and sideboard, and, at the far end, floor-to-ceiling windows overlooking Lake Michigan.

Claire asked, "Where would you like to sit?"

"Let's work at the table," Zach replied, heading into the dining room.

"So we're really going to do it." Claire sat across from Cassidy and began twisting her ring.

"You seem a little nervous," Cassidy said. "Are you sure you want to go through with this?"

"I guess maybe I'm afraid of what I'll find out. But I'd rather know than not know."

"This is a big step you're taking. Of course you're

afraid.'' Cassidy paused. ''You understand I'll need permission to tell Zach anything that seems relevant. And I'll also need you to sign this consent form.'' She removed an envelope from her new black purse and handed it to her client.

Claire read the words on the form. ''I'm really going to be exposed, aren't I?'' Gazing at Zach, she asked, ''Can I look the story over before you turn it in?''

''Reporters never let anybody censor their work.''

Claire rubbed her left hand up and down her right arm. ''I don't know. I really want to do this but it's so scary to think of everything being right out there in print.''

''How 'bout if I let you see just the parts Cass thinks you might have a problem with?''

Cassidy frowned at her husband. *And if I guess wrong, she can be mad at me.*

''Well…'' Claire's delicately arched brows drew together. ''I guess I can live with that.'' She signed the form.

Handing her a business card, Cassidy said, ''Here's the name of another therapist I know. I've already checked and she can see you right away.'' Cassidy looked at her watch. It was getting on toward nine and she knew Claire hadn't been sleeping well. ''We can't cover everything in one session, so let's just get in as much as we can before ten and then quit.''

''Tell me about your courtship,'' Zach said, taking out his notepad. ''Where did you and Max meet?''

''It was the Success in School program that brought us together. That's a tutoring agency for inner city kids. We met at the monthly support meeting. I'd been volunteering for the past year, Max'd just started. About six months ago he sat down next to me, and after the meeting was over, he asked me to lunch.''

''Then what?''

''We started going out. I liked him a lot but I tried to take it slow. I don't have a good track record with men and

I wanted to make sure I wasn't repeating my old pattern."
She looked nervously at Cassidy.

"Did Max pressure you when you tried to slow the relationship down?"

"That was one of the things that made me feel safe. He was always understanding, never tried to control me."

"Did Max have any enemies that you were aware of?"

"No," she shook her head vigorously. "He had all kinds of friends. He was generous and helpful with everybody. People just loved him."

Too good to be true, Cassidy thought, not for the first time. *Nobody's the paragon Max appeared to be.* She gazed through the glass wall at lights on the lake. There were several small dots representing individual boats, plus a long line of attached lights, the windows of a cruise ship, crawling across the surface like a centipede. Above the lake hung a silvery quarter moon.

Cassidy said to Claire, "It's easy to idealize someone you love. But there were a few glitches, and Zach needs to know about them."

Claire swallowed, then got herself a glass of water. "The only thing I'd call a glitch was the money."

"How was money a glitch?"

"There were a few times we'd be at expensive restaurants and he'd discover he didn't have any credit cards on him. And then I'd offer to pay. Cass kept saying it was a red flag but I didn't see it as a problem. He always traveled in style, seemed to have plenty of money." Claire rubbed both hands over her face. "But I was wrong. It's much worse than I ever imagined." Gulping from her glass, she gazed downward and continued in a voice barely above a whisper. "I should have told you at my session today, but I was so upset I couldn't talk about it."

Not unusual for clients to leave out the embarrassing stuff. And if you were in their place, you'd probably do the same.

Claire hesitated, then picked up her story again. "This

is something I found out yesterday when I was helping Max's mother and sister clean out his condo. I figured they were having as bad a time as I was, so I offered to give them a hand.''

Cassidy folded her arms on the glossy white table. ''There was something at his condo?''

''I was going through his desk. Since I'm a financial officer at my company, I thought I ought to handle the paperwork. Well, I opened his bottom drawer and it was crammed with unpaid bills and credit card statements.'' Claire bit her lip. ''I couldn't believe it. He had twenty-eight cards and owed more than a hundred-and-fifty thousand dollars. All but three of the cards were maxed out, and he wasn't even making the minimums on most of them.'' Blinking back tears, she clasped a hand over her mouth. ''Oh Cass, I should've listened to what you said about the red flags. I felt just awful when I found out what a mess he was in with money. Especially considering how much he'd spent on my ring and the honeymoon cruise.''

''What a shock!'' Cassidy reached out to touch Claire's arm.

''None of the expenses was out of the ordinary, just a lot of them—a new computer, clothes from Nordstrum and Bloomies, car maintenance, that sort of thing. But I couldn't find any sign of the twelve thousand for the ring or the ten thousand for the honeymoon. In fact, there wasn't room on any of the cards for either of those things. So I have no idea how he managed to pay for my diamond,'' she held up her left hand with the glittering stone on her third finger, ''or the cruise tickets.''

Zach asked, ''Did you get any sense that he was using drugs or gambling? He could've dropped his paycheck at the casinos and then been forced to charge everything else.''

''I don't think he wasn't doing either of those things— but you never know, you never know. He smoked an occasional joint, but as far as I could tell, that was the extent

of his drug use, and he didn't even buy lottery tickets."
Claire stared out at the lake for a moment, then looked at
Cassidy. "There was something even spookier. We found
dozens of items with sales tags still on them. Shirts, jackets,
underwear. Here he owed all this money and he kept buying
things he didn't even use."

Classic spendaholic.

Zach said, "You never saw any of this before?"

"I think he must've been ashamed of it. He kept all the
unused clothing in his extra bedroom and I didn't go in
there very often."

"How did his mother and sister react?" Cassidy asked.

"They made jokes about it. Said Max was single-
handedly keeping the economy alive."

Zach jotted notes on his pad. "Did Max ever say anything to you about his debts?"

Claire shook her head. "He said the new restaurant was
doing great, that we wouldn't have to worry about money."
She twisted her hands together. "I can't get over the fact
that he had this huge problem and never told me about it."

*I wouldn't imagine that men like Max tell anyone about
their debts—especially not prospective brides.*

"Do you know of anyone he borrowed from?"

"Well, I lent him money a couple of times and once he
paid me back. He said it was a cash flow problem."

Which, of course, she never mentioned to me. "Anybody
else?"

Claire shook her head. "You think he might've been
killed over a bad debt?"

"If it was over money," Cassidy said, "why do it at the
wedding? Think how much easier it'd be to shoot him in
a dark alley or a parking garage. Somebody picked the
wedding for a specific reason and if we could figure out
what that reason was, we'd probably have the motive."

Claire's face paled. "Someone who couldn't stand losing
me. My ex."

Zach tapped his pen against his pad. "Or someone who

couldn't stand losing Max. Claire, what do you know about the women from Max's past?''

"The only woman he ever talked about was his business partner, Susan Freeberg. He said she had the hots for him but she's twenty years older so she couldn't have thought anything would come of it.''

Cassidy pictured the stony-faced woman at the wedding.

Zach said, ''Or someone who really wanted to make you suffer.'' He leveled his eyes at Claire. ''Can you think of anyone who might've done this to hurt you?''

Claire's skin went even paler. She whispered, ''No, she wouldn't do such a thing.''

Cassidy covered Claire's hand. ''You think Erin might've done it?''

''No!'' Claire shook her head. ''She'd never do a thing like that.''

Leaning back in her chair, Cassidy said, ''I think we must be on the right track. A person who couldn't stand losing either Claire or Max. Or a person who wanted to torture Claire. Or—one other possibility—a person who wanted to watch the murder with impunity. It could be a wedding guest who really wanted to see him die.''

Zach gazed at her admiringly. ''That's very good.''

She worked hard to keep the smugness off her face. Then she glanced at Claire, who looked visibly shaken, and her smugness disappeared.

''What's the matter?'' Cassidy asked softly.

''It's so hard to think that one of these people I know—one of our friends—could've killed Max.''

''Yes, it is hard,'' Cassidy said, remembering how terrible she'd felt when someone from her past had threatened Zach. ''Well, I think we've done enough damage for one night. We need to go home and let you get your mind off all this.''

''Before you leave, I've written out the names and numbers of some people you might want to talk to.'' She stood up. ''Let me get them for you.''

Claire left the room, reappearing a moment later with a sheet of paper and a cell phone. Sitting down again, she showed the paper to Cassidy. "The names on top are Max's friends, followed by our immediate families, and then Hank here at the bottom."

"This will certainly help us along." Zach pushed his polished white chair back from the table.

"Here's the person I think you should start with." Claire placed her finger on Julie O'Connell's name.

Julie, sister of Max, astrologer, flower-child, poet. The one who wasn't sure Max and Claire should get married.

"She's a little flaky, and you can't believe everything she says, but she and Max were pretty tight, and if you catch her in the right mood, she could tell you a lot. She always seemed to be hanging around in the background. People talked in front of her as if she wasn't there."

"We'll definitely get in touch with her." Cassidy started to take the paper but Claire hung onto it.

"Let me call her now and tell her you're doing a story on the murder. If she hears it from me, she'll be more likely to co-operate." Claire punched numbers into her cell phone. When Julie answered, Claire made a strong pitch to get the younger woman to agree to answer their questions. After a pause, Claire said in a sharp voice, "Well, I *want* you to talk to them. Don't you think it's important to find Max's killer?"

Cassidy blinked in surprise. It was a tone she'd never heard from Claire before.

Another pause, then Claire continued cajolingly. "Please say you'll talk to them. Zach's being very nice. I'm sure he wouldn't put anything in the paper you wouldn't like."

By the time the conversation was over, Claire had wrested an agreement from her almost sister-in-law.

SIX

TOFU AND VEGGIE BURGERS

A UNIFORMED DOORMAN held the plate glass door for Cassidy and Zach as they stepped out into the chilly night air, a sharp breeze from the lake causing Cassidy to clutch her goosebump-ridden arms across her midsection. *Typical spring day. Too hot in Oak Park, too cold in the city. How does anybody ever know what to wear?*

A taxi stopped at the curb, letting out a gray-haired man in a tuxedo and a much younger woman in a fur coat. Claire's building was located on the inner drive, just west of Lake Shore Drive. The swish of traffic from LSD, four lanes zipping along in both directions, created a constant background hum.

As the Subaru headed home, Zach remarked, "I thought you said Claire was such a sweetheart."

"Nobody can be a sweetheart all the time." *One problem with therapy. People tend to bring their good parts into the office, leave their bad parts outside the door.*

"You said 'glitches' plural. What were the ones Claire didn't want to talk about?"

"There were two. The first was, Max told Claire his new business partner had a thing for him and he wanted Claire to stay away from the restaurant so as not to rock the boat. Essentially, he kept the fact that he was seeing her a semi-secret until they announced the wedding date. Claire did get to know his friends and family but she wasn't allowed to step foot in the restaurant.''

"And she didn't have a problem with that?"

"She bought his story. And for all I know, it's true. Which would certainly put Susan's name high on our suspect list."

"What else?"

"The fact that the whole thing happened so fast. Claire talked about taking it slow, but the truth is, they'd known each other a mere five months when they decided to get married, and then they set the date just a month out."

An elegantly coiffed white-haired woman walking a Greyhound crossed in front of them, the animal so thin Cassidy thought it appeared on the verge of starvation. *Just looking at that emaciated creature makes me want to go search for a convenience store and buy peanut butter cups right now. To make sure food is always at hand.*

"Did you try to stop her from jumping in so fast?"

"I talked about giving it more time but she didn't listen. I was uneasy about the marriage but I tried to convince myself it'd be okay. I didn't see any of these flaws as necessarily fatal. You and I had a lot more going against us than Claire and Max did."

"The money is definitely a fatal flaw."

"Yeah, but I didn't know it was as bad as it was. And even if I had, given how insanely in love Claire was, she probably would have married him anyway." *Just like you married Zach even after his teenaged son appeared and Zach himself was implicated in his old flame's murder. Love really does turn our brains to mush.*

Cassidy rubbed her thumb across her garnet ring. "So let me see if I understand how this credit card gig works. No matter how much Max owed, as long as he paid the minimum balance on each of his cards, he could keep getting new ones?"

"That's pretty much it."

"Why does anybody bother to have a job when we could all just accumulate credit cards?"

"Eventually the system breaks down. People end up owing so much they can't keep up their minimums and then their credit rating tanks. Apparently that'd already started to happen with Max."

"But somehow he came up with money for the ring and the cruise."

"He probably had some source of extra income. And—since he never mentioned it to Claire—I'd have to assume it was illegal. Embezzlement maybe. Or identity theft. Or blackmail."

"But if he had a source of illegal funds, why wouldn't he make his minimum payments?"

"Who knows? Maybe he was a better chef than he was a thief."

CASSIDY, FINISHED WITH her morning petting session but not yet dressed, called Max's sister, Julie, to set up a meeting.

"I've been staying at Mom's place in Hinsdale ever since the shooting," Julie said. "You know, to give her a hand." The younger woman's voice sounded as dreamy as the red-brown eyes Cassidy had gazed into at the wedding. "But I don't think it'd be a good idea for you to come to the house. Wait—I know—we could meet for lunch." Julie suggested a small café in back of a health food store in downtown Hinsdale.

Tofu and veggie burgers. Won't Zach love that?

Can't make Zach the health-food heavy. You don't have any more of a taste for seaweed and soy than he does.

After her shower, Cassidy returned to the bedroom to find Zach on the phone with his editor. Pulling black cotton pants and a magenta top out of the closet, Cassidy listened as Zach pitched the wedding-murder story.

"John gave me a go ahead," Zach said, hanging up the receiver. "He doesn't expect me to solve the murder, but he'd be happy to get an in-depth piece on the victim as well as the events leading up to the shooting."

"I notice you didn't mention I was working with you."

"Unless you insist on a byline, he may never need to know."

She frowned. "So you use the same I-just-won't-mention-it approach with your editor that you do with me."

"I hardly ever do it with you anymore. You've nailed me too many times."

THEY ENTERED A small health food store and threaded their way through narrow aisles to a brightly lit, all-white space at the rear: a counter to the right, a half-dozen mostly empty tables in the center; a blackboard on the wall with a menu on it. Cassidy and Zach parked themselves in plastic chairs at a Formica table.

Staring at the menu, Zach said, "We don't actually have to eat here, do we?"

"I think we probably should."

Fifteen minutes later Julie appeared, her strawberry-blond flyaway hair creating a halo around her pixie face. "Hey!" Joining them at the table, she stared at Cassidy's bruises. "What happened?"

"I fell on the sidewalk," Cassidy lied, not wanting all the sympathy her mugger story evoked. "It doesn't feel half as bad as it looks."

A waiter came to take their orders. Julie recommended the white-bean vegetarian chili with herbal tea and they all picked that.

"We were at Claire's house last night when she called," Cassidy said. "We'd really like for you to talk to us, but we don't want you to do it just because you feel pressured by Claire."

Zach, who didn't care why Julie talked, shot Cassidy an annoyed look.

"Oh, Claire gets a little snappish sometimes but I don't let it bother me. I still consider her my sister even if she isn't married to Max. Claire isn't fully evolved yet but I see her moving toward the next plane.'' She gazed at Cassidy. ''And you're one of her guides.''

Zach said, ''Since you agreed to meet with us, I take it you're willing to talk about Max.''

The waiter brought herbal tea, corn muffins, and steaming bowls of white chili to the table. The fruity scent of the tea filled Cassidy's nostrils. Zach asked the waiter to provide salt and pepper as well.

Resting her elbows on the Formica, Julie wrapped both hands around her cup and held it in front of her mouth. ''I guess I'm okay talking about Max. But Cass has to let me do her chart.''

''What?'' Cassidy felt her spine stiffen. ''I don't understand. What does my chart have to do with Max?''

''I'd just like to do it.'' Julie offered a wispy smile.

''Why me? Why not Zach?''

''Because you and I are connected to Claire and that means we're connected to each other.'' Julie took a sip of tea. ''We both have the mission of moving Claire to the next level.''

Zach shoveled a spoonful of chili into his mouth. ''Amazing. This stuff is delicious, even if it is vegetarian.''

Ignoring Zach's comment, Cassidy asked the astrologist, ''How exactly are you helping Claire evolve?''

''I watch over her. I make sure no harm befalls her.''

Cassidy clenched her teeth, trying to hold back the words that wanted to come out. *Don't say it. Saying these words will not help you build rapport.* ''So, um…if you were watching over her, why didn't you foresee the murder and stop it?''

''It's all part of the mystery, Cass. For some reason we'll never understand, this is what was meant to be.''

The great catchall excuse that allows God to be all powerful, all good, and never take the blame for anything. Religions have gotten great mileage out of this one since the beginning of time.

"So, how did you happen to take on this mission to watch over Claire?"

"It was assigned to me in a chart I did for myself. You see, Claire has this major obstacle to overcome. She has to either play the victim or turn on other people and victimize them."

"She victimizes people?"

"Well, maybe that's a little strong. But she picks on people. She does it to me because she thinks I'm more vulnerable than she is, even though I'm not."

I could buy that. Anybody who's been abused themselves is likely to pass the abuse along to someone else.

Julie waved her spoon in the air. "She needed Max because he was good to her and didn't mistreat her like the other men did. She needs you to get her to see her part in it. And she needs me to help her learn not to pick on people who are weaker than she is."

Except for the airy-fairy language, I could almost agree with her.

Zach said to Julie, "So Cass has to agree to have her chart done before you'll tell us about Max?"

Tilting her head, Julie wrapped a tendril of hair around her finger. "I need to learn more about Cass, and the best way to do it is to cast her chart."

Surprised at the ripple of anxiety in her stomach, Cassidy asked, "What do I have to do?"

"Just tell me the hour, date and place of your birth."

She provided the information.

Julie touched a finger to her lips, then said to Zach, "You threw Cass a surprise fortieth birthday party. You caught her completely off guard and she was so pleased that you did it."

Don't like people knowing things about me I didn't choose to tell them.

"Stop that," Zach said with a smile. "You're disrupting my belief system. Creating cognitive dissonance." Pushing aside his polished bowl, he took out a notepad.

"So," Cassidy said to Julie, "how does this horoscope business work?"

"I'll call when I've finished your chart. But we can start talking about Max now." She paused. "Here's something I think you should know. You saw Garrett—Max's best man—at the wedding, didn't you? The dark-haired handsome guy."

Cassidy nodded.

"Well, Garrett says he moved to Chicago with his daughter a couple of years ago. He's a single parent, like Claire. And Max says he met Garrett shortly after he moved here. And then right away Max got Garrett a job at the Chicago restaurant where he was the chef, and then when Max moved on to the Naperville restaurant, he took Garrett with him. But the part I don't believe is that they didn't know each other before."

And she got that from her charts.

Zach said, "You think they're lying?"

"Well, I'd hate to say that."

"But you don't believe them."

"The reason is, I was in my old bedroom at my mother's house, and I heard Max and Mom talking out in the hall. Max told Mom that she had to be very careful never to tell anybody that he and Garrett used to be roommates at college."

"So, Max and Garrett had a secret, did they?" Zach looked at Julie. "Where did Max go to college?"

"Notre Dame. Dad wanted him to be a lawyer, but he dropped out in his junior year and went to chef school instead."

"And your mother would've known his roommate?"

"She visited Max at college all the time. But I was so busy with my own life I never went to see him."

"You have any idea why Max and Garrett would want to keep this thing quiet?"

Julie curled strands of hair around her finger again. "I

think Garrett wants to keep everything quiet. He wouldn't tell me his birthdate or anything.''

I'm with Garrett. Not wanting unauthorized horoscopes does not a sinister character make.

"What's Garrett's last name?" The lines between the base of Zach's nose and his jaw had deepened, an indication that Garrett had snagged his interest.

"Hillard."

"One other thing that's puzzling," Zach said. "We know Max had some pretty hefty debts, and yet he always seemed able to get his hands on whatever money he wanted, including the money for Claire's ring and the cruise tickets. Do you know of any sources of income he might've had besides his job?"

Julie smiled vaguely. "Max was good to his friends and his friends were good to him."

Speaking in riddles—part of the astrologer job description?

Zach's brows drew together. "Could you elaborate on that?"

"His friends helped him out."

"You mean he borrowed from his friends?" Cassidy asked. *Deadbeats like Max usually don't keep friends very long. They go through them like locusts through a field of wheat.*

Julie crumbled a portion of her muffin into her empty bowl. "He did favors for people. And they showed their appreciation by helping out when he was short."

"You seem a little reticent," Cassidy said softly. "Is this hard for you to talk about?"

"I loved Max a lot. He was always good to me. I mean, almost always."

Except for what? You better not ask. Push too hard and she's likely to shut down on you.

"He talked to me all the time, included me in whatever was going on. Even if he didn't take me seriously, he was always warm and sweet. I didn't like that red-faced cop, so

I didn't tell him much. But I do like you and I think it's possible you might be able to track down the killer. It's just a little embarrassing, trying to explain Max to people who didn't know him.''

Leaning in closer, Cassidy put her hand on Julie's arm. "I wouldn't want to have to explain Zach to anybody either.''

Julie let out a breathy little laugh. Zach crooked up the corners of his mouth at her.

"So," she continued, "could you maybe give an example of the kind of favors Max did?''

"Okay, here's one. This happened in high school. The principal suspected one of Max's buddies of breaking into the school and Max gave the guy an alibi.''

Zach asked, "Was the kid guilty?''

"I don't know. But Max was very loyal to his friends and he might've covered for him even if he was. Anyway, about a month afterward, the friend bought Max a new video game.''

Zach's eyes narrowed. "Look, I believe Max was basically a good guy. And I can understand your not wanting to cast him in a negative light. But is there any possibility he might've blackmailed the kid into buying him the game?''

Drawing her head up straight, Julie sent Zach a withering look. "Max would never do anything like that. His friends meant everything to him.''

"I'm sorry if we've offended you," Cassidy said. "It's just that we don't have a clear enough picture of Max. Do you think your mother might talk to us? I'm sure she'd be able to help us fill in the blanks.''

"She probably would if I asked.'' Julie shook her head. "Mom's not doing so good. What happened at the wedding—well, it was almost too much for her.''

"Is she seeing a therapist?''

"She'd never do that. Mom thinks people should take all their problems to the church. She's always been way deep into Catholicism and it used to bother me that she wouldn't accept my beliefs as equally valid. But now I'm glad she's got her faith. It's all that keeps her going."

Wonder if astrology has the same effect. For all you know, it does.

Julie's gaze drifted to a cat-shaped clock, its tail serving as pendulum, on the wall behind the counter. The astrologer wore numerous beads and rings but no watch. *Guess keeping track of the time is for us less-evolved creatures who live by the clock.*

"Ooops!" Julie said. "I'm late for an appointment." Standing, she smiled down at them. "I'll talk to Mom and give you a call."

"So soon?" Cassidy said in dismay. "I wasn't finished yet." *Need to find out why she said they shouldn't get married.*

"You can ask anything you like when I do the reading."

After she was gone, Zach asked, "Why all the reluctance to let her do your chart?"

Cassidy took a bite out of his untouched muffin. "I don't want to know what's coming. I'd rather be surprised."

"I thought you didn't believe in it."

"I don't. But if she forecasts something negative, I'll start to worry."

The waiter left the bill. Checking it over, Zach said, "I believe they just tell you the good stuff."

"Then I'd get my hopes up and be disappointed. Even though my most mature self doesn't believe in astrology, I have some young parts that are very big on magical thinking." Popping the remainder of Zach's muffin into her mouth, she washed it down with his tea. "Wasn't that spooky how she knew about the birthday party?"

"Lots of husbands throw surprise parties for their wives' fortieth."

"Several of my clients have reported in about their astrological adventures. In every case, the astrologer gained credibility by telling the client something she didn't have any right to know. But the predictions never came true.''

"So there you go." He laid down some bills.

"But how do they come up with things like the birthday party?''

"You're talking to the wrong guy. I'm a nonbeliever, remember?'' They started toward the door. "And so, by the way, are you.''

Most of me is. But I have a few traitorous parts that would love to think that somebody out there has The Answer.

SEVEN

SHOWDOWN AT THE OK CORRAL

ZACH DROPPED CASSIDY OFF at the house, then drove on down to the Post. With no clients until six, she took out the vacuum and applied herself to cleaning her office and waiting room. She pruned the coleus that sat on the wicker table, then sucked up dirt and cat hair from the stained rug.

Zach's right. This old house is almost a lost cause. Office needs new carpeting, paint's peeling in every room, kitchen ought to qualify for disaster relief funds. Only sensible thing is to start fresh in a better neighborhood.

What do you mean, better? Everybody on our block is wonderful. How could any neighborhood be better than this?

Could be farther from Crime City.

She was putting the vacuum in the closet when the front doorbell rang. Opening the door, she saw her wiry little grandmother on the porch, a lopsided Marilyn Monroe wig on her head, a pet carrier in her hand. Cassidy stared at the small wrinkly face, the normally bright eyes looking rheumy, the pug nose a splotchy shade of red.

"Gran, what's wrong? Have you been crying?"

"Not crying, sniffling." With her free hand, she dug a tissue out of the pocket of her khaki pants and blew her nose.

Cassidy's gaze moved to the pet carrier. "What are you up to, anyway?"

"Aren't you going to invite me in for a cold drink or something before you make me tell my sad story?"

"If I let you bring that carrier into my house, will I regret it?"

"Well…" Gran shifted her weight, "you might. But you're gonna have to let me in anyway 'cause you're too kind to slam the door in my face and too curious to send me off without hearing my tale of woe."

Cassidy lowered her brow at her grandmother, who had not a self-pitying bone in her body. "You're setting me up."

"I suppose I am, but it's for a good cause."

Gran settled on the paisley sofa in the living room. In front of the sofa stood a glass coffee table, and across the room, a matching paisley loveseat. Two small blue armchairs sat at a right angle to the sofa. The air in the room was stuffy and swollen with humidity.

As Gran set the carrier on the floor beside her tennis shoes, the box began uttering a series of small mews.

Standing in front of Gran, hands on hips, Cassidy regarded the carrier uneasily. "I don't think I'm going to like this sad story of yours. And Starshine's going to like it even less."

"Why don't we have something to drink first."

Cassidy went into the kitchen, returning a few minutes later with two glasses of iced tea. Placing them on the table, she seated herself in one of the blue armchairs.

"Why take on a kitten when you know you're allergic?"

"I had to, or Lillybeth would've refused to go into the hospital." Gran blinked her puffy eyes and wiped her nose. "Uh, I'm surprised Starshine isn't down here throwing hissy fits."

"You came by during her afternoon nap. If she realized I'd let another cat onto her property, she'd be right here in our faces raising hell." *For all you know, her sensors went off the instant the carrier crossed the threshold and she's already embarked on her revenge campaign. Peeing in the plants, shredding your best dress, depositing hairballs on the comforter.*

Straightening her white-blond hair, Gran said, "Lillybeth called at six this morning. Said she thought she had pneumonia but couldn't go into the hospital 'cause she didn't have anybody to leave Roscoe with." Gran patted the top of the carrier.

"She couldn't find anybody?"

"She's outlived all her family and most of her friends."

"Oh." Cassidy noticed sneaky little feelings of sympathy oozing up inside her. Frowning down at the mewing carrier, she asked, "Why didn't you simply offer to feed Roscoe at Lillybeth's apartment?"

"She wouldn't hear of it. You see, she got him when he was only two weeks old. Bottle fed him 'round the clock. Now he hardly lets her out of his sight. The minute she sits down to watch her soaps, he's right there in her lap. She figured he'd feel abandoned if he got left in an empty apartment."

"So you thought you'd bring him here and we could keep him." Cassidy tried to inject a note of sternness into her voice but she could feel her resistance melting.

Gran sipped from her glass. "I started off with the idea that a few sneezes and a runny nose wouldn't kill me. So I took a handful of antihistamine but then I fell asleep and when I woke up Roscoe'd climbed to the top of my drapes and was all in a panic 'cause he couldn't get down. I had to get out the step ladder to rescue him."

"Oh dear." Cassidy pictured Gran on a wobbly ladder struggling to unhook a Velcro kitten from her drapery.

"I tried to think of somebody else who could take him, but all the cat people I know already have their quota. I even considered your mother but you know how she is."

If any cat dared to shed a single hair in Mom's absurdly clean apartment, she'd have a conniption.

Knowing she had lost, Cassidy said, "Okay, let's see what he looks like."

Gran took a kitten, its fuzzy black fur punctuated by a white stomach and mustache, out of the carrier. Wrapping both hands around his body, she kept his claws contained so he couldn't scratch her. He appeared to be about three months old. The kitten's wide, frightened eyes fastened on Cassidy. He opened his mouth and hissed.

Poor thing's terrified.

"Why don't you let him loose so he can familiarize himself with his surroundings."

Gran released the kitten and he began sniffing his way around the edge of the sofa. Watching Roscoe, Cassidy remembered what it had been like living with Starshine's three terrorist offspring before she found adoptive homes for them. Half the time she'd been crazy about the kittens; the other half she'd been frantic over their housewrecking ways.

Roscoe sprinted across the room, climbed to the top of the loveseat, and made a huge leap onto a pink mouse Starshine had left in the middle of the room. Grabbing it with all four paws, he wrestled it to death.

He's so adorable. She wondered if she ought to go through the motions of consulting Zach but decided it wasn't necessary. He'd been every bit as sappy about the kittens as she was.

"Okay," Cassidy said with a sigh. "We'll take him. Any idea how long Lillybeth'll be in the hospital?"

"I'll be visiting her tonight. Maybe I'll find out something then." Gran reached over to pat Cassidy's leg. "I sure do appreciate you bailing me out like this."

"You've done so much for me, how could I not?" *Should've said yes the minute I spotted Gran's drippy nose.* "The only reason I hesitated is that Starshine has consistently failed her sharing lessons."

As if on cue, the calico came thumping downstairs and into the living room. The kitten instantly let go of its toy, locked eyes with Starshine, and went into a low crouch. Starshine raised the fur along her spine, lashed her tail, and growled. Taking tiny steps, she slowly approached the intruder. Roscoe hissed. Starshine sat tall and took a swipe at him. The kitten stood on all fours, puffed himself up, arched his back, and hissed again. Starshine turned abruptly and ran upstairs. Roscoe made a leap in the calico's direction, then came high-stepping on long thin legs back toward Gran.

Oh oh, this is not the way it's supposed to go. Roscoe should've shown his belly and let Starshine win. Kept the hierarchy intact. Now we've got the showdown at the OK Corral. Or worse, Starshine outgunned on her own turf. Cassidy felt a sudden pang, wondering if the calico would ever forgive her.

"Maybe I better get out of here before you change your mind," Gran said, holding a hand out to Roscoe, who rubbed his fluffy black head against it. "But you know, I've purely fallen in love with the little devil. If I didn't have these allergies to protect me, I'd probably turn into one of those weird old ladies with a houseful of cats."

As Gran got to her feet, Cassidy reached for her arm. "Before you go, there's something I want to tell you about."

"Does that mean we get to dish some dirt?" Gran settled back on the sofa, a sparkle coming into her watery eyes.

"Well, not exactly." Cassidy paused. "Zach wants to move. Because of the mugging and also because the house needs so much work." Cassidy's gaze followed Roscoe. Having climbed to the top of the loveseat again, he threw himself off in another death-defying Evel-Knievel leap.

"That's good news, isn't it?" Gran studied Cassidy's face, apparently trying to ascertain whether she was supposed to be for or against the idea. "I mean, it seems like it'd be a big improvement to live in a house that's all spiffied up instead of a wreck like this."

Cassidy felt hurt at hearing her beloved house referred to as a wreck, even though she'd used the same word herself many times.

"What's the matter?" Gran asked. "You don't look so happy about it."

"I don't know what I want. Sometimes I think I'd like a nice safe neighborhood where I don't have to worry about who might be lurking in the alley. Other times, I can't bear the thought of leaving my house."

"But Zach wouldn't like it if you made him stay, would he?"

"That's the dilemma."

Roscoe darted over to Gran's feet and began climbing her pantsleg. Gran scooped him up and held him in her lap, where he tucked himself in and purred rambunctiously.

Cassidy curled her fingers beneath his chin. "You and Grandpa had a good marriage, didn't you?"

"We got along most of the time, which is about the best you can hope for."

"How did you handle it when you wanted opposite things?"

"Well, William was pretty good about letting me have my way. But then I'd have to give in sometimes so he didn't think I was ruling the roost. Even though, if you came right down to it, I was. But why ask me? We just had ourselves an old-fashioned marriage. You're the expert on how things work today."

"Yeah, I'm the expert all right," Cassidy said miserably. "I know that people have to compromise and if the same person wins too often, the marriage is headed for trouble." *Which means—this time it ought to be Zach's turn.* Picturing herself atop a load of furniture in the back of a pickup, she felt her stomach knot.

"So then you know what you should do?"

"I guess."

After Gran left, Cassidy carried the litter box, which Gran had delivered along with the kitten, upstairs, the kitten bouncing along beside her. *This child has a bad case of separation anxiety.* She deposited the box in the den, the room to the left of Zach's office. In former incarnations, it had been a junk room, a kitten nursery, and a crash pad for Bryce. Teaching himself carpentry, Zach had rehabbed it into a recreation center, with a big-screen TV, two recliners, and floor-to-ceiling bookshelves.

She sat in her desk chair to watch the newest temporary addition to their family. *How on earth are you ever going to appease Starshine and keep this little guy happy at the same time? If you shut Roscoe in the den, he'll be beside himself. If you don't, Starshine'll hate you.*

The kitten raced over and tried to climb Cassidy's legs, bare beneath the cuffs of her grape-colored shorts. Carrying him to the bed for a petting session, she said, "I don't need a bloody road map on my legs to go with the sullen palette of colors on my face."

Minutes later Starshine jumped onto the bed. Her eyes went first to the kitten, then to Cassidy's face. Ears twisting backward, the calico turned away in disgust.

Now you've done it. Who knows what it'll take to win her back after a betrayal like this.

Starshine fled and Cassidy went after her. Heading into the kitchen, she glimpsed the calico scooting down the basement stairs. As Cassidy followed, she saw Starshine slip through the cat flap in the basement window and disappear.

Staring at the calico's exit point, Cassidy wondered if there was any risk of Roscoe leaving through the cat door. *Not hardly. You had to shove Starshine through at least ten times before she was willing to try it on her own. Cats don't like to push things with their heads.*

EIGHT

WHY ME?

WITHIN THE NEXT half hour, Cassidy received two calls: the first from her six o'clock client, who rescheduled for the following week; the second from Julie, who reported that her mother would be available to see Cassidy and Zach anytime up until seven, when her TV programs began. Cassidy considered the client cancellation a stroke of luck, since it freed her up to visit Max's mother.

Amidst all the body-blows and kicks-in-the-pants that fate delivers, every now and then she blows you a kiss.

Cassidy called Zach to make sure he'd be home in time to get to Irene's house by six. She also informed him that they'd taken temporary custody of Roscoe and Starshine had left home in protest.

"A kitten? One we don't have to keep forever?" He sounded pleased. "That's sort of like being grandparents, isn't it? We can enjoy the kid for a while, then send him home to mother."

"The only downside is, we may never find our way back into Starshine's good graces."

"Her urge to eat beats out her urge to sulk every time."

When Zach arrived, Cassidy shut Roscoe in the den in hopes that Starshine would return if the kitten did not have free run of the house. As she headed down the stairs, she heard plaintive cries from above.

CASSIDY AND ZACH spent the next hour crawling through rush hour traffic out to Hinsdale, a community about fifteen miles southwest of Oak Park. The housing stock was similar to the village's, although the meandering streets and open spaces gave it more of a suburban feel.

Should be glad Zach's talking west Oak Park instead of someplace like Hinsdale. Should be thankful and agree to move simply because it's what he wants. Look at all he's given up for you—his city condo, his habitation of bars, his whole sleazy lifestyle. Should be willing to forgo a small thing like your house just to even the score.

Zach parked in front of a tricolor Victorian, the yard overflowing with flowering plants. As they climbed the steps to the spacious front porch, Cassidy admired the flower boxes, vividly abloom, lined up along the wide plank railing.

The door was opened by a woman Cassidy recognized from the wedding, thin, in her fifties, with a smooth cap of iron gray hair above a weathered face. Garbed in a freshly pressed shirt and pants, she stood with her shoulders squared, her back as straight as a signpost.

"Your yard's beautiful," Cassidy said. "Especially the flower boxes."

The woman's thin features tightened. "Julie's been watering them. She thinks it cheers me up, but it doesn't. I wish she'd just let them die."

She wants her plants to die? Well, what do you expect? She just lost her son.

"Irene O'Connell?" Zach asked.

The woman nodded, staring at Cassidy's bruised face. Cassidy quickly told her the story about her fall on the sidewalk.

Zach introduced himself and Cassidy, then said, "I believe you told Julie you'd be willing to talk to us."

Irene gazed at Zach, her eyes the same shade of blue as Max's but without the warmth. "I told Julie I would, but now I'm not so sure. What do you plan to say about Max in this article of yours?''

''All I can do is quote other people.''

''Nobody'd have anything but good to say about him, so I guess there's no harm.'' She held the door wide. ''Please come in. I hope you won't mind talking in the kitchen. I'm in the middle of making soup.''

They followed her through a corridor, eighteenth century paintings on the wall, small antique tables beneath the art. Everything perfectly aligned. Not a speck of dust. *The good Catholic mother, doesn't miss a beat, even though her son is dead.*

The aroma of simmering beef greeted them as they came into the kitchen, a large square room, lots of natural light, a pot cooking on the stove, a butcher block island in front of the sink. Atop the island, a couple of knives, piles of peeled vegetables, and a half-empty wine bottle, a nearly full glass standing beside it.

''Smells wonderful,'' Zach remarked. ''I love homemade soup.''

''This was Max's favorite. Julie's a vegetarian. She won't eat it.'' Irene chopped carrots. ''There's no reason to be cooking at all. But I have to do something, and making soup was all I could think of.''

Irene drank a portion of her wine.

Not offering us any. Some part of her rebelling against Miss Manners' rules.

Pointing her knife at Zach, Irene said, ''Before you start with your questions, I have one for you. Why did this happen? All my life I've tried to do the right thing, and here I am with my beautiful son taken away from me. What's the sense in that?''

Zach rested his hands on his belt. ''That's a question for your priest.''

''My priest tells me God works in mysterious ways. Julie tells me it's because of the planets.'' Irene cut a potato into small cubes. ''Sometimes I think it's my fault. I didn't do

ight by my kids, either one of them. Didn't insist they go
o mass every Sunday. Or check up on how often they made
onfession. If I'd brought them up better, maybe Julie'd
ave a husband and children by now. And Max wouldn't
ave wanted to marry a divorced woman with a crazy ex.''

*As much as Catholic guilt is a boon to therapy, I still
ate to see people concoct ridiculous reasons to beat them-
elves up.*

Oh, and you've never done it?

''You don't really think you caused any of this, do
ou?''

''Sometimes. But then I start thinking it's the ex-
usband's fault. What's the matter with the police? Why
on't they arrest him?'' Grabbing a parsnip, Irene brought
he knife down hard, splitting it in two.

Zach took out his pad. ''I realize the odds are that the
x is behind it, but I still need to cover all the bases. Do
ou know of anyone else who might've wished Max
arm?''

''I don't see how you can even ask such a question. If
ou'd done your homework, you'd know that everybody
oved him.'' She lifted the lid of the pot, adjusted the flame,
nen returned to her post behind the island. Raising her
lass, she took a long swallow.

Cassidy moved a half step back from the island. ''Sev-
ral people have told us that Max was generous and kind
nd always good to his friends.''

Irene's gaze softened. ''That's exactly how he was.''

''But even the best-loved people have an occasional dis-
greement.''

''Not Max.'' Irene scooped the chopped vegetables into
colander and added them to the pot. ''Well, there was a
ttle friction between him and his former boss, Nicky An-
rews. But Nicky was completely out of line and he came
o see it himself soon enough.'' She began cutting up a
arge stalk of celery.

Nicky Andrews. Oh yeah, the glad-handing guy with the long white ponytail.

Zach jotted a note. "There was some kind of problem between Max and Andrews?"

"Max worked for Nicky in Chicago before he got this great opportunity to open his own place in Naperville. Nicky didn't want to let Max go, but of course he had no right to try and hold onto him. So Nicky was irritated for a while, but he got over it. By the time the wedding rolled around, they were back to being friends again."

Zach said, "There's one other thing, and that's Garrett Hillard."

Irene fumbled with the bottle, topping off her glass.

Cassidy said, "Julie seems to think Garrett and Max were roommates at college."

Irene met Cassidy's gaze, an angry light showing in the older woman's eyes. "Julie means well but you can't always believe what she says."

"You think she's lying?"

Putting the knife down, Irene straightened her shoulders and looked off into space. "Did you know Julie was adopted? She was almost five when she came to live with us, and even though we tried our best to bring her into the family, I don't think she ever felt like she quite belonged. Almost from the beginning she made up stories. The psychologist said it was her way of getting attention, of making herself feel special. Unfortunately, she never outgrew it." Irene picked up the knife again. "Now, if you're finished, you can see yourselves out."

ZACH DROVE NORTH on Route 83, a four-lane highway that passed through a stretch resembling an artificial canyon, the walls made of concrete sound breakers that rose about eight feet high on both sides of the road.

"So what do you think?" he asked. "Is Irene lying about Garrett?"

"That would be my guess."

"Tomorrow I'll call the registrar at Notre Dame and see if they had a Garrett Hillard and a Max O'Connell enrolled at the same time."

Leaving the concrete walls behind, they moved into an area made up of wide open spaces, a few huge mansions standing tall on the rolling green land.

Cassidy gazed at Zach, who appeared as calm as ever. *Things never get to him the way they get to you.* Seeing the rawness of Irene's grief and anger had made her feel all shivery inside. In the space of a breath, with no warning, Irene's life got blown apart.

"You know that ubiquitous, 'why me' question? What kind of answer do you come up with in the privacy of your own mind?"

"I never bother with questions that don't have answers."

"Why me...I hear it from clients all the time. Why do bad things happen to good people?"

"Beats me."

"I'm sure there are times when it's entirely random. Shit happens and it's nobody's fault. And there also are times when people simply bring it on themselves. They play with a loaded gun and end up dead. But most of the time, I think it's somewhere in the middle—some combination of bad judgment and bad luck. We influence things. We play a part in what happens to us." She stared at the far-flung mansions whizzing by. "If we ever get down to the truth of it, I'll bet it turns out that Max contributed to his death in some way."

WHEN THEY RETURNED to the house, Starshine met them at the door, jumped onto the counter next to her bowl, and said *mwat.* Cassidy dished up food, then waited to see what kind of mood the calico would be in after she'd filled her tummy. Zach went directly up to the bedroom.

Starshine gobbled most of her food, leaving just enough to form a crust at the bottom of her bowl, then washed her face and dashed upstairs, with Cassidy trailing behind. Ignoring the constant mewing from the den, the calico made straight for Zach's lap. Cassidy sat in her chair a few feet away, aware of a small stab of rejection. The calico rubbed her head against Zach's arm, purred loudly, then looked straight at Cassidy, her cold yellow eyes telegraphing an I-don't-need-you-anymore message.

"Looks like we have a love triangle on our hands," Zach said. "She's punishing you by throwing herself at me."

"Couldn't you at least take my side?" Cassidy asked in a cranky voice.

"What, and miss my chance to have catly love heaped upon me? Oh well, I really do have other things to do." He dumped Starshine on the floor. "Since it's only seven-thirty, there should be time to catch up with either Garrett or Nicky later tonight." He took out Claire's list of phone numbers. "The one who really intrigues me is Garrett. If it's true that he and Max had some reason for keeping their prior connection a secret, I want to know what it is."

"Doesn't seem likely he'd lay it out to a reporter."

"No, but the first step is to nail down the version he concocted for public consumption, then see where we can tear holes in it."

As Zach dialed on the cordless, Cassidy listened in on the desk phone, an image forming in her mind of the best man's darkly brooding face. When Hillard picked up, Zach explained that he was working on a story about the shooting. "I'm talking to people who were close to Max, trying to get as much background as possible."

"We don't need any more press coverage. It'll stir things up. All I want is to put this tragedy behind me."

"Both Claire and Max's mother are in favor of doing the story. I think they see it as part of the healing process."

Healing process? Zach never uses jargony phrases like that. Must've nearly gagged him getting it out.

"Well, don't expect me to help you with your story," Hillard asserted. "It's too ghoulish for my taste." The phone clicked down.

Zach swiveled in Cassidy's direction. "That was a bad move. Garrett obviously doesn't know how to handle the press. You want to avoid negative publicity, you answer questions head on and create an appearance of openness. That gets reporters off your case. The 'no comment' approach only eggs us on."

"So how do we proceed?"

"Let's sic Claire on him. I'll call Nicky first to see if he's inclined to pull the same shit, then you call Claire and have her explain to Garrett that if he refuses to talk to us, we'll question everybody in town who knows anything about him, including his babysitter."

Cassidy got a bad taste in her mouth. "That sounds really awful, you know? Shouldn't Garrett have the right not to talk to the press without being threatened?"

"We have good reason to think that something was going on between Max and Garrett. Something sufficiently dicey they felt a need to cover it up. Are you willing to just forget about it?"

Cassidy moved her head from side to side. *Garrett's right to privacy or your right to question him. Which is more important?* Knowing that she was not making the righteous choice, she said, "Okay, I'll call Claire."

Leaning back in his chair, Zach laced his hands behind his neck. "I told you before, you have too many scruples to be an investigator. You ought to just back off and leave it to me."

"I said I'd call Claire."

Zach phoned Nicky, who suggested they meet at Kincaid's around nine o'clock, after the dinner crowd had thinned out. Then Cassidy talked to Claire, who agreed to do her best to twist Hillard's arm.

NINE

COGNAC AND A TOUCHY FEELY GUY

AS ZACH SLID DOWN the ramp onto the Eisenhower, Cassidy remarked, "If I wanted to put out a contract on someone, I wouldn't have the slightest idea how to locate a hitman."

"The only safe way is through a mob connection."

"I wouldn't know how to locate a mobster, either."

"You have an amazing talent for tracking down killers, but murder's not your forté. You wouldn't be any good at it."

"But you would?"

"Oh, I expect I could arrange a murder if I wanted to, but I'd never have any reason. I'm not doing anything illegal. You, Bryce, and Gran are the only people I really care about. And if anybody seriously pisses me off, I just walk away."

The trick to not being murderous. Make sure nothing matters very much.

But Zach's just fooling himself—things do matter. His job. The people he mentioned. Most of all me. Anybody did serious damage to me, Zach just might take him out.

He handed the Subaru over to the valet parker in front of Kincaid's, then led Cassidy into the restaurant, an old factory building transformed into a brightly lit, understated dining room. Basement-level, with exposed brick walls, square posts holding up the beamed ceiling, and painted pipes running overhead. The large open space filled with tables, only two of which were occupied.

They started down the half flight of stairs, Nicky, standing at the bar that ran along one side of the room, waved them over. He looked exactly as she remembered him. Wide-shouldered body, youthful jovial face, white ponytail hanging halfway down his back.

Giving them a broad smile, he said, "Well, Zach, and uh...."

After supplying her name, Cassidy told him about the fall on the sidewalk.

Nicky slapped Zach on the shoulder, then reached for Cassidy's hand, covering it with both of his own.

A real touchy-feely guy. But not necessarily sensitive. More like he wants to grab your attention and hold it than he wants to get to know you.

The restaurant owner picked up his snifter from the bar. "I'm having cognac. What about about you?"

"Sure, we'll have that," Zach replied without consulting her.

"Yeah baby!" Nicky gave a thumbs-up gesture. Instructing the bartender to pour two more and make them generous, he waited until they had their drinks, then led them to a small table surrounded by easy chairs. After they were seated, Nicky wrapped a beefy hand around his jaw and said to Zach, "So you're writing about the murder."

"Not just the murder. The life and death of Max O'Connell."

Nicky looked from one to the other. "And the two of you are working on this together?"

"Yeah, we're collaborating."

Nicky shook his head, obviously not understanding why a reporter would bring his wife along on interviews.

The reporter is including his wife because his wife refuses to stay in her therapy office where she belongs.

"Amazing. You two can actually work together and stay married?"

"So far we've managed to pull it off."

"Good luck to you. I couldn't stay married to either of my ex-wives, even when we left each other strictly alone. But then they were both models and you know how models are—they never stay put very long."

If he knows models don't stay put, why keep marrying them?

Nicky sipped his brandy. "Before we get into it about Max, what do the cops think happened to that girl from Le Barre?"

"Either fell into the lake or somebody killed her."

"Gives me the willies, you know? Things always happen in threes. I was at Le Barre when the girl disappeared, then I was at the wedding when Max got shot. So now I keep thinking, what next? When's the other shoe gonna drop?"

Zach took a large swallow, set the snifter on the table, and folded his hands across his chest. "Le Barre's right across the street, isn't it?"

"Yeah, it's a funny thing. We got our own bar right here, but after closing, we all troop across the street and spend our money over there. Most nights after eleven you'll find a bunch of us bending our elbows under the competition's roof."

People who work in drinking establishments must rate high on the liver-transplant scale.

"So," Zach said, "we heard you were pissed at Max for jumping ship."

"Damn straight I was," Nicky said in an amiable tone. "The little prick messed me over good. First he tried to hide the fact that he'd set up a partnership with Susan Free-berg. Well, of course I got wind of that. But then, when I confronted him, he said the rehabbing of the Naperville building was going real slow and he begged me to let him stay on here another six months. I was stupid enough to agree, and then a few weeks later he ups and quits without notice. So there I was with no chef in my kitchen just because I tried to give the kid a break."

Sounds to me like a major-league dirty trick. For alpha-male Nicky to just blow it off would be almost like Nicole's family welcoming O.J. back into the clan.

"You're not still mad?" Cassidy asked.

"Aaaw." Nicky shrugged his large shoulders. "Who can hold a grudge against Maxie?" He leaned forward to check Zach's drink. "Looks like you're getting empty there, dude." Twisting his head toward the bartender, he yelled, "Hey, Dave."

The guy behind the bar poured more cognac for the men. Putting a hand over her glass, Cassidy scowled at Zach's newly filled snifter. *This stuff's too strong for guzzling.*

"So," she said to Nicky, "why couldn't you hold a grudge against Max?"

Nicky shrugged again. "Maxie couldn't stand to have anybody pissed at him for very long. He just kept coming back like a little puppy, wagging his tail and slobbering all over you, till you couldn't hold out any longer."

Zach said, "Seems like Maxie spent a good deal more than he earned. Any idea where the money came from?"

"He hit up the staff fairly often. Usually small potatoes—fifty bucks here, twenty there. He was such a nice guy, people didn't have the heart to turn him down."

Such a nice guy? Except he jerked his boss around? So what does nice guy mean in the restaurant biz?

"What about you?" Cassidy asked. "Did you lend him money?"

"Hey! Do I look like a bank?" Nicky started punching his right fist into his left hand. "Maxie may've put something over on me when he quit, but I'm not so stupid as to hand out money to my employees."

Zach said, "We heard he did favors for people and they gave him money in return."

"Yeah, he'd do anything for his friends," Nicky said in a cynical tone. "You need a ride to the airport at three A.M.? You want somebody to watch your kid for a couple of hours? Maxie's your man."

"You know of anyone with a grievance against him?"

"Nah, he had a knack for getting along with people. Look at me. He managed to worm his way back into my good graces even though by all rights I never shoulda talked to the little prick again." He swallowed cognac, stared into space a moment. "Well, there was Luke. That happened so long ago I almost forgot about it." Nicky jerked his head toward a waiter taking dessert to a couple in the far corner. "About a year ago they had a falling out. Max and Luke were real tight for a while. Nobody could figure it out since Luke's a lot younger and doesn't have any money, but for some reason, Max started hanging with him. It lasted, oh, maybe three months, then all of a sudden Luke got a hair up his ass, didn't want anything to do with Max. Never did say why. Whatever it was, we weren't able to pry anything out of Maxie either. Which was pretty surprising, considering Max was never one to keep things to himself."

"You think we could talk to Luke?"

"Fine with me, but don't expect him to tell you anything."

Nicky intercepted Luke on his way back to the kitchen and brought him over to their table. He was slender, with well-groomed white-blond hair, startlingly dark eyebrows that rose like little tents above his eyes, and a neatly trimmed goatee.

"This is Zach Moran, reporter for the Post," Nicky said. "And his wife, Cassidy."

They stood to shake hands with the waiter, who looked to be in his early twenties. He didn't appear to notice the bruises on her face.

"I want you to sit down with these guys and answer all their questions. Just make sure you don't say anything that'd reflect badly on anyone here. Especially me. And don't worry about that last table. I'll finish up."

Now here's a guy who understands perfectly how to handle the press.

Bribe them with brandy, talk freely, give an appearance of transparency. Does it so well it almost makes me not trust him.

Zach said to Luke, "Let's go over to Le Barre. I'll buy you a drink."

"What? You're gonna go next door and pay for drinks when I been feeding you free booze here?"

"It'll be easier for Luke to relax away from the job."

And out from under the watchful eye of his boss.

Zach emptied his snifter. "Thanks for the drinks."

"Yeah baby!" Nicky slapped him on the back. "You be sure and come back soon for dinner."

The atmosphere at Le Barre was entirely different from the spare, muted ambiance of the restaurant across the street. Le Barre was dim and raucous, the smell of smoke and beer heavy in the air. Threading their way through the crowd were waitresses in tee shirts that clung to their chests like a second skin, leaving nothing to the imagination.

Zach found an empty table and the three of them sat around it. Atop the table were two beer bottles, a heaping ashtray, and a cocktail napkin scribbled with illegible notes. A waitress with tightly contained breasts the size of grapefruit whisked the table clean.

That bra looks about as much fun as a medieval torture device. Thank God therapists are expected to be asexual and Zach prefers a natural look to Wonderbras.

The waitress asked for their orders.

Zach requested two bourbons, which Cassidy quickly amended to a bourbon and a cabernet. Luke ordered a Sam Adams.

Zach folded his arms on the table. "I'm trying to get a fix on Max. I plan to do a piece on what kind of guy he was—how he might've antagonized someone enough to get himself shot."

Hunching his shoulders and keeping his eyes lowered,

Luke rubbed his index finger against his thumb. "I don't have anything to say."

The waitress brought their drinks. Watching Luke take a swig from his beer, then settle in with both elbows on the table, the bottle dangling from one hand, Cassidy was aware of an unusual degree of fluidity in his movements. *Bet he's dynamite on the dance floor.*

"We know you and Max were on the outs," Zach said. "How 'bout if we do the interview on background. That means anything you say'll be kept strictly confidential."

Luke shook his head. "I really don't want to discuss it."

If I had him in my office, I could say, "What about discussing Max would be a problem for you?" But that question doesn't fit with bar talk.

"If you don't want to comment on Max, how 'bout filling us in on Andrews? What's he like to work for? How well does he get along with the staff?"

Luke concentrated on tearing the label off the Sam Adams' bottle. "Nicky's all right. Better than most. Sara's kid was sick last week and he let her take paid time off."

"Yeah, but there's a downside to everybody. What is it with Andrews?"

"Nicky likes to be in control. But then he's the boss, so why shouldn't he be?"

Cassidy asked, "What happens when he's not in control?"

"We had a waiter who was very good with the customers, but he wouldn't push drinks the way Nicky wanted him to, and that guy was outta there, like right now."

The creases between the base of Zach's nose and his jaw deepened. "But Andrews was willing to forgive and forget where Max was concerned?"

Luke raised his eyes briefly. "Yeah, that came as a big surprise. After the way Max ripped Nicky off, I'd've expected Nicky to drop him completely. The two of them even got into a fistfight right here at Le Barre. 'Course they were both a little polluted at the time."

"How exactly did Max rip Nicky off?"

"He promised the boss he wouldn't leave for at least six months, then he wangled a large cash advance, and as soon as he had the money in his hands, he was gone."

Well, and Nicky said he didn't give money to Max. So why didn't he tell us the whole story? Because he wants us to think the fight'd blown over when it hadn't? Could Nicky've been pissed enough to want Max permanently gone?

Zach asked, "Is there anything more you can tell us about the problem between your boss and Max?"

"That's all I know."

Zach swallowed the last of his bourbon. "Well, it's about time for us to take off. What about you? You going to hang around a while?"

"Not me. This place gives me the creeps. I haven't been back since the night that girl disappeared."

"You were here that night?"

"Yeah," Luke said in a defensive tone, "but I didn't have anything to do with her."

Zach handed the claim ticket to the car parker, who dashed off to retrieve the Subaru. To Cassidy he said, "Did you notice that Luke's gay?"

"Gay? What makes you say so?"

"The fact that he's a waiter. The way he moves." Zach's eyes narrowed. "Remember Nicky saying nobody could figure out why Max was hanging around this young guy who didn't even have money? If Max was gay himself, that would explain it."

The Subaru pulled up to the curb. The valet hopped out and Zach handed him a bill.

"Okay," Zach said, "I know the drill. You're going to insist on driving because you think I've had too much to drink, even though I think I'm fine." He walked around to the driver's side and opened the door for her.

Facing him over the car door, she said, "Actually, I think

you're fine too.'' She knew Zach could put away large quantities of alcohol without so much as a slur. ''However, I have no idea what number you might blow on a breath-alyzer.'' Sliding behind the wheel, she adjusted the seat for her shorter legs.

Zach got in on the passenger side. ''That's okay. I don't mind you driving.'' As she pulled out onto Clark Street, he continued. ''So what did Claire have to say about their sex life? Was Max enthusiastic about doing it with women?''

''She didn't talk about it much. Which I took to mean it was okay.'' Cassidy stopped behind a Lexus at a light. ''But why would anybody who lives in Chicago and works in the restaurant business want to stay in the closet, much less get married?''

''Maybe Max couldn't face his Catholic mother. Or maybe he wanted to get his hands on Claire's six figure income.''

''I suppose it's possible. But I don't see how it leads to any kind of motive for murder.''

They drove several blocks in silence, then Cassidy said, ''I keep thinking about that poor girl who disappeared. Were either Nicky or Luke suspects?''

''After we bumped into Andrews at the wedding, I went back and looked over my notes. The police ended up with about ten people who couldn't verify their whereabouts after the girl was last seen. I know Nicky wasn't one of them and I don't recall seeing Luke's name either.''

''I don't suppose Max was in Le Barre that night?''

''Not likely. The cops did their best to reconstruct the list of people who were present and Max's name wasn't on it. Of course it's always possible he was there and no one saw him.''

TEN

RUNNING AWAY FROM HOME

THEY WENT IN THE back door and headed toward the stairs at the front of the house, the sound of nonstop cat cries floating down from the den where they'd left Roscoe. *Does he have some sort of computerized chip that makes him into a perpetual mewing machine? Or does he rest up while we're gone, then start pumping out his lonesome kitty blues the minute we walk in the door?*

Coming into the bedroom, Cassidy saw Starshine curled up on the waterbed. *Well, good. She's willing to coexist with the cry-baby kitten as long as we keep him locked up.* Spotting Zach, the calico jumped down and began rubbing against his ankles. When he sat in his chair, she instantly commandeered his lap.

"Nobody's better at withholding and punishment than Starshine," Cassidy said.

"Not exactly subtle, is she?" Zach nodded toward the blinking light on Cassidy's desk. "We've got a message."

Garrett's voice, sounding annoyed, came from the answering machine. "Claire convinced me I'd be better off giving you the straight dope myself instead of letting you gather misinformation from other people. Tomorrow's Institute Day at my daughter's school so I'll be home. Give me a call in the morning and we can set up a time."

"Well good," Zach said. "One more person we can

check off the list.'' He scratched behind Starshine's ears as she gazed adoringly into his face.

Glowering at the two of them, Cassidy said, ''I'd better go check on Roscoe.''

She crossed the hall, carefully opened the door, and cradled the kitten in her arms. Climbing her chest, he nestled against her neck and purred in her ear. She started toward the bedroom. *I'll show Starshine. Two can play the same game.*

You shouldn't be lowering yourself to Starshine's spiteful ways.

Yes, but I can't let her think she's won.

Cassidy carried Roscoe into the bedroom. Starshine growled, holding her ground on Zach's lap for about thirty seconds, then raced off downstairs. Cassidy sat in her chair. ''So now we're faced with a dilemma. Which cat gets to sleep with us tonight?''

''If Starshine gets deposed from her place on the waterbed, she'll take it as a major insult.''

Removing Roscoe from her shoulder, Cassidy settled him in her lap.

''You want to lock this poor bereft kitten in the den and let him cry all night just so Starshine doesn't get her feelings hurt?'' *Considering how gleeful she is about trampling on mine, I think I could stand to see her suffer a little.*

''If we let Roscoe stay with us, we'll have to shut Starshine in the basement or she'll be up here howling outside the door as soon the light goes off.''

Cassidy gave him a tight smile. ''I think you should be the one to lock her up. So we can share the bad guy role. That way I won't have to hate you for taking her away from me.''

Zach reached over to slide his forefinger down Roscoe's back. ''If I have to choose between the two females in my life, I'd rather stay on the good side of the one I have sex with than the one that climbs on my lap and purrs.'' He eaded downstairs to impose the overnight lock-up on Starhine.

Later, after Cassidy and Zach were in bed, Roscoe curled p against the back of her neck. *This cat likes necks so uch, I wonder if he's part vampire. And if he is, will I ake up with bite marks and a strange thirst for blood?*

At three A.M. she felt something pulling at her hair, then eedlelike claws pricking her arm. Rising on one elbow, he grabbed the kitten and moved him to the foot of the ed. He came prancing back and jumped on her face.

As dippy as you are about cats, you're not going to turn ourself into a sleep-deprived zombie just to keep this one appy.

Depositing the kitten in the den, she tuned out his cries nd returned to bed.

Picking Roscoe over Starshine was definitely a bad call.

STARSHINE DIDN'T show for breakfast.'' Zach carried two ugs of coffee into the bedroom, handing the purple cat ug to Cassidy, who was sitting up in bed trying to ignore ie woebegone cries from the den.

Plunking into his desk chair, he added, "She could be lking in the basement, but considering how much she)esn't like to miss a meal, it's more likely she took off rough the cat door and hasn't come home yet."

"Oh shit." Cassidy felt a pang of guilt. "I shouldn't ave sent her away just because I wanted to get even."

"Is that why we did it? I thought it was because we were eling sorry for Roscoe."

Cassidy sucked in her bottom lip. "You think we should) looking for her?"

"I think we should assume she'll be back on her own henever she gets hungry enough." Swiveling toward his :sk, he unfolded the newspaper.

Half an hour later the phone rang and Cassidy picked up her desk.

"This is Darnella Roberts." Darnella, who lived on Cassidy's block, had saved her from feline overpopulation by adopting two of Starshine's kittens.

"Good to hear from you, Darnella. How you doing?"

"Fine except for having an extra mouth to feed. My husband opened the door to get the paper this morning, and there was the mother of our two monsters sitting on the porch, pretty as you please."

"Oh, I'm so glad you found her."

"Your calico marched straight into our house, located the cat food, and chowed down. But the greeting she got from her two grown children didn't seem to please her at all. Actually, I don't believe they recognized each other. My cats started hissing and growling, and your cat scurried back to the door and said she was ready to leave. But I figured she'd gone AWOL and it'd be a good idea to report her whereabouts to her official keeper."

"Thanks for letting me know. I'll be right down to get her."

That's how she ended up with me. She appeared on my doorstep, walked into my house, and took over. Now it appears she's decided—if we insist on keeping Roscoe—she'll just go find herself a new family. One where she doesn't have to share.

Hope Lillybeth recovers soon.

CASSIDY HAD a second cup of coffee with Darnella, then scooped up a docile Starshine, who seemed relieved at being removed from the presence of her forgotten offspring, and went home.

Once they were back in the bedroom, the calico, apparently in a forgiving mood, bundled herself on Cassidy's chest, squinted her eyes, and purred, despite the squawls from the den.

Zach, wearing a black tee imprinted: BEER: NOW CHEAPER THAN GASOLINE, swiveled toward her. "I scheduled our meeting with Garrett for six this evening. I also have a real estate appraiser coming at one. Since you probably don't want to show the appraiser around, I decided to work from home so I can do it.''

Cassidy's mouth compressed in a thin line. "Why didn't you tell me?''

"Because of that look you just gave me. I knew it was coming and I wasn't eager to see it.''

"You thought I'd be less pissed if you just sprang it on me?''

"I like to put unpleasant things off as long as possible.''

"But we haven't decided yet. A decision means you and I both agree we want to move. You said we could take as long as we need.''

Zach replied in a gentle voice, "If I don't get started, you'll just wait around and hope I forget about it. But this isn't going to go away. I really want to move.''

Cassidy gazed at a corner of the ceiling above Zach's head where the paint was crumbling. *Well, what can you say? He nailed you. Fact is, you were thinking if you procrastinated long enough, he'd get over his aversion to living in your wonderful house.*

She glanced at her desk, piled high with unprocessed paper. "I don't have any urge to deal with the embarrassment of watching a stranger inspect my messes. So I think I'll go grocery shopping at one.''

"Fine with me.'' Zach pulled out the list of numbers Claire had given them. "I'm going to set up a couple more interviews for this evening. Maybe the ex-husband and the business partner.''

Cassidy asked, "Did you call Notre Dame yet?''

Zach indicated that he hadn't.

"I can do it.'' *Anything to keep my mind off real estate matters.*

A polite female voice at the registrar's office gave her Max's attendance dates.

"Do you show a Garrett Hillard enrolled at the same time as the O'Connell boy?''

"I have no record of anybody by that name.''

"Well," Cassidy swiveled to face Zach, "either Julie was lying like her mother said, or 'Garrett Hillard' is an alias."

SHORTLY BEFORE ONE, Cassidy drove to Dominick's, a supermarket on Lake Street, and began trolling the parking lot in search of an empty space. *Here it is, middle of a Friday afternoon, and half of Oak Park is out grocery shopping. Why aren't all these people chained to their desks from nine to five so I can have the store to myself?* Locating a slot in the far corner, she stepped out into the warmth of a near-perfect spring day, the sun high overhead in a deep blue, puffy-cloud sky. *The good thing about living in the Chicago area is that a day like today is always a gift. Even with real estate appraisers and hitmen lurking in the background, you can't not appreciate it.*

After she finished shopping, she dug out her keys, hoisted her plastic bags, and headed toward the Toyota. About five yards from it, she came to a sudden halt, the sound of blood pulsing in her ears. A black man, medium height, bulging shoulders and arms, clad in baggy jeans and a sleeveless tee, was leaning against a post about ten feet to the rear of her car. She tried to swallow but her mouth was too dry. No other people were in sight except for a couple of elderly shoppers headed into the store.

The man scanned the parking lot, his gaze sweeping past her.

Obviously waiting for someone else.

As she started walking again, the man moved a short distance away.

See? This is just a post-traumatic stress reaction you're having.

"Hey, Cassidy McCabe," a gravelly voice called out from behind her. She whirled around. The man had covered the distance between them and was now so close she could smell his rancid breath. "Got a message for you."

Her left hand tightened around the bags. Her right hand,

fingers clutching her keys, moved in close to her body. "From who?" she squeaked.

"You tell your old man he got to drop that story the two of you be writin'. He don't drop that story, somebody gonna drop you."

Memorize his face. Maybe you can find him in the mug books. Buzz-cut hair, high cheekbones, prominent nose, chiseled lips and chin. Totally different features from the bared-tooth man. This guy might've made it as a Wesley Snipes double if he hadn't aspired to thughood instead.

"He don't drop that story, he be scrapin' you off the pavement again."

Again? Does that mean he knows about the mugging?

The man started jogging away from her. She kept her eyes glued to his figure as long as she could, until he turned east on South Boulevard and disappeared.

Sitting behind the wheel, she sucked in air and waited for her hands to stop shaking. When she'd composed herself to some degree, she drove home, parked next to her back gate, and tried to think. One idea stood out clearly in her mind: she would never allow any wannabe gangster to stop her from anything.

But Zach might feel differently. Threats against him would never phase him, but threats against her might make him want to quit. She briefly considered not telling him. *Oh no you don't!* During their first year together, they'd both jeopardized the relationship more than once by withholding information. Since then they'd learned their lesson and didn't keep things from each other any more.

Okay. She drew in a breath. *You have to tell him. And then you have to convince him not to back down.*

She found Zach in the kitchen with a slender young woman in business attire. Standing in the doorway, Cassidy said, "There's something I need to talk to you about."

He took one look at her face, then said to the real estate appraiser, "We'll have to continue another time." They showed the woman to the door, then went upstairs to sit in their desk chairs, bodies angled toward each other.

A small shiver running down her arms, Cassidy told Zach about the man in the parking lot, making it clear he wasn't the same person as the mugger. "I suppose the first thing I ought to do is go look at the mug books."

Zach leaned forward, legs spread wide, hands on knees. "The cops won't see this as urgent. The most they'll do right now is take a report."

Cassidy felt some of the tension in her neck drain away at hearing Zach talk about it so calmly. "It was just a verbal threat, after all. I don't think we need to make too much out of it."

Zach gazed at the west window for about three beats, then brought his eyes back to hers. "I know you won't like this, but I think we should let the investigation go."

Just what you thought he'd say. Indignation rushed through her, a cold breeze that blew away the fear. "We've never let ourselves be scared off anything before."

"Yeah, but seeing you knocked out in the alley has put things in a different light. I don't think I ever before realized on a gut level just how vulnerable you are."

"How can you say that? Just because I got mugged doesn't mean I'm this delicate person. Look at all the dangerous situations I've made it through alive. I've even managed to save your ass on occasion."

"How long do you think your luck's going to hold? Besides, this doesn't look like a solvable case to me. Why take the risk of you getting hurt when we probably won't accomplish anything anyway?"

Propping an elbow on her desk, she leaned toward Zach. "If this were unsolvable, there'd be no reason for anybody to threaten us. In fact, the appearance of this thug means we must be getting close to something. We can't stop now. If we do, the killer wins by default." Not that our investigation guarantees that he won't win.

Zach went to the window and stood, hands on hips, staring down at Hazel, then returned to his chair. "I didn't want you involved in the first place," he said, an edge to his voice. "Now I want out and you're trying to argue me down. Can't you for once just give in?"

Quitting was simply not an option for her. Leaning her forehead against her palm, she said, "Zach, please, if you insist on stopping because you think I'm too vulnerable, I'll feel like a lesser being. Like some kind of damsel in distress that has to be protected. These are things I've fought all my life not to feel."

"So—once again—what you want is more important than what I want."

"We have to be equals. That's what this whole marriage is built on."

"But we're not equals. You always get your way."

A sort of fierceness came over her. Standing, she paced beside the waterbed. "Zach, don't do this to me. I won't be in a marriage where my husband has the right to decide what I can and can't do."

"When have I ever decided anything for you?"

Sitting again, she reached across and wrapped her hand around his wrist. "You haven't. That's one of the things I love most about you. You've been wonderful about not interfering, even when the choices I make are hard on you. But asking me to let that bully scare me off—well, you should understand how I feel about that."

"Yeah, I do. I feel the same way when people try to push me around." He stared into space for a moment, then looked at her again. "Okay, we'll continue as is, but I want you to take some precautions. Will you agree not to go out at night unless I'm available to walk you to the garage? And to call me on the cell phone when you're coming home? And if you leave the car unattended, to check the back seat before you open the door?"

Are you really going to let him walk you to the garage? You have to give in sometimes. Besides, the truth is, you aren't Zach's equal in your ability to defend yourself.

"Okay, I can live with that."

Zach settled back in his chair and exhaled.

He deserves a best-husband award for putting up with you.

"Well," Cassidy said, "I guess the next item on the agenda is to tell the cops about the parking lot thug."

She called the police department. A beat officer listened to her story, then informed her that a detective would contact her later.

Lacing his hands behind his head, Zach said, "First a mugger, then a thug to warn you off the case. Both of these guys must've been hired by the killer."

Cassidy spent nearly a minute trying to figure it out. "I don't see how the mugger could've been. He jumped me before we'd even thought about getting involved in Max's murder. And he didn't issue any warnings. Why would the killer send somebody to rough me up unless he was trying to make a point?"

"It doesn't make sense, does it? But this second guy knew you'd been mugged. How would he know that if the two were unconnected?"

"Wait—I've got it. The killer heard about the mugging and wanted to play off it. He figured if I'd already been hurt by one black guy, sending another to deliver the warning would make it doubly frightening."

"Well, that could be it."

"You know, the more I think about it, the more I see the logic in sending someone who'd remind me of the mugger. I saw this guy standing by my car and immediately freaked because I've developed an association between rough-looking black men and getting beaten up."

"If what you're saying is true, you must've told somebody about the mugging who either is the killer or knows the killer."

Cassidy searched her memory. "The only person I mentioned it to is Claire." Picking up the phone, she said, "I'll give her a call." When Claire answered, Cassidy told her about the parking lot guy and what he'd said.

"Oh, Cass, that's terrible. I couldn't stand it if you got hurt too." She paused. "I don't know, I don't know. Maybe you should give up the investigation."

Cassidy reassured her client that she could take care of herself. *Which, of course, is patently untrue since you just let some idiot beat up on you in your own alley.*

"I know you didn't mean any harm," Cassidy said, "but you must have told somebody about the mugging."

"I can't think who it would've been." A long silence. "Wait, now I remember. I was at Irene's house and Julie was there too. They were talking about the questions you and Zach asked and for some reason I brought up the mugging."

"Those are the only two people you told?"

"I'm sure I didn't mention it any other time."

Cassidy called Julie and Irene. Both women denied having told anyone else. Cassidy turned to Zach, "Claire, Julie, and Irene—the three women who loved Max the most. I can't imagine that any of those women would've hired the hit. Or hired a thug to threaten me."

"It doesn't seem likely." Zach narrowed his eyes in thought. "Did you tell Claire the mugger was black?"

"I don't remember my exact words but I probably wouldn't have mentioned his race. However, I am fairly certain I told her it happened in our alley, so she might have assumed the guy was black."

Cassidy creased her brow and sighed. *Everything's a tradeoff. You love where you live, but living here means you always have to keep your guard up—especially when you encounter thuggish looking black guys in your alley.*

ELEVEN

ROOMMATES AND PRIVACY INVASION

LATER THAT AFTERNOON Cassidy and Zach drove into the city for their meeting with Garrett Hillard, the man Julie said had once been Max's roommate. Hillard's yellow brick apartment building was located in Wicker Park, a largely gentrified neighborhood that still provided some low-cost housing.

Climbing to the third floor, they found Hillard, a good-looking man of medium height, waiting for them in one of the doorways. His complexion was olive-toned, his hair thick and black, his eyes an arresting shade of blue, his jaw framed by a short dark beard.

Looks broodish, a Heathcliff type.

Lines of irritation creased his face. "You're wasting your time. I don't know anything about the murder."

Zach replied pleasantly, "However, I believe you did agree to meet with us."

"All right. You can come in."

They filed into the living room, a young girl with long straight hair watching them from a loveseat. Across from her, a television with creatures from The Lion King on its screen.

Squatting in front of his daughter, Hillard said, "You remember, I told you some people were coming and you'd have to go into your room while we talked."

She grabbed his arm. "Please, Daddy, this is my favorite part. Don't make me go now."

"I know you don't like stopping videos in the middle, but I'll make it fast. Then, after the movie's over, we'll go out for pizza." He stood and placed his hand on her shoulder.

"No, please, I'll turn it down."

"I'm sorry, Ashley, but you have to go to your room."

Patient, firm, empathic. Could be a poster boy for good parenting.

When Ashley started toward the hall, Cassidy could see that the girl wore a brace on the lower part of her right leg. Dressed in a bright attractive outfit, she was obviously a well-tended child.

Hillard followed his daughter. "I'll just be a minute."

While he was gone, Cassidy studied the room. A gray-striped sofa and loveseat. A window flanked by scarred wooden bookcases, the shelves crammed with fat volumes. Although the upholstered furniture appeared new, the unwashed window and grayish walls lent a grungy appearance to the space. No art, no decoration, no doodads. The only personal touch came from Ashley's toys and a photo display hanging in two perfectly straight, horizontal lines on the wall near the door.

While Zach parked himself on the loveseat, Cassidy took a closer look at the photos. They all starred Ashley. In one, Hillard was pushing her in a swing; in another, the two were playing catch.

Cassidy, whose father had disappeared when she was five, felt a sudden pang. She blinked, drew in a breath, then went to sit beside Zach, her leg touching his. *Having a husband who treats you like gold makes it almost all right that you didn't have a father.*

Hillard returned and sat in the center of the sofa, a pack of cigarettes, a lighter, an ashtray, and a Coke can on the glass coffee table in front of him. "Ashley's taken care of for the moment, but I promised I'd have you out the door in half an hour.''

"She's a lovely girl," Cassidy said, "and you're so good with her.''

Hillard awarded her a bashful smile.

"Are you raising her all alone? Or does she have a mother who participates?''

Lighting a cigarette, Hillard took a deep drag, then exhaled through his nostrils. He picked up the Coke, swirled it, and set it back down.

"Is this difficult for you to talk about?''

"It's not my favorite topic.''

Cassidy waited.

"Oh hell, why not?'' Hillard took another drag, then deposited his cigarette in the corner of the square glass ashtray. "My wife and I were living out in the Bay Area and she took off with another man. She was a dancer. He was a tour director. She decided he was her soul mate and I wasn't.''

"Being left for somebody else—that's always tough.'' Cassidy remembered how she'd felt when her first husband had done it to her.

"It shouldn't have come as any surprise. I mean, I already knew she was bored with being a wife and mother.'' Taking a swig of Coke, Hillard set the can down precisely inside the ring it had left and began twisting it in a slow circle. "We met right out of high school. Both planning careers in the theater, only she made it and I didn't. Anyway, she wasn't interested in custody or visitation, which left me free to go wherever I wanted. So a few months after the divorce, I packed up and moved. I figured neither Ashley nor I needed to live with all the reminders.''

"It must've been terrible for your daughter, having her mother abandon her like that.''

"Like I said, I didn't want any reminders.''

"But why come all the way to Chicago?'' *Never known*

anyone to pick Chicago over California, where weather like today is a given instead of a gift.

Jiggling the lighter in one hand, Hillard said, "My grandparents used to live here. I spent summers with them as a kid, so I have some fond memories."

"You've known Max how long?" Zach asked.

Hillard kneaded the short beard framing his jawline. "'Bout two years."

"How did you and Max come to hook up?"

"I'd just moved to Chicago and was bartending at this dump on Clark Street. Somebody in the hospitality industry threw this big bash, and the word just kind of went around. So I attended the party and that's where I first saw Max."

"Then what?"

"That night at the party I was complaining about this sleazy place I worked, and Max right away said he'd see what he could do for me. At the time I didn't think much of it, but a week later his boss called and offered me a job."

Max doing favors. That fits. "Sounds like Max really came through for you."

"He was the best." Hillard's voice went low and husky. "This has to be so hard on Claire and his family."

"You must miss him."

Hillard nodded. His intense blue eyes starting to glisten, he quickly looked away.

Cassidy said, "Max had a large cadre of friends, guys he went way back with. And yet he chose you to be his best man. Any idea why?"

"Did you know he brought me in as manager at the Naperville restaurant?" After Cassidy nodded, he continued. "A lot of nights the two of us ended up having a drink together after everyone else left. We got to be pretty tight during those evenings at Cypress."

"Well then," Zach said, "since you two were such good friends, maybe you can tell us how he managed to pay for the honeymoon cruise and a big rock of a diamond—given that he was so far in debt.''

Hillard frowned. ''What is this—an exposé on Max? I can't believe Claire would go along with that.''

''I have no interest in making Max look bad. It's just that he'd run out of credit and he was still spending as if he had the keys to Fort Knox. When I come across anomalies like that, I want to make sense out of them.''

''Well, I don't have any answers for you. I just figured he made everything work by juggling credit cards. And so what if he did? If living beyond your means was a crime, half the population'd be in jail.''

Instead of a stigma, indebtedness now seems almost like a badge of honor. Whoever dies with the most credit cards wins.

Zach gave Hillard an appraising look. ''To what extent was Claire's income a factor in Max's decision to marry her?''

''Not at all.'' Hillard shook his head vigorously. ''Max was crazy about Claire from the day they met. He talked all the time about how lucky he was to have this warm, beautiful, intelligent woman in his life.''

''Well, I'm glad to hear it. Claire will feel better knowing he wasn't after her money.'' Zach glanced down at his notepad. ''Now let's see…you said you grew up in the Bay Area.''

Hillard took a drag on his cigarette, then started jiggling his lighter again. ''My family moved there when I was in tenth grade.''

''After high school you met your wife.''

''Yeah.'' Lowering his head, Hillard carefully lined up the items on the table.

''Then you went to college.''

''Acting school.''

''I heard you went to college. That you and Max were roommates at Notre Dame.''

Hillard's head jerked up. ''Who told you that?''

"I just heard it around."

"Somebody's bullshitting you, man. I never met Max before that party two years ago."

AFTER LEAVING Hillard's apartment, Zach said they had some time to kill before their next appointment. "We passed an espresso bar a couple blocks down. Let's go wait there."

Cassidy and Zach went inside to get their coffee, then carried large ceramic cups out to an umbrella table on the sidewalk. The late afternoon sun cast long shadows, but a thin band of light remained on the east side of the street where they were sitting.

"So," Cassidy asked, "what do you think? Is Garrett really Max's roommate under a phony name?"

"It's my hunch that the moniker on our best man's birth certificate isn't 'Garrett Hillard'."

Knowing that her latté was probably still too hot, Cassidy raised the cup in both hands and took a small sip, nearly burning her tongue. "Why do I think he's lying?" She replayed the interview in her mind. "It's not that he was resentful. Given the way we coerced him, that's entirely understandable. It's not even that he seemed nervous. That's pretty natural too." She paused. "It's the way he told that story about his wife. Considering it's not his favorite topic, he went into way more detail than necessary. It's as if he were trying to convince us—something people usually don't do when they're telling the truth."

Zach nodded. A cardinal landed in a parkway maple. Cassidy's breath caught at the sight of bright red feathers.

She took another sip, finding that her latté had cooled to an almost drinkable temperature. "So the next question is, what's Garrett trying to hide?" She squinted in thought. "Maybe Max and Garrett were lovers, then Max dumped his old boyfriend for Claire. That would explain killing him at the wedding."

"I didn't get any sense that Garrett was gay."

"If he's remained firmly in the closet his whole life, I doubt that you would."

"The problem with the gay theory is, it doesn't explain Garrett's taking on a new identity. Conducting a secret relationship wouldn't require an alias."

"It'd have to be more than just a name change, wouldn't it? He probably couldn't get away with giving an employer his real social security number attached to a false name."

"The IRS catches people when they do that. So you're right—he has to have a new number as well as a new name. And the only reason I can think of for taking on a new identity is to hide out from the law."

A lump formed in Cassidy's stomach. "Child abduction."

"It could be anything. Embezzlement, assault. But yeah, child abduction does make sense considering he's got his kid with him."

"Oh shit." She wadded her napkin into a tight ball.

"What's the matter?"

"I hate to think of that poor girl being taken from her mother. Anytime the bond between a mother and child is broken—even if the mother's abusive—the child is damaged by it."

Zach folded his arms on the table. "Who knows what reason he may've had? But our problem's the murder, not Hillard's crime. So let's assume he needed to disappear and his good old buddy Max helped him do it. Then later, when Max's credit card scam fell apart, guess who he'd be most likely to hit up?"

"Blackmail." Rubbing her fingers along her jaw line, she thought it through. "The only piece that doesn't fit is the wedding as crime scene."

"You said it might be somebody who wanted to watch Max die."

"Max blackmailing Garrett makes a good theory, but we'd have to prove that Garrett isn't who he says he is before we could take it to the police."

"I'll run a background check," Zach said. Then, shaking his head, "No, I think I'll have Izzie do it." Izzie was a P.I. Zach used on occasion to research news stories. "Internet privacy invasion takes a little time and I'm already putting way too much of it into this investigation. You should see the backlog on my desk."

Said the case was unsolvable, but he wouldn't be working so hard on it if he didn't believe we're going to catch a killer in the long run.

"I'd like to learn more about researching the Web," Cassidy said. "I could get Gran to help. She's turned herself into a real techie."

"It'd take you a lot longer than Izzie, and if I get a story out of this, I can expense his fee."

"But I'd really like to try my hand at it, and Gran'd be thrilled to have the chance to do some detective work."

"Is there anything your grandmother doesn't do?"

"I believe she draws the line at brain surgery." Straightening her napkin, Cassidy dabbed at the corners of her mouth. "But getting back to Garrett, don't we need his social security number to run searches on him?"

"I'll buy it from Izzie."

"Izzie has everybody's number?" Omigod! Privacy is dead. Big brother rules.

"There are brokers who sell them. P.I.s get them all the time."

"Well then, you get me the number and I'll see what we can come up with." *You just lamented the loss of privacy, now you can't wait to take advantage of all the ways to invade it.*

Cassidy gazed at the cardinal preening in the tree. "Your theory about Garrett makes sense, but there's something that doesn't feel right. You saw how tender he was with his daughter? And how his eyes misted over when we talked about what a good friend Max'd been? Garrett's defensive on the surface, but underneath I think he's a pretty soft guy. It's hard to imagine he could be tough enough to commit premeditated murder—especially of a close friend.''

''You know, you have this tendency to see everything through rose-colored glasses. Most people aren't nearly as nice as you like to think they are.''

I'll take my rose-colored glasses any day. They ward off that depressing cynicism Zach seems to favor.

''Finish your coffee,'' he said. ''It's time to go visit Claire's ex. Now what line of work did you say he's in?''

''Professor of geography at the U. of I.''

TWELVE

THE EX-HUSBAND'S VERSION

"CLAIRE'S SAID such wonderful things about you." Hank Linden, a trim well-built man with thinning sandy hair, greeted Cassidy in the entryway of his Dearborn Park condo. His liquid brown eyes gazed warmly into hers. Then he pumped Zach's hand and gave him a welcoming smile as well.

"Come in and make yourselves comfortable."

Cassidy and Zach moved on into an earth-toned room with a bike hanging from the ceiling against one wall. They sat on a contemporary sofa with a cherry wood table in front of it.

Linden lowered himself into an armchair. "Your timing's perfect. I just got out of the shower after leading a Sierra Club hike along the Prairie Path. Have you ever walked that trail? It's really quite an experience."

"We're not the outdoorsy types," Zach said.

"So," Cassidy asked, "what did Claire tell you about our purpose here?"

"She said you might be able to identify the killer and get me off the hook." Closing his eyes briefly, he shook his head. "My life's been a nightmare ever since it happened. The police keep harassing me. Molly's refusing to visit. My friends look at me out of the corners of their eyes as if they think I'm a mad psycho killer."

Cassidy felt a stirring of sympathy. Reminding herself of what Hank had done to Claire, she quickly stamped it out.

"You know who we are?" Zach asked.

He better know, since we're not allowed to explain my connection to Claire.

"You're a reporter from the Post and your wife is Claire's therapist."

"Cass already knows your history with Claire but I don't. So why don't you start by filling me in."

Linden said to Cassidy, "All you've heard so far is Claire's version. Which isn't, by any means, unbiased."

"Nobody's objective. Especially two people who've been through a divorce."

"Of course," he said, a slight tone of condescension creeping into his voice. "But you have to remember, Claire's a little on the hysterical side. Some might even call her a drama queen."

Here we go. What's-wrong-with-Claire time. Hank's true colors coming out.

"About your marriage," Zach prompted.

"Yes, well…this isn't the easiest thing to talk about, you know." He drew in a breath. "At first we were very much in love and very happy together. But Claire has this tendency to take on more than she can handle. After her promotion, she started putting in a lot of extra hours on the job. It got so the only time I saw her was on weekends. And then, as if she wasn't overloaded enough, she decided she had to have a baby. I didn't see how she could give a child the attention it needed and continue working such long hours, but she insisted if she didn't have a baby, she'd never be fulfilled. When Molly was born, Claire threw herself into mothering and there was no time left for me. I tried to talk her into giving up her job but she refused. She thought she could have it all. We drifted farther and farther apart. I still loved her, and I'm convinced she loved me, but the marriage just seemed to die."

Interesting how he left out the part about the constant stream of verbal abuse. Cassidy's stomach knotted in anger, but she took a deep breath and got her therapist part in control. "Does that mean you think the divorce was all Claire's fault?"

"No, of course not. Both people always contribute."

"So what was your part?"

Irritation flickered across Linden's face. "I wish I knew. I've never been able to figure it out."

Nail him to the wall the way I would if he were playing games in a therapy session? Considering he needs us more than we need him, can't see any reason not to.

"After the divorce, you weren't able to let go, were you? You followed Claire around and called her in the middle of the night until she was forced to take out a restraining order."

"I was worried about her. She was so depressed, I was afraid she might hurt herself. I was watching over her."

Oh right. Waking her up every night was a way to protect her.

"When she told you she was getting married again, didn't you say you'd never let anybody come between you?"

He stood and walked to the window, then turned to face them, a look of desperation in his eyes. "Why are you asking these questions? I didn't kill Max. I thought you believed Claire when she told you I was innocent."

Zach sat straighter. "We need to understand exactly what happened, and it would help if you'd start by explaining what you meant when you said you'd never let anybody come between you."

Returning to his chair, Linden ran a hand over his sparse hair. "I'm sorry. It's just that the police have been all over me about that comment. The only reason I said it is, I honestly believe Claire and I belong together. Someday she's going to see it too and come back to me."

Amazing how people can believe what they want to believe. This is two steps beyond rose-colored glasses.

Slumping forward, Linden clasped his hands together between his knees. "We may have made our share of mistakes, but we can learn from them and next time we'll do better."

"Okay," Zach said, "let's hear your side of it. Tell us why the cops are wrong in picking you as their prime suspect."

Hank let out a deep sigh. "I didn't have any reason to kill Max. I really think Claire will come back to me on her own. Even if she'd married that lowlife chef, I was convinced she'd end up leaving him for me. And besides, I'd never have him killed in front of my daughter. Claire says Molly's been having night terrors. If I were going to hire someone to shoot Max, I'd make sure my daughter was nowhere around."

"How did you know it was a hitman?" Zach asked.

"Claire told me."

Cassidy wondered if there were any truth in what Linden had said. "If you didn't do it, who else might have?"

He gazed into the middle distance. "It's probably somebody connected to Max. Somebody I don't even know. Although I have had some thoughts that it might be Erin."

Cassidy pictured Claire's heavyset sister with her frozen smile.

"Why Erin?" Zach asked.

"She was always so jealous of Claire. Claire was prettier and more successful and had better luck with men."

Claire had luck with men like Clinton had luck with interns.

"There were times when Erin couldn't handle it. Shortly after I started seeing Claire, Erin broke into my apartment and slashed everything up."

Cassidy blinked in surprise. "Why would she do that?"

"Because I dropped Erin when I started dating Claire." Linden's pale brows drew together. "Didn't she tell you?"

So humbling to find out from other people what your client failed to disclose. "I didn't know you dated Erin."

"I met her in the Sierra Club. I didn't have anyone in my life at the time so I took her out casually for a while. Then she brought me home to meet the family, and Claire and I were an instant take. I had no idea Erin was so much more serious than I was."

"How did you know it was Erin who trashed your apartment?"

"She called later to apologize. Said she didn't know what'd gotten into her." He paused. "Since I felt a little guilty over dumping Erin and going after her sister, I decided not to report it."

"But you must've told Claire."

He shook his head. "We'd just started dating. I was afraid if she knew how upset her sister was, she might not keep seeing me."

After asking a few more questions, Cassidy and Zach rose to leave.

Linden stood also. "Any chance I could get you to sign a petition to stop some communities out west from building a landfill on a site migrant birds use as a stopover?"

Zach rested his hands on his belt. "I've been following that issue and I'm not so sure the landfill's a bad idea."

"I'll sign." Cassidy, who knew nothing about the particulars, felt an urge to protect all the undeveloped land on the globe.

THEY LEFT Linden's condo and boarded an unoccupied elevator. As the doors slid close, Zach pulled Cassidy up tight and gave her a long open-mouthed kiss. Snuggling closer, she glued herself against him, a hot tingling sensation radiating through her body.

He whispered in her ear, "Have I ever told you about my fantasy of doing it in an airplane?"

Cassidy smiled. *Can't quite picture the logistics, but the idea certainly has its appeal.*

They retrieved the Subaru from the parking garage, paying twenty dollars to liberate it, and drove north on Dearborn through the Loop. Rush hour was over and traffic moved freely, an orange light from the sodium vapor street lamps suffusing everything with a warm glow. Glittering towers rose on all sides, and the sky overhead was a dark purplish blue.

"We're due to meet with Max's business partner at the Naperville restaurant in a couple of hours. Let's find ourselves a steak house and have dinner before we head west."

"Fish would be healthier."

"Ah, but I need red meat. To make sure I have the vigor I need to jump your bones later tonight."

That red-meat excuse is as lame as the-dog-ate-my-homework. Zach never doesn't have enough vigor.

Noticing that the temperature had dropped, Cassidy folded her bare arms beneath her breasts. "What did you think of Hank?"

"I didn't believe much of what he said, and I also didn't like the way he dumped on Claire. He's still got the best motive, although if the police haven't succeeded in digging up any evidence, there's not much chance we'd be able to either."

"What about the guy who tried to threaten us off the case? Linden sees us as his salvation. He'd have no reason to try and stop us from investigating."

"He strikes me as a pretty slippery guy. It's possible the eager welcome was all bullshit. Maybe he does have something to hide and he's afraid we'll find it." He paused. "The guy's so full of himself, it'd be a pleasure to put him away."

"Not for me it wouldn't. Not considering how hard it'd be on Claire and Molly."

Zach glanced her way. "You said he was emotionally abusive. I hear that term all the time, but I'm not exactly sure what it means."

"It doesn't have an exact meaning, which makes it hard

to know for sure when it's happening. If a guy tells a woman he loves her, then proceeds to belittle her and find fault with everything she does, I call it abuse. The payoff for the abuser is control. The more he beats his partner down, the more she'll do anything to avoid displeasing him.''

Zach shook his head. "And the reason women put up with it?''

"It's not just women who are victims. Men get abused too. And the reason they stay is that the abuser starts off as the perfect lover. He adores his partner, showers her with attention, makes her feel like the most desirable woman in the world. Then the compliments shift to criticism, but she keeps hoping—if she does everything right—he'll adore her again. It's paradise lost. The victims keep trying to find their way back to it.''

"There's one other thing," Zach said. "When Hank was spouting all that nonsense about wanting to protect Claire and knowing she'll come back to him, was he trying to con us? Or is he delusional?''

"I'd say delusional.''

THIRTEEN

A REPORTER GROUPIE

AS CASSIDY WALKED into Cypress with Zach behind her, the first thing she noticed was Garrett Hillard standing at the host's station.

He smiled a professional smile. "Good to see you again. Let me get Susan. I know she's expecting you." He headed across the room toward a golden-haired woman chatting with the bartender. Nearly closing time, two lone men at the bar, the tables empty.

Cassidy instantly approved of the décor. Purple napkins standing like little tents on crisp white cloths. Widely spaced tables. A row of high-backed, polished wood booths against the wall to their right. A whimsical, pastel-toned mural depicting the planets and stars on the wall to their left.

Susan walked briskly in their direction. She was a plump, attractive woman in a low-cut, short-skirted, electric blue dress that looked fantastic on her, even though she was a tad too old for it. At a distance, she'd appeared to be in her thirties. Up close, the lines in her neck and face made it evident she'd passed the half-century mark. Cassidy thought Susan was the stony-faced woman from the wedding, but the expression she wore now was so amiable, Cassidy couldn't be sure.

Susan held out her hand to Zach. "Well, you must be the reporter from the *Post*."

Zach introduced himself and Cassidy.

Cocking her head, Susan gave Cassidy an infectious smile. "So, do you always follow your husband around when he works on stories?"

Ouch! She's calling you a reporter groupie.

Looking Susan in the eye, Cassidy said, "No, not always."

The restaurant owner laughed. "I'm sorry, that wasn't very nice. But it seems so odd—a husband and wife doing interviews together."

"Cass knows a few of the people involved," Zach said. "I thought she could open some doors."

Susan gave him a disbelieving look, then shrugged and said, "Let's go sit in one of the booths."

Once they were seated, she beckoned to a waiter who removed the place settings and took drink orders. Clasping her hands loosely on the table, Susan displayed fingers encrusted with a large assortment of gold rings.

Never could understand how women are able to do anything with all that clunky metal on their hands.

"So, what kind of story are you writing?" Susan asked.

"A piece about the shooting, with particular emphasis on Max—who was this guy and why would someone want to shoot him on his wedding day."

The waiter brought their drinks. Susan stirred the ice cubes in her Evian water with a heavily adorned finger. "Are you hoping to outwit the police and track down the bad guy before they do?"

Zach explained why he considered the murder unsolvable.

Giving him a sly smile, Susan lowered her chin and looked up coquettishly. "So if I answer your questions, you won't be secretly probing to see if I have a motive?"

"Waste of time. You can't prosecute on motive. You have to have evidence, and there isn't any."

"Well then—" Susan sucked on her finger, then stirred

her ice cubes again ''—if I let you interview me, will you give the restaurant a nice plug?''

"I do news stories, not P.R."

She made a pretense of pouting. "Then why should I talk to you?"

"Because you like to see your name in the paper."

"Well, you're right about that." She looked at Cassidy. "Are you going to interview me too?"

"I expect to get a question in here and there."

"I don't mean to be rude, but I can't understand why you'd want to follow your husband around like this. You must have a career of your own. You don't look like a person who doesn't have a life."

This is a reversal. For once the person asking intrusive questions isn't me.

"I'm a psychotherapist. And yes, I do have a life."

"Well, I guess it doesn't bother you to go around with Zach on his interviews. I'm just really different. One of the reasons I never married is, I couldn't stand the idea of giving up my independence."

"You never wanted to marry?"

"My mother was appalled, but no, I didn't. I was like those men who get right up to the brink, then run like hell. Marriage always seemed to me like a cell door slamming shut."

"So the man I saw you with at the wedding wasn't your husband?"

"Oh no." Susan waved a hand in dismissal. "Vincent's just a good friend."

"The reason I noticed you was that you looked like you didn't want to be there. Like you were mad or something."

"I had a ferocious headache. But I wouldn't have missed Max's wedding for anything. At least that's how I felt before the shooting."

Taking out his pad, Zach asked, "How did you and Max happen to set up a partnership in the first place?"

"Are you familiar with the Cypress in Chicago?"

He nodded.

"I opened that first restaurant fifteen years ago. A while back I started thinking about expanding into the 'burbs, but I wasn't in any hurry to do it." She pulled at the diamond stud in her ear. "Max, on the other hand, was so eager to move into an ownership position he was nearly wetting his pants over it. Of course he didn't have any capital, so he had to find someone like me to bankroll the deal. At first I wasn't interested. I didn't think he had anything to offer."

Smiling to herself, she shook her head. "But I finally decided he had enough draw as a chef to make it worth doing business with him. So I told him I'd back him if he could come up with the place. He found this building, oversaw the rehabbing, and pretty much ran it—along with Garrett, of course."

Cassidy said softly, "I understand there was more between you and Max than just a business partnership."

"Oh? What makes you say so?"

"Max told Claire she couldn't come to the restaurant because he didn't want you to find out he was seeing someone else. He said that you," Cassidy paused, searching for a delicate way to say it, "were interested in him."

"I was interested in Max?" Susan let out a booming laugh. "Sorry, honey, it was the other way around."

"You're saying Max was the pursuer?"

"Well, he pretended to be anyway. He sent flowers, took me out, spent a lot of money. He was good in bed so I went along with it for a while, but I never took him seriously."

Cassidy's stomach sank. *If he pursued Susan for a partnership, does that mean he pursued Claire for her money? She finds out he was just using her, it'll break her heart.*

Rubbing her thumb over her garnet ring, Cassidy asked, "Then you weren't jealous?"

Susan tossed her golden hair girlishly and laughed again. "Sexually he'd served his purpose. I was done with him.

So as long as he did a good job running the restaurant, I didn't care who he fucked.''

Cassidy's brow creased. "Then why tell Claire she couldn't come near Cypress?"

"Maybe he had something going with one of the waitresses. Or a customer."

God, I hope not. Already have too many sleazy things I have to tell Claire.

Susan looked across the room. Following her gaze, Cassidy saw Hillard beckoning to his boss.

"If you'll excuse me a minute."

Cassidy watched the zaftig restaurant owner move rapidly across the room in stiletto heels that would have sent Cassidy sprawling. *Late at night, at least ten years older and fifty pounds heavier than I am, she still has a bounce in her step. Wonder what vitamin she takes I don't.*

When Susan returned, Zach asked what she knew of her manager's history. She repeated the same story Hillard had told them.

"So," Cassidy said, "how did the partnership work out?"

"A little rocky at first. Well, that's the way it always is, starting a new business. But after everything settled down, I was glad to have Max as a partner. The customers loved him and he put together an exceptional menu."

Zach rattled his ice cubes. "It appears he ran up so much debt he was in severe financial straits. Can you give us some idea what kind of money he was making?"

"He took home enough he could've paid his bills and had money left over if he hadn't been such a spender."

"We suspect he had some source of outside income. Any possibility he could have been embezzling from the restaurant?"

Pressing her lips together, Susan shook her head. "You think I'm dumb enough to let Max anywhere near the books? I made sure he kept his distance from the business side of things, and I also watched the computer system like a hawk. He may well have had larcenous impulses, but he never got the chance to act on them."

"Can you think of any other way he might've been making a little extra on the side?"

"Knowing Max, he was probably selling his body. And getting top dollar for it too." Susan laughed her boisterous laugh. "No, seriously, I don't have any recent information. Of course I ran a credit check on him before I signed the contract, but that was eight months ago. Back then, he had a lot of debt but was making the payments. You know, it doesn't surprise me to hear he was in trouble. He was too much of an optimist. Never saw problems coming, always thought things were better than they were. And the way he liked to shop!" Shaking her head, she said in a nostalgic tone, "I used to tell him he had girl genes."

"You were pretty fond of him, weren't you?" Cassidy asked.

"We had our problems, but Max is the kind of guy you can't not like."

Bet I could've not liked him. "What was it about Max that made him so irresistible?"

"Well, I don't know. I guess it was his interest in people. He liked everyone so much you couldn't help but like him back. Whenever I talked to him, he put everything else aside and focused his whole attention on me. He really listened. Do you know how rare that is?"

Considering that's how I make my living, I think I do.

As Cassidy and Zach drove north on Naperville Road, he said, "I couldn't find any obvious holes in her story. I'd have to guess she was telling the truth."

"You were just dazzled by the short skirt and the cleavage."

"Distractions like that do make it hard to focus."

They drove a while in silence, Cassidy watching the lampposts flit by.

Zach glanced at her. "Did it bother you that Susan jumped you for being glued to my side?"

"I had one twinge of feeling fatally female, then I reminded myself that submissiveness is not one of my character flaws."

"Well, I wanted to tell you—even though I'm not happy that you've gotten yourself involved in another murder, I don't mind having you with me on interviews. I wouldn't want to do this on a regular basis, but now and then I kind of like it that we can work together."

Cassidy felt a warm interior smile flow through her.

ZACH TURNED INTO the driveway, stopping briefly to let Cassidy disembark before pulling into the garage. Hugging herself against a sharp breeze, she hurried toward her back gate. Overhead, a canopy of thick leaves from the parkway elms blotted out the stars.

Starshine rolled on the sidewalk to greet her.

"Come on inside," Cassidy said, walking around her. "I'm not standing out in the wind to provide chin scratches tonight."

With Starshine on the counter fussing at her, Cassidy spooned food into the calico's bowl, then descended the basement stairs to lock the cat flap in the window.

When she returned to the kitchen, Zach was putting out more food.

"I just fed her."

"She told me she hadn't eaten all day."

"I closed the cat door so she won't be able to invade some other house tomorrow morning."

"You spoiled her game."

Cassidy gritted her teeth. "You never set any limits."

"You're overprotective," he said, gathering her into his arms.

She leaned back to look into his blue-gray eyes. "You're the one who's overprotective. With me."

"Nope." He shook his head. "Given the fact that you're a danger-magnet, no amount of protectiveness would be too much. Besides, I'm doing it for me, not you. I don't want to be widowed at an early age.''

Having been terrified herself when Zach was the target of an unknown stalker, she knew what he meant.

"Well," he let go of her, "I'm ready to call it a day."

As they left the kitchen, the calico ran ahead of them. About the time they hit the living room, Cassidy could hear Roscoe singing his sad song from above.

"Tell you what," Zach started up the stairs, "I'll pet Starshine. You go minister to the baby in the den."

Starshine trotted into the bedroom, tail held high, Zach following. Cassidy stood in the doorway and cast a wistful glance at the calico as she jumped into Zach's lap.

Before Roscoe, you were Starshine's primary love object. Roscoe's cute but it's not the same.

Sighing, Cassidy turned toward the closed door across the hall, which was now rattling and thumping as the kitten threw himself against it. Guilt oozed into her chest. *You shouldn't've left him in the den all day. He needs way more attention than he's getting.*

She opened the door, ready to grab Roscoe when he came out, but a black streak hurtled between her legs and darted into the bedroom. Racing after him, Cassidy saw Roscoe spring onto Zach's lap. The calico bared her teeth and hissed. Slithering out of Zach's hands, she hopped onto his desk, then made a giant leap for the top shelf of the wall unit above the desk.

She grabbed at the shelf, sliding off and bringing a stereo speaker crashing down onto the desk with her. Zach jumped to his feet and tried to get hold of the calico, who lashed back at him with her claws. Roscoe raced across the room and into the closet, where he hid beneath a row of slacks that hung nearly to the floor. Starshine went zipping down the stairs.

Heading out of the room, Zach said, "You take care of Roscoe. I'll get Starshine."

When Cassidy entered the walk-in closet, all she could

see was the end of Roscoe's tail sticking out from under her slacks. She got down on her hands and knees, pulled him out, and went to sit with him on the bed. Purring happily, he climbed her chest and nestled against her neck.

Zach came back into the bedroom. "She went into hiding in the basement."

"Well, of course. That's what she always does when she's mad."

They both knew that once the calico disappeared into the maze of cat-sized cubbyholes in their nether region, she was almost impossible to find.

Reaching toward the ceiling, Zach stretched. "I've had enough excitement for one day. Let's go to bed."

"Roscoe's had less than five minutes' petting time. Even though he doesn't sleep through the night yet, maybe we should let him stay with us."

Zach leveled his gaze at her. "You're nuts."

She felt a sense of relief that he was stopping her from doing something stupid. "Okay, I'll put Roscoe back in the den."

After the kitten was attended to, she joined Zach in bed, scooting her back up against him in a spoon position. He wrapped an arm around her and held her close.

"What was that you said about jumping my bones?"

He yawned. "I can't remember."

Several seconds passed, then Cassidy added, "Last night we had too many cats. Now we have none."

Zach nuzzled her shoulder. "You always have me."

Having Zach was wonderful. Feeling his body wrapped around hers anchored her and gave her a sense of well-being. But she still missed the sound of a soothing purr from the spot between their heads where Starshine usually slept.

FOURTEEN

ONE STEP BACK FROM THE BRINK

FRESH OUT OF the shower, wearing nothing at all, Cassidy came into the bedroom and removed a bra and underpants from a drawer.

Zach, in a black tee shirt and jeans, sat at his desk reading the Saturday paper. Looking up, he smiled his slow easy smile. "Do you have to get dressed? Maybe we could go back to bed for a while."

"This is an idea whose time came and went last night."

"We were both tired. It would've had to be a quickie. What we really ought to do is plan an evening just for us." He gave her a look that made her wish she could go back to bed. "But you have a client at—let's see—nine o'clock, don't you?"

"How'd you know?"

"You're not still in bed with a second cup of coffee."

"Since Starshine isn't doing laps this morning, there's no point lolling around." The calico had come up for breakfast, then retreated to the basement again, neglecting her usual routine of running upstairs for a beginning-of-the-day cuddle.

"How long will your sessions run?"

"From nine to noon."

"The appraiser's coming at ten. She'll be in and out before you're done."

Zach wants to move. I don't. And we're not even talking about it. We're acting like one of those communication-impaired couples I see in therapy.

"Just so long as your appraiser doesn't walk in on one of my sessions."

"She's all done on the first floor. Even though the house'll clearly go as a fixer-upper, it's spacious and solidly built, so we shouldn't have to drop the price too low." He paused. "I don't suppose you've started looking at real estate ads yet."

Turning her back on him, she stared into the closet. All of her professional outfits appeared overdue for the cleaners. *Almost nine. Have to get dressed. Don't think about the house.* She seized on a pair of burgundy pants and a matching flowered silk shirt.

"I'm going into the office after the appraiser leaves. What with all the time I've been spending on Max's murder, I'm a little behind on other things."

"Fine." She bit off the word.

"I suppose you're pissed because I'm going ahead with the appraisal."

She turned to face him. His head was drawn up straight, his expression rigid and unyielding. *This is one time he's not going to roll over for you.*

"I'm pissed because you're acting as if we'd made a decision and we haven't."

"I'm just gathering information. So when the time comes, we can make an informed decision based on facts, not feelings."

"We're deciding where we want to live. If that isn't about feelings, I don't know what is."

"An appraisal doesn't commit us to anything."

"No, but you could have held off till we'd had more time to talk."

His voice turning cool, he said, "I've already made it

clear where I stand. I'm just waiting for you to do the same.''

Oh Lord, don't want to move, don't want to fight, don't even want to think about it.

She said, ''Let's not get into a tug of war over this.'' *How can you avoid it when you want opposite things?*

''Look, I hate to fight a lot more than you do.'' He leaned forward, arms on knees, his body language telling her he was ready to drop it.

Crossing the room, she kissed him lightly on the mouth. He smiled his easygoing smile again.

One step back from the brink but the battle's far from over.

The back doorbell rang, signaling that her nine o'clock client had arrived. Picking up her calendar, she took a quick look at herself in the full-length mirror on the closet door. Her curly cinnamon hair lay on her shoulders in permanent disarray. A faint spot showed on the front of her shirt, and her low-heeled pumps were one step away from the Good-will bag. *If there were a most disheveled contest, you'd definitely be a contender.*

She glanced at Zach, who was reading the list of names Claire had given them.

''Who's this Erin person?''

''Claire's sister.''

''Would you see if you can set up a meeting with her for tonight?''

''Sure.''

HER SESSIONS OVER, Cassidy ate a handful of peanut butter cups, then went up to the bedroom to check the answering machine. One message, a familiar deep voice. ''This is De-tective Wharton. I see you're having problems again. I'll need you to come into the station and tell me about the incident in the Dominick's parking lot.'' He reeled off a number Cassidy knew by heart because of her many dealings with the Oak Park police.

Oh shit. Not Wharton. After what happened last fall, he probably thinks you have a menacing-character fetish. Wharton was the cop who'd worked with them when an unknown person was making attempts on Zach's life. Having lied to the detective at the outset of his investigation, they'd earned themselves a well-deserved place on his list of least-credible persons.

She went to her desk to make phone calls. *Gran, Erin, and Wharton. From the one who likes me best to the one who likes me least.*

When Gran answered, Cassidy said, "I'm working with Zach on a story and I'd like you to help me do some cyber snooping."

"Oh goody! I've been surfing the Web a whole bunch lately and this'll give me a chance to see if I can get where I want to go."

"You're so good at jumping in and trying things on the computer. I'm not nearly as adventuresome as you."

"I always figure—what's the worst that could happen? I s'pose I might get my wires crossed and blow up the house, but I'd rather do that than die in bed."

"Dying in bed doesn't sound so bad to me." Cassidy remembered how warm and safe she'd felt the night before lying next to Zach.

"I've already planned how I want to go out," Gran said gleefully. "I want to be dancing on the table at some big party—"

"Topless?"

"Hah! If I uncovered any part of this scrawny old body of mine, everybody'd go running for the door. So anyway, I'm dancing on the table and I make this big dramatic leap into the arms of a lover, only he drops me and I break my neck."

"But not till you're a hundred and five!"

"No, of course not." Gran cackled, sounding like a little bantam rooster.

"So tell me about this story you and Zach are writing. And how'd you get him to let you in on it, anyway?"

"Do you remember that article in the *Post* about the groom who got shot?"

"I sure do. But Zach didn't write it, did he?"

"No, but now he's doing an in-depth piece about the victim, and I'm working with him because I can help with some contacts."

"Well, I'd sure be tickled to get in on it. There's nothing I like better than digging up the dirt on other people."

Cassidy smiled to herself. *Gran gobbles up other people's business like a dog wolfs kibbles. She's absolutely flagrant about it, but nobody ever seems to mind.*

"So," Cassidy asked, "where should we log on? Your computer or mine?"

"Why don't I come to your house so I can get in a visit with Roscoe?"

"Sounds good. I have to go out for a while but I'll call you when I get back. Oh—by the way—any word on Lillybeth?"

"She's getting better but it's slow. Us old folks don't bounce back the way you young people do."

Cassidy dialed Erin's number and a woman's voice answered. "This is Erin Dubuque speaking."

Erin's voice sounded so much like her sister's that it brought Cassidy to a momentary halt. Then she introduced herself, going on to say, "I believe Claire may have told you who I am." *And if she hasn't, this confidentiality limb I'm out on is about to break underneath me.*

"You *used to be* Claire's therapist," Erin said in a reproachful voice, "but you've turned her over to some new person she doesn't know at all."

Cassidy forced herself not to say the defensive words forming in her mind. "I get the impression you're not happy with that."

"Claire's barely making it from day to day. You abandoned her just when she needs you the most."

Heaviness settled on Cassidy's shoulders, the feeling that came over her whenever she thought she might've done something wrong. "Did Claire tell you why I had to stop seeing her?"

"She wants you to play detective, and for some reason I don't understand, you can't be both her therapist and her investigator at the same time. She has this crazy idea that you and your husband will prove Hank innocent, which isn't going to happen because everybody knows he did it. As her therapist, you should've had better sense than to go along with this outlandish request of hers."

Cassidy drew in a shallow breath. "Well, Erin, you may be right, but we still need to see you. Would it be okay if Zach and I came by your place sometime this evening?"

A short silence. "As much as I don't think this is going anywhere, I did promise Claire I'd talk to you. But I won't be free until eight. There were three days last week when Claire was too depressed to make it into work, so she's gone in today to catch up, and I'm babysitting Molly."

"I'm sorry to hear she's having such a tough time." *But she'd still have to grieve, even if she hadn't switched to Maggie, even if she were seeing me every day of the week.*

"I know you care about her. I just think this investigation is a big mistake."

Cassidy propped her feet on the radiator and stared out the west window. A mother pushed a stroller down the sidewalk on the opposite side of Hazel, a flock of other children running along beside her. A modern version of the old woman who lived in a shoe.

Most sane people would agree with Erin. What was

wrong with you, that you didn't have the sense to tell Claire no? Giving in to your own urge to investigate. Being selfish, just like you were with Zach when you insisted he let you in on the investigation.

Cassidy allowed herself five minutes of hair-shirt time, then reached for the phone again. *Time to call Detective Wharton, another person who's been known to scold you. For someone who hates disapproval, you certainly bring on your share of it.*

"Well, Ms. McCabe," the detective said, "we meet again."

CASSIDY SET the security system and stepped outside. Although the afternoon air felt sticky and warm, dark clouds filled the sky and the light was a gunmetal gray. Standing on her back stoop, she scanned the street between her house and the garage. The sixty-something man in the corner house across Briar was trimming his bushes. Two unoccupied cars sat at the curb.

Muggers—like rats—do not come out in the middle of the day. Yes, but parking lot thugs obviously do.

Keys in hand, phone in her purse, she made herself pick up her feet and start moving. Heading to the far corner of the garage, she looked down the alley. It was as uninhabited as the cars.

She drove west on Briar, intending to take Ridgeland south to Madison, and Madison east to the village hall, which sat atop the basement-level police station. Drawing up at a stop sign, she glanced into her rearview mirror and saw a battered sedan directly behind her Toyota. The driver, a black guy in a ball cap with the brim pulled to the side, was alone in the car, the light too dim to distinguish his features. She rolled a few feet forward to get a look at his license. The plate was missing.

Her chest tightened. Her heart started to race.

Are you going to let this creep scare you into a coronary? I'm so damned sick of thugs pushing me around. It's the middle of the day, houses all around, what can he do?

With shaking hands, she put her car in park, took out her cell phone, and started walking toward the sedan. She had taken only a few steps when the car went zooming backward to the intersection behind them and turned south.

She wiped her sweaty forehead. *Oh shit—he's watching the house. But not looking for a confrontation. At least not now he isn't, but who knows what he'll be looking for the next time you see him.*

FIFTEEN

CYBER SNOOPING

DETECTIVE WHARTON, tall and ruggedly handsome, skin the color of ebony, led her into the long narrow room that housed the detectives' unit. He sat her in front of his desk, took the chair behind it, and moved his black-framed glasses from the top of his head to his nose. "Okay, now tell me about this mope you ran into at Dominick's yesterday."

His voice courteous and cultured. His dark eyes probing her suspiciously.

The price you pay for having lied to him last time. She recounted the parking lot incident, then went on to tell him about the driver of the battered sedan. "Unfortunately, I couldn't begin to identify the make of the car."

"Did you recognize him?" Wharton asked. "Are you sure it was the same person?"

"I told you I didn't get a good look at the driver's face. But why put the car in reverse and stomp on the accelerator if it wasn't the same guy?"

"He might've thought you were a plainclothes cop stopping him for the missing plate."

"He knew I wasn't a cop. Cops wear suits and drive Fords, not ten-year-old Toyotas."

"All right, Ms. McCabe," he said with exaggerated politeness, "I will include in the report that you believe the offender tried to follow you today."

Don't antagonize him. He has every reason not to trust you.

Wharton shifted in his chair. "The offender threatened to hurt you unless your husband dropped the story he's working on. So, what story is that?"

"It's about Max O'Connell, the groom that got shot on his wedding day."

"That's an unsolved murder, isn't it? And it happened a few weeks back." He stared at her for several seconds. "So, what is it you're not telling me this time?"

She kept her face blank. "Zach's researching a story about a murder. That's what he does. He covers the crime beat for the *Post*. Why this guy decided to pick on me is anybody's guess."

"So you and your husband aren't mixing it up in police business again, is that right? There's no chance the two of you might be trying to close the case on your own." He raised his glasses to the top of his head.

Cassidy pulled herself up straight. "I know everyone in the department has heard all the stories about Zach and me interfering with the police. And that you all think we're a menace to society, even though we have solved a few crimes. Now I'm here to report a verbal assault. Does the fact that I pissed you off last time mean I'm going to receive differential treatment today?"

"No, of course not." His face grew more attentive. "We treat everybody the same."

Like hell you do.

Tapping his pen against the pad in his hand, he added, "I'll need the names of everyone your husband's interviewed."

"Zach's at his office now. You can call him there." She gave Wharton the number.

After the detective had taken her through her story two more times, he led her into a small room filled with camera and computer equipment. "We're going to do a compu-sketch," he said, pointing to a large monitor. They took their seats in front of the keyboard. Settling his glasses on his nose, the detective began to create a picture of the man who had threatened her. "Was his face wider or narrower? What kind of hair did he have?"

Focusing on the mental image in her brain, Cassidy answered Wharton's questions.

"So," he said, rolling his chair back, "you think that's it?"

"Looks exactly like him." *Gotta get a copy. This is a low priority for the cops. They're not going to spend nearly as much time showing the sketch around as you and Zach would.*

"Well, then, Ms. McCabe, I believe we're finished. You see any sign of this guy, don't hesitate to call 9-1-1. We won't put up with any of our citizens being harassed."

Cassidy leaned back in her chair and crossed her legs. "Before I go, I'd like a copy of the sketch. Zach needs to see it so he'll know who to look for."

"No can do. This is official police property. Tell your husband to come into the station and I'll show it to him."

"No, no." Smiling, she laced her hands together in her lap. "I have to have my own copy. My memory for faces is very poor. After a couple of days, I might not recognize him myself without it."

Wharton's mouth flattened into a tight line. "It's police policy. I can't give this out."

Policy—the word people use to justify slamming a door in your face.

"This is *my* offender. I'm the one he threatened. I should have a right to the sketch." She lowered her brow. "Doesn't the freedom of information act apply here?"

He started to shake his head.

"If you don't give me a copy, I'll march upstairs to the village manager's office and lodge a complaint. I will also mention the sarcastic way you talked to me when I first came in."

The village manager went to great lengths to keep Oak Parkers happy, because when they weren't they wrote letters to the editor, harassed the manager at meetings, and generally made his life miserable in every nonviolent way known to man. The local citizenry was well aware of its rights and never allowed anyone to abridge them.

Wharton's broad chest slowly rose and fell. "Let me see what the commander says." He was gone about five minutes. When he returned, he silently tapped a couple of keys, waited as the printer whirred, lifted the copy from the machine and handed it to her.

"I hope you're not planning to conduct your own search. The last thing you need is more bad press with this department."

"Thank you," she said sweetly and left.

"SO," GRAN SAID, "the guy you want to get the goods on is Garrett Hillard. And the reason we're doing it is, you think he might have created a false identity for himself."

Cassidy and Gran sat in matching swivel chairs in front of a long, built-in table in Zach's office, a spare room across from their bedroom. When Zach first moved in, he'd set up his computer equipment on a fifties-style dinette table. Then, about a year later, he decided to teach himself carpentry and rehabbed both spare rooms for a den and his office.

"Have you had any experience gathering data on people?" Cassidy asked.

"Well, actually, I did try it once." Roscoe climbed to Gran's shoulder and began chewing on her short, silvery wig. She took it off, exposing a pink scalp with sparse tufts of white hair.

"Maybe I should give him this ratty old thing." Gran flapped the wig in front of Roscoe so he could play with it. "He might think it's another kitten that doesn't move around much."

"He's got lots of other toys."

"But he might get lonely, considering Starshine won't give him the time of day."

"The reason she won't is, he keeps attacking her." *Starshine wouldn't go near him unless he was completely immobilized and smelled like tuna.*

"So maybe he needs this old wig here to cuddle up with."

Roscoe jumped from Gran's shoulder onto a piece of twine Zach had dropped on the hardwood floor. The kitten pounced on it from several different directions, then trotted around the room with the twine dangling from his mouth.

"Tell me about the time you tried to get information on somebody."

"Well, I was curious about this guy I met in my metal sculpture class."

"Metal sculpture? Don't you have to use a blowtorch? Why on earth would you be interested in metal sculpture?"

"'Cause the other classes were full of old ladies."

"So you did a search on this guy?"

"I'd invited him over for dinner a couple of times and he said he was a lifelong bachelor, but other than that he was pretty vague about his past, so I thought he might have some skeletons rattling around somewhere. Then I got this spam in my mailbox telling me I could find out anything about anybody, and I decided to check him out. But by the time I got the report back, I wasn't curious anymore."

"Why not?"

"Well, he started coming for dinner without waiting for

an invitation and he just talked my ears off. He never said anything about his past but he'd tell me what he ate for breakfast and when he did his laundry and what programs he watched." Gran's face tightened in disgust. "These old geezers who live alone turn into nonstop talking machines. So I decided the reason he'd never gotten married was that he talked everybody to death, and the reason he didn't say anything about his past was that he didn't have one."

"How'd you get rid of him?"

"Told him I'd gone stone deaf and the restaurant was closed. Then I got the email report and it was just as boring as the guy himself." Gran rolled her chair closer to the table. "Well, we better get started. Do you have Google in your favorites?"

With coaching from Gran, Cassidy typed in search words, then scrolled through pages of sites. "The biggest problem with the Internet is, there's too much of it."

"I usually just go surfing. And let me tell you—I've wandered into some pretty strange places. Why, I hardly even get embarrassed anymore when I see beach-ball-sized boobs and men with huge thingies. Then there was this site called Out-of-Species-Dating, but I decided I probably didn't need to know about that."

After several more tries, they landed on Vitalrec.com, a Website that provided birth, death, marriage, and divorce records for a fee.

"A death record," Cassidy said as she typed in Hillard's name and the social security number Zach had obtained from Izzie. "Just what I was looking for."

"But you know he's alive, don't you?" Gran paused. "Oh, I get it. You think he took some dead guy's social security number."

"That's the easiest way I'm aware of to change identities."

"Is this all you're looking for?" Gran asked. "I got a lot more out of that program I used."

They hunted around a while longer and came across a Website that, for a larger fee, provided background checks on dating partners, including criminal records, former addresses, and the names of people who'd lived with the person being checked on.

"Well," Gran said in an exuberant voice, "with all this information, you oughta be able to tell for sure if that old Garrett Hillard is who he says he is."

"And if he's not, he must be Max's former roommate."

SIXTEEN

SIBLING RIVALRY

"I DON'T LIKE THIS one bit," Zach said, his face turning grim. He sat on the paisley sofa, swigging from a bottle of beer. Cassidy, the compu-sketch in her hands, was seated in the armchair to his left. She'd just filled him in on the day's events: her encounter with the battered sedan and her visit to the police station.

"I was pretty upset when I first saw the car," she said, "but the more I thought about it, the more I decided it wasn't all bad."

"How is it not bad?" Emptying his bottle, Zach set it on the glass table in front of the sofa.

"The fact that he ran away. It doesn't look like he wants to do anything more than scare me."

Zach's brows drew together. "If he did intend to do you bodily harm, he wouldn't make his move during daylight hours in the middle of Briar."

"Well, but at least I got a copy of the sketch."

"I have to admit, that's pretty amazing." Zach took it from her. "The only time I've managed to get my hands on one of these is when the cops wanted some offender's face plastered all over the front page."

"This guy's obviously a link to the killer. Now that we have the sketch, maybe we can track him down and get him to tell us who hired him."

"Beat it out of him with rubber hoses," Zach said with

a smile. "Okay, here's what we'll do. As long as we're going into the city to interview Erin, we can eat at Kincaid's afterward, then wait till the place clears out and show this face to everyone who works there."

"Sounds good."

"But before I do anything else," Zach stood, the sketch in his hand, "I'm going to take a walk around the neighborhood and see if I can find any old beaters with guys behind the wheel that look like this."

"SORRY I WAS SUCH a bitch on the phone," Erin said, standing in her condo doorway. Cassidy was surprised again at the similarity between Erin's voice and Claire's.

"I'm not usually like that," Erin added, leading them into her living room. "It's just that I'm so worried about Claire."

Cassidy felt a stab of guilt. "We'll be finished with the investigation before long, and then I can start seeing Claire as a client again."

"Please sit down." Erin waited while Cassidy and Zach settled on a sofa draped with gold and blue shawls, then she lowered her large frame into an armchair across from them. Although the furniture was faded, Erin had used colorful fabrics and artifacts to brighten the room: a blue and red rug hanging above the armchair, a shelving unit filled with vividly painted pottery, billowing golden drapes drawn across the window.

Zach held his pad in his hand.

"This is an interview, isn't it?" Erin said uneasily. "You're going to ask personal questions, and if I answer them, embarrassing information will appear in the newspaper." She shook her head. "I can't imagine what Claire was thinking when she agreed to let you do a story."

"You know why she did it," Cassidy said.

Erin turned her large green eyes on Cassidy. "She wants closure, but it's never going to happen. Hank had Max shot and he's going to get away with it, just like he's gotten away with every other rotten thing he's ever done.''

Except for her luminous eyes, Erin was a study in plainness, with her broad face, square chin, and drab brown hair. The only thing she'd done to enhance her appearance was attire herself in a loose, ankle-length dress that camouflaged her extra pounds.

With such an angelic beauty for a sister, can see why Erin would choose not to compete in the looks department.

Cassidy said, ''I gather there's no love lost between you and Hank.''

''I watched him destroy Claire's confidence. I saw how he broke her down. It seemed like a minor miracle when you finally convinced her to leave. I went with her to sign the lease for her apartment, and right up to the last minute, I was afraid she'd back out.''

''I know you two are extremely close.'' *In a strange, convoluted sort of way that I don't quite have a handle on.*

''I'm the person Claire can always count on. The one who takes Molly when the nanny doesn't show, the one Claire calls in the middle of the night, the one who does the laundry when she can't get out of bed.''

''You've been like a second mother to her, haven't you?''

Erin pushed one side of her jaw-length hair behind her ear, where it stayed briefly before coming loose again. ''Claire feels things too intensely. She's too fragile. When we were kids, she was always falling apart, and it was my job to put her back together again. Mom would have done it if she could, but she had to work long hours just to put food on the table.''

Sounds like Erin wouldn't mind talking about her family. And I wouldn't mind hearing what the older sister thinks of the father the younger sister has on such a pedestal. A father who's ten years deceased but still lives on inside Claire's head.

"Wasn't your dad home a lot?" Cassidy asked. "Claire told me he was a musician and didn't work regularly."

Cassidy noticed that Zach was giving her a quizzical look. *Has no idea why I'm pursuing the paternal thread.*

Her jaw tightening, Erin said. "I'm sure you already know quite a bit about our father."

"I know what Claire said. But two people from the same family seldom see things exactly the same way. I'd like to hear what your take on him was."

Erin stared at Zach. "If I talk about my father, is that going to end up in your story too?"

Cassidy jumped in before Zach could answer. "Your father has no connection to either the newspaper story or our investigation. I'm only asking because I like to have the broadest possible context for doing therapy. The more I know about Claire's childhood, the better equipped I'll be to help her."

"Oh. I guess that makes sense." Folding one hand into the other, Erin began alternately squeezing them in a gesture that bore some resemblance to hand-wringing. "Dad adored Claire. He called her his little princess and showed her off to all his friends. That is, he adored her except when she did some normal kid thing like cry, or fall down, or get her dress dirty. Then he'd go on a rant about how stupid she was, what a disappointment she was, that sort of thing. That's when she'd fall apart and I'd have to pick up the pieces."

"What was he like with you?"

"I was the lucky one. I wasn't even on his radar screen."

So that's why Erin doesn't wear makeup or get her hair styled. Being plain is safer than being pretty.

"But didn't you sometimes resent all the attention Claire got?"

A sort of blankness came over Erin's face. She stared at the wall behind their heads. "I've always had it easier than Claire. She's the one who gets abused and depressed. I get left alone, and that's how I like it."

Her voice soft, Cassidy asked, "When Claire was three and you were seven, didn't you try to smother her with a pillow?"

"I was just playing," Erin replied in a flat monotone. "I didn't know she could get hurt."

"Well," Zach said, sitting straighter, "it was interesting to hear about your father, but it seems we've gone a little off topic here. What I really want to pick your brain about is Max and Hank."

Cassidy's mouth went tight with irritation, but she quickly squelched it. *How long do you expect Zach to sit and wait around while you explore family dynamics?*

"Let's start with Max," Zach continued. "What did you think of him?"

Becoming more animated, Erin said, "I hardly knew Max, but I was skeptical about the wedding. Every man Claire's ever been involved with has turned out to be abusive. Why would Max be any different?"

"Well, then, let's talk about Hank. What makes you so certain he was behind the shooting?"

"Hank's totally self-absorbed and he'll do anything to get what he wants. And what he wants, obviously, is Claire. The one good thing about Max was, when Claire was with him, Hank couldn't get to her. But now that Max is gone, Hank's regaining some of his control. He's convinced Claire that he's innocent, and he's even got her feeling sorry for him."

Zach said, "We talked to Hank yesterday and he told us something of the history you two have together."

Erin's face paled. "What did he say?"

Cassidy replied, "He told us he dated you before he met Claire. And that you trashed his apartment when he dropped you."

Turning her head sharply away, Erin said nothing.

"Why did you do it?"

"I don't know," Erin responded in a faint voice. "Something came over me and I just did it. I've never done anything like that before.''

When people get violent, they don't usually start with trashing an apartment. They start with small things and work their way up.

"Hank said you were jealous of Claire," Cassidy stated.

"That's not true," Erin said, still looking away from them. "I like being alone. I'm glad I don't need men the way Claire does. Men just make your life miserable.''

"If you're not jealous, why do you sometimes pick fights with Claire? Why do you say things to hurt her?''

"Claire's too sensitive, I told you that already." A brief silence. "I only do it to bring her down a peg. When she starts thinking she's better than I am. She's not always nice to me, you know. Here I've spent my whole life picking up the pieces for her, and then she gets snippy on me. So I slap her out of it. It's for her own good.''

"You *physically* slap her?''

"No, of course not. I just meant…I bring her to her senses, that's all.''

Conflict between sibs—not exactly uncommon. Except Erin's wrapped her whole life around her sister. And if her sister were to succeed in getting herself together, what would be left for Erin?.

"You said you've never done anything like trashing Hank's apartment before, but I don't think that's true. I think you've done similar things in the past.''

"No, nothing like what I did with Hank's apartment. Just little things." Erin stared at the wall behind them. "One time I broke my father's watch. But why should men get away with hurting you and never have to pay?''

As he pulled out into traffic, Zach asked, "How crazy is Erin, anyway?''

"I can't be certain from just that one interview. Erin could be simply an overzealous caretaker who uses her sister to fill up the emptiness in her own life. Or—and this is more likely—she could be a borderline who swings back and forth between extreme love and extreme hate."

Zach glanced at Cassidy. "Trashing Hank's apartment. Breaking her father's things. What's the connection between violence and overzealous caretaking?"

"People who go way overboard on caretaking almost always have a lot of rage. They develop all this resentment that they're pouring so much energy into another person's needs and ignoring their own."

"So why didn't Erin just turn Claire over to you and get on with her life?"

"She probably never had a life and doesn't know how to get one."

Cassidy sighed. "And besides, look at the payoff she gets out of mothering Claire. It allows her to feel one-up, saintly, and wise. Considering how little else she has going for her, she's not about to give that up."

"How does Erin have time for all this caretaking, anyway? Doesn't she have a job?"

"She's a technical writer. She can work at home whenever she wants so she has maximum flexibility.

Cassidy gazed at the car in front of them. The trunk was tied down with rope. A taillight was broken. The license plate hung from one screw. A half dozen stickers in the rear window exhorted sinners to repent. The left turn signal came on, and the car turned right from the left lane.

"Did you know Erin was this warped going into the interview?"

"I knew Claire leaned on her sister too much and I've been working to get her to be more independent. But I didn't realize Erin was as over-involved as she is." Cassidy shook her head. "The problem with individual therapy is, you only get one person's perspective."

"Well, I'm with Hank. I think Erin has a big problem with jealousy, and I also think she's nuts enough to do something like hire a hitman."

"Claire will have a terrible time if it turns out her sister is the killer. Even worse than if it turns out to be Hank. But I have to agree. Erin is a possibility. And, in fact, she has a double motive—her jealousy over Claire's wonderful marriage, and her need to keep Max from coming between them.''

SEVENTEEN

A Feminist Power Spike

CARRYING A BRIEFCASE with the sketch in it, Zach led the way down the half flight of stairs into Kincaid's well-lit, basement-level dining room. When they'd been there before, the place was almost empty, allowing Cassidy to appreciate its muted atmosphere and understated design. On a Saturday night at nine, the clatter of voices reverberating off hard surfaces made her wish she'd brought earplugs. She noticed Nicky Andrews standing near the kitchen door. He gave them a broad wave.

Zach asked for a table.

The sleekly dressed woman at the host's station said, "It'll be about fifteen minutes. You can wait in the bar if you like."

Zach headed toward the polished-wood bar, with Cassidy grudgingly trailing behind him.

You are so not with it. You don't like sitting on a bar stool sucking up alcohol before dinner. You don't like trendy places where you have to shout to be heard. You don't like being packed into a room so crowded you have to walk sideways and grease your behind to get between the tables.

Zach, on the other hand, would be perfectly happy to spend every Saturday night of his life in a place like this. It led her to wonder once again if she and her husband had anything in common.

By the time the host called Zach's name, Cassidy had sipped half a Coke, while Zach had guzzled his bourbon and looked as if he were thinking of ordering another.

The host, a tall woman in a long black dress with a slit up the front, led them to a table in the middle of the room where they sat at right angles from each other. A cherubic, round-faced waitress who could have passed for fifteen asked for their drink orders.

"We'd like to see the menus first," Cassidy said, jumping in before Zach could order a second drink.

"I'll get them right away."

After the waitress left, Zach said amiably, "Very clever, the way you cut me off at the pass. But not necessary. All I'm planning to get is wine with dinner."

She laid her hand over his. "Maybe this marriage can be saved after all."

Gazing out over the dining room, Cassidy watched their waitress as she threaded her way to the host's station, where she stopped to talk to the slit-skirted woman who stood there. Joining them, Nicky draped a casual arm across the young waitress' shoulders.

"Do you see what Nicky's doing?" Cassidy's brow creased in irritation. "Isn't that sexual harassment?"

"I'd say it's more avuncular than sexual. That's just how Nicky is. He puts his hands on everybody, including me."

"But he's the boss. He shouldn't be touching young female employees."

"Sexual harassment's in the eye of the beholder. You're just having some kind of feminist power spike, so you see his behavior as harassment. Since I generally don't get up in arms over things like that, I see it as nothing more than Nicky's gregarious nature coming out."

"I am not having a feminist power spike. What Nicky's doing is wrong and you know it."

The waitress patted Nicky's cheek.

"Even if the victim likes it?" Zach said, his voice amused.

"They both need sensitivity training."

The waitress returned and handed them menus. Cassidy studied the list of entrées.

"What do you suppose this tuna with wasabi mashed potatoes and peapods in a sake-ginger-lemongrass sauce is?"

"You'll have to ask the waitress. I'm going to play it safe and order the steak and fries."

"You keep mainlining fat grams, you may have to exercise to avoid blimping out," she said, knowing how much he hated any form of physical activity that had no purpose other than keeping the body fit.

"Thus spaketh the woman who lives on peanut butter cups."

Shaking her head, Cassidy looked up to see a slender blond waiter pass their table. "Isn't that Luke?"

"That's him all right. According to Nicky, the only person who ever managed to hold out against Max's puppy-dog ways."

Closing her menu, Cassidy watched Luke pass through the swinging doors into the kitchen. "I'd like to take a crack at him. Try to build some rapport."

"You think you can get him to open up?"

"Not here in the restaurant I won't. But if I can get some conversation going, make him feel comfortable with me tonight, maybe I can get him to tell me about his fight with Max at some later time."

"Does that mean you don't feel the need to hover over my shoulder while I show the sketch around?"

"I believe I could resist that." A sharp twinge in her abdomen reminded her that it was a couple of hours past her usual dinner hour and her stomach wasn't happy with the delay. After another five minutes, she saw the waitress approaching their table. "Well, at last. I was beginning to think the restaurant might close around us before we got to order."

A short time later a bottle of wine and a basket of crusty

Italian bread arrived. Cassidy devoured three slices, then took a large swallow of Merlot. Her stomach appeased, she leaned back in her chair, let out a sigh of satisfaction, and watched Nicky Andrews make his way toward them.

"I'm glad he waited till I got something to eat," she told Zach. "I'm much less likely to yell at him for touching his waitress now that I'm not on the verge of starvation."

Stopping at their table, Nicky rested a hand on the empty chair across from Cassidy. "Hey, you took my advice and came back for dinner. You're gonna love the food here. After Max disappeared on me, I hired a chef who's twice as good and actually works for less—but don't tell him I said so. In the long run, turns out Maxie did me a favor. So, what'd you two order, anyway?"

"The tuna," Cassidy said.

"Excellent choice. Wait till you see it. This guy's really good at presentation." He crossed his arms over his chest. "What about you, Zach?"

"The T-bone."

"Aw, Zach, you got no imagination. When you come here, you oughta try one of our more exotic creations."

"Next time." Zach pushed his chair a few inches back from the table. "Sit down for a minute, will you? I've got something to show you."

The broad-shouldered restaurateur seated himself next to Zach, who took out the sketch and laid it on the table. "You ever see this guy?"

Nicky gazed at the picture. "Looks like one of those jobbies that comes out of a cop shop."

"It is."

"So what's the deal? Is this a clue you've got more going on than just a story?"

"Sorry, I can't go into any of the details. But I need you to look at the face and tell me if you've ever seen this guy."

"Always a one-way street with you reporters," Nicky grumbled good-naturedly. He gazed at the sketch again.

"Can't say for sure. Got so many people in and out here, I can't begin to remember all the faces."

Zach returned the sketch to his briefcase. "As soon as the place clears out, I'd like to take it around to your employees."

"You can show it to the staff all you want but don't go near the customers. They might think we're harboring criminals or something." Nicky started to get up.

Remembering Susan's depiction of Max as a lady's man, Cassidy said, "There's something else I'd like to ask about Max."

Nicky settled back in his chair.

"How was Max with women?"

"You mean, did he like them? Sure he did. Who doesn't? Well, half my waiters don't, but you know what I mean."

Zach folded his arms on the table. "So Max wasn't gay or bi?"

"Not so far as I could tell. But sometimes people fool you. There were a couple of guys I didn't catch on till they showed up with full-blown AIDS."

"That's not exactly what I was asking," Cassidy said. "What I wanted to know is whether or not Max was a Don Juan type? Or more of a one-woman guy?"

"Well, Max was a charmer, so naturally he had chicks all over him. He probably could've had a different broad every night if he wanted to, but I don't think he ran around that much. You gotta remember he had this strict Catholic mom. She threw all this morality at him, and it seemed to me that some of it stuck."

This the same person Susan was talking about? Or is Nicky's sense of morality a little askew? Cocking her head, Cassidy offered a playful smile.

"C'mon, Nicky, 'fess up. Was Max really such a good boy? Or did he just seem good in comparison to you?"

Nicky flashed her a grin, his dark eyes holding hers an

instant too long. Just as she was starting to feel uneasy, he looked away.

"Hey, I don't claim to be any role model where chicks are concerned. I got burned in two divorces and I'm not looking to marry again. But hell, I'm not any monk either. I just take it where I can get it and don't pretend to be any better than I am. But Max, he was the marrying kind. He couldn't wait to stand in front of a preacher with Claire." A somber look coming over his face, Nicky punched his right fist into his left hand. "What a lousy shame some bastard had to go and blow his head off before he even got to enjoy his wedding night."

Cassidy rested her chin on her fist. "What do you think, Nicky? Was Max faithful to Claire or not?"

"I couldn't say for sure. But if I had to guess, I'd say he was."

And if he wasn't, I'd rather not know. And most of all, I'd rather not have to tell Claire.

Zach looked toward the kitchen. "I believe that's our dinner coming."

"Yeah baby! You come get me later, Zach, and I'll introduce you around." Nicky ambled off in the direction of the bar.

Cassidy ate half her large dinner, which was every bit as good as Nicky had claimed, then asked a busboy to wrap the leftovers. By the time he returned with her doggie bag, it was going on eleven and the restaurant was nearly empty.

Zach pushed back his plate, which held not a scrap of edible food.

"Okay, I'm off to show the sketch."

Cassidy fastened her gaze on Luke. He spoke to a foursome at a table across the room, then headed into the kitchen. Emerging a short time later, he stood near the host's station to chat with the youthful waitress who'd served Cassidy and Zach, then wandered around talking to a few other people, finally ending up at a computer station not far from Cassidy. He leaned against it, his left arm draped across the small shelf, his legs crossed at the ankles, one foot resting on its toe. His body was so gracefully arranged he could have been posing as a model.

Walking up to him, Cassidy said, "Zach's busy showing the police sketch around and I've been sitting alone at that table for ages. What I really need is somebody to talk to. So if you could find it in your heart to keep me company for a while, I'd be forever in your debt."

If you were as lacking in self-reliance as you just claimed, you'd probably need to take yourself out and shoot you.

Luke rubbed his goatee. "Um…I'm not very good at small talk."

Cassidy beamed her brightest smile. "I assure you, I can talk enough for both of us."

He ventured a small smile in return and followed as she retraced her steps.

Propping both elbows on the table, she laced her hands together. "The restaurant business has always seemed glamorous to me. I have this image of the staff leaving work at midnight and partying until dawn every night of the week."

"I guess a few people do that." He gazed at some point beyond her left shoulder.

"I'd never hold up myself."

"I'm not into it much either. People usually go in groups—I don't have that many friends."

"Well, a lot of people are a little shy."

His face flushing, he picked up Zach's discarded napkin and wrapped it around his hand. "I didn't know it showed."

"It doesn't. It's just that it seems like you have a lot going for you, so I figured—if you don't have many friends, it must be because you're shy."

"I have a lot going for me?"

"Sure you do. You're good looking, easy to talk to, a hard worker." *As if you knew anything about him.*

"Yeah, but all I'm doing is waiting tables. My parents are constantly on my case about it. They think I'm wasting my life."

"Well, there must be some reason you're doing what you're doing." These were not empty words. Cassidy possessed a deeply held belief that when people failed to live up to their potential, it was because some part of them wouldn't allow it.

"A reason? Like what?" He stretched the napkin out, then wrapped it around his hand again.

"Do you like waiting tables?"

"The money's good. The tips really add up. But I'm not going any place."

He stared into space for about three beats. "I'm still living at home with my parents."

"So what would you like to do instead of being a waiter?"

He shrugged. "I haven't a clue."

Cassidy felt an urge to dig deeper but feared that too many questions would scare him off. "You know, I was over thirty when I went back to school to get my master's in social work. Figuring these things out can take time."

She noticed that her husband was sitting on a bar stool watching her. "Well, it looks like Zach's finished with the sketch." They both stood up. "I appreciate your rescuing me from boredom. It's one of my least favorite things."

The waiter looked directly at her for the first time. "Nice talking to you."

Well, you've succeeded in priming the pump. Here's hoping you can get some water out of it next time. She started across the room toward Zach, who met her halfway.

"Any luck with the sketch?"

"No, but I wasn't really expecting to get any hits the first time out. I've got plenty of places left to try—the Naperville restaurant plus all the bars in Chicago."

"All the bars in Chicago?" she said with dismay.

He smiled. "You should know by now how tedious investigations are."

Out on the sidewalk the air was chilly, making Cassidy wish she'd remembered to bring a jacket. Across the street, Le Barre's neon sign winked at them.

"You want to try there?"

"That place is going to take a little time. Think I'd rather wait till I can get an earlier start."

ZACH SAID, "Well, we made it home before midnight. So how 'bout we have a glass of wine and listen to some music?"

What nice code words. So much better than "you wanna do it?" or "how 'bout a roll in the hay?"

Standing near the cartoon-plastered refrigerator, she said, "Before we were married, it didn't matter how late it was. Morning, noon, or night—anytime was fine."

"I thought we got married so we could get some rest." Removing two stemmed glasses from the rack in the dining room, Zach poured wine, then gathered her into his arms. Nestling his face in her hair, he asked, "You miss the old days when we were doing it every chance we got?"

"Sometimes. But overall, I prefer the comfort of marriage."

Upstairs Zach slid a Rory Block CD into the player, drank half his wine, then began undressing Cassidy. Slowly he removed her blouse, slacks, and shoes, his hand brushing against her bra, his finger sliding down inside her underpants. She felt as if her skin were melting in all the places he touched her.

Glancing in the mirror, she frowned at her boring white cotton underwear. *Even though your figure isn't bad, you can't show it off to advantage without something exotic and filmy to package it in.*

"I need to get over being intimidated by Victoria's Secret."

"Let me pick out some things for you. Victoria's Secret doesn't bother me at all."

She decided not to ask how many other women he'd shopped for there.

Zach took her hand. "Come dance with me." Leading her into the empty space in the middle of the room, he slid his hands around her back as she looped her arms around his neck and pressed her body against his. Rory Block's whiskey voice wove itself around them, ensnaring them in its deep contralto web.

EIGHTEEN

ASTROLOGY AND LOOPHOLES

SITTING UP IN BED, Cassidy was aware of a sense of languor and contentment. *Afterglow—like melt-in-the-mouth chocolate after a sumptuous meal. Good thing it's Sunday and I don't have to worry about wiping the silly smile off my face.*

She spent some time in the den with Roscoe, then returned to the bedroom where Starshine and a mug of lukewarm coffee awaited her. Cassidy settled back on the bed, and the calico climbed onto her chest, squinted her eyes, and stretched her chin for scratching.

Pulling a tee shirt from his drawer, Zach said, "This business of juggling cats is getting tiresome. I think we should institute an open door policy. Let Starshine and Roscoe work out their differences."

"But he'll attack her."

"He's just a kitten. The worst that'll happen is her pride will be wounded."

"You say that as if a blow to one's pride wasn't one step down from mortal injury. I can't stand it myself, and I'd hate to see Starshine go through the humiliation of being chased around her own turf by a pint-sized kitten."

Zach leveled his eyes at her. "I'm letting Roscoe out."
Hate it when he overrules me like that.
Yeah, but how else can he get you to do what he wants?

This is not worth a fight. Especially not with the battle about the house about to crash down on you.

Zach opened the door to the den and Roscoe came running into the bedroom. Unaware of Starshine's presence, he toppled the wastebasket, then dived into the pile of loose paper spilling out of it.

Fur standing along the ridge of her spine, Starshine moved slowly to the foot of the bed and hissed. Although the calico could easily have disappeared, Cassidy understood her need to take the offensive. She would have done the same herself.

Roscoe launched himself at Starshine. Racing to the opposite side of the bed, the calico jumped down and darted out the door, the kitten in close pursuit.

Cassidy went bolting after the cats. By the time she hit the stairway, they were gone. Dashing through the living room, she heard piercing screams ahead of her and a phone ringing in the background. As she entered the kitchen, she saw Roscoe prancing in front of Starshine, who was backed into a corner, terrible noises coming out of her mouth.

You should lock that vicious little usurper back in the den.

No—Zach's right—you should stop trying to control everything and let them work it out.

Cassidy gripped her arms across her chest and watched. Roscoe jumped at Starshine and drew quickly back; jumped again, coming a little closer; then threw himself at her in a major attack. The calico reared up on her hind legs and smacked him soundly. The kitten moved away. Arching her back, Starshine took mincing steps toward him and slapped him again. He turned and fled. The calico executed a little victory dance, then sprang onto the counter. Gazing at her human, she awaited praise.

Cassidy felt a thrill of triumph. Raising one fist, she said, "Power to the distaff side. We shall overcome."

Don't you think you're over identifying just a little?

After lavishing compliments on Starshine, Cassidy went

upstairs to see where Roscoe had landed. She found him washing himself on a recliner in the den. *A dose of humiliation is good for youthful upstarts. But you and Starshine should never have to endure it.*

When she returned to the bedroom, Zach handed her a used envelope with a phone number scribbled on it. "Julie called while you were running after the cats. She's ready to do your reading."

Sitting in her desk chair, Cassidy stared through the side window at leafy maple branches, the sunlight bringing out a vivid palette of greens. She still didn't like having astrology foisted on her, but at least it would give her a chance to ask Julie about her I'm-not-sure-they-ought-to-get-married comment at the wedding.

But you'll have to be nice. You can't disparage astrology and expect her to open up to you.

Cassidy returned Julie's call.

"I'd like you to come to the house this morning," Julie said in her ethereal voice. "Mom's out so there won't be any interruptions."

"Could we hold off until noon?" Cassidy asked, thinking it would be nice to take a shower, get dressed, and eat before she left.

"The latest we can start is eleven. I'll explain when you get here."

Cassidy looked at her watch. It was now ten and it would take half an hour to get there. *Looks like breakfast will be peanut butter cups in the car.*

As she hung up the phone, Zach said, "Why don't I drive? To make sure the parking lot guy doesn't give you any trouble."

You should let him, a small voice whispered. You don't want anybody hurting you ever again.

She shook her head. "I have to be able to face these things on my own."

"That's nuts. Having some thug threaten you and follow

you around isn't the sort of thing anybody should have to face on their own.''

"I need to do it because... '' she faltered, trying to make sense of her feelings ''...because I brought this on myself by getting involved in the investigation.... And because I'll lose my confidence if I let you do too much protecting. I'll start seeing myself as a wimp.''

Before Cassidy left, Zach searched the neighborhood for a battered sedan.

"HEY CASS,'' Julie greeted from the open doorway of the tricolor Victorian.

"The flowers are gorgeous,'' Cassidy said, referring to the blossoms sprouting from the wooden boxes on the porch railing. ''Your mother told us you were the one keeping them alive.''

Julie offered a dreamy smile. ''She complains about it and tells me to stop watering them, but I can't just let them die.'' The astrologer brought Cassidy inside the house. "Follow me, we're headed up to my room.''

Stepping from Irene's pristine living quarters into Julie's kaleidoscopic bedroom was like going from a symphony orchestra to a mariachi band. There were bright green café curtains at the windows; large contemporary paintings with vivid splashes of red and yellow on the walls; colorful pillows piled high on the bed; and shiny glass beads festooned across the picture frames.

Julie gestured toward a straight-backed chair in front of a heavy wooden desk. ''Have a seat.''

As the two women took their places, Cassidy noted a computer-generated sheet of paper on the desk's surface: concentric circles and mysterious symbols, with black and red lines drawn inside the innermost space. *That must be the actual horoscope.*

"Well, let's begin.'' Julie touched a finger to her lips. "The reason I needed you here at eleven is, I didn't want to start the reading during a void of the moon.''

Don't ask. Whatever she says, it'll just make you want to argue.

Handing Cassidy a sheet with dates and times on it, Julie added, "These are all the times in June to watch out for. You never want to start anything during a void of the moon. Any action you initiate then is destined to go nowhere. If you schedule a client's first session during one of these times, the therapy is bound to fail."

So it doesn't matter whether my clinical work is good or bad—it all depends on the moon. Keeping her voice neutral, Cassidy thanked Julie, folded the timetable, and slipped it in her purse.

Looking down at the sheet on her desk, Julie continued. "I'm going to tell you what I see in your chart, and I need you to let me know if I'm right or not."

"I thought you said the charts never lie."

"They don't. But I could be a bit off in my reading. There's always the possibility of human error."

Sounds like a loophole wide enough to accommodate that moon you're not supposed to start things in the void of.

"Well, Cass, I see that you're quite health-conscious. You exercise regularly, watch what you eat, and generally keep yourself fit."

"I wish that were true, but the fact is, I stuff myself with chocolate and I'm kind of a slug when it comes to physical activity."

Julie raised her red-brown eyes, which appeared not the least daunted by Cassidy's response. Moving on, she said, "You're a warm, understanding person. People are drawn to you. You always try to see things from the other person's point of view."

Cassidy nodded. *Considering I'm a therapist, that wasn't much of a stretch.*

Tilting her head, Julie added, "But you have an opposite side—a self-centered side—that's also very strong."

Ooops! She nailed you on that one.

"And both sides get you into trouble. Your compassionate side causes you to get over-involved with other people's problems, and your self-centered side makes you fight too hard to get what you want.''

Cassidy sat very still. A small shiver ran down her arms. She nodded slowly.

Warming to her subject, Julie elaborated on the problems Cassidy encountered because of the internal conflict between these two warring parts. She was mesmerized. *How could Julie know these things about you? She can't. There's no way the position of the planets at your birth molded your personality.* But saying this to herself did not stop her from hanging on Julie's every word.

The younger woman paused to take a breath. "You're also a bit of a loner. You have some close friends, but you need a lot of time to yourself as well.''

That true? More or less. But not to any large degree. Cassidy gave a minimal response and Julie went on quickly to her next pronouncement.

"You're a highly structured person. You like everything planned out in advance. Your house is always in good shape.''

Cassidy worked to keep a smile off her face. "I don't think that one quite fits.''

"In about six months your therapy practice will see a sharp increase, and within the year you'll double your number of clients.''

Some part of Cassidy began to jump up and down with anticipation. She tried to tell the jumping part that she didn't believe in astrology, but it continued its excited dance nonetheless.

"There's something else coming that's not so good,'' Julie said somberly, "and this will happen before the month is out.''

Cassidy's stomach started to twitch. "What is it?''

"A crisis of some kind, but it's not at all clear what it'll be.'' Julie met Cassidy's gaze. "I can't tell if it's a health issue, or connected to one of your clients, or a relationship problem.''

The parking lot guy beating me up? Claire turning suicidal? A fight with Zach over moving? You have potential crises all over the place.

"But it can't be too bad, can it?" Cassidy reminded herself again that she didn't believe in astrology. "If my practice is going to double, I must get through it and be okay.''

"I'm sure you will," Julie agreed, but her eyes looked troubled.

At the end of the hour, she laced her hands together on top of the chart.

"Well, Cass, I feel a much stronger connection to you now. This reading has created a bond between us, and the more our relationship evolves, the better we'll both be at helping Claire. Sometimes I think the three of us—you, Claire, and me—were sisters in a former life.''

Personally, I take my religion from the beer commercial that says you only go around once. Cassidy nodded and smiled the way she did in therapy when clients made outrageous statements.

"I realize you had your doubts coming in, "Julie said, "but I'm sure this reading has given you something to think about.''

"Some of what you said was right on target." *Faint praise. C'mon, you want to stay on her good side.* "It was very informative. I got a lot out of it.''

Julie tilted her head. "I like to help people. That's the reason I became an astrologer in the first place.''

"There's one other thing you could do." Cassidy pressed a fist up under her chin. "Remember at the wedding when you said you weren't sure that Max and Claire should get married? I'd like to know what you meant by that.''

"No, I can't." Julie started breathing in short gasps. "I can't talk about it.''

Leaning forward, Cassidy asked, "What would be so bad about telling me?"

"I just can't. I'm not supposed to. I don't even like to think about it."

"Who said you're not supposed to?"

"My mother told me not to say a word."

"So your mother doesn't want you to talk about it?"

Julie fixed her gaze on one of the windows. "I don't want to either. I never should've said anything."

"But you did. And there was some reason you wanted me to know or you wouldn't have said it."

The astrologer tugged at a stray piece of hair. "I wanted to warn somebody."

"Julie, I think this is important. You need to tell me."

"What difference does it make? Max is dead." Julie's eyes filled. She went to her nightstand and grabbed a handful of tissues, then sat behind her desk again.

"You really need to tell me."

Dabbing at her eyes, Julie stared at the window for a long time. "Will you promise not to tell anybody?"

"If there's any possibility this is connected to Max's death, other people will have to be told."

Julie sucked in air through her mouth. "My brother molested me. When I was eight and he was ten. The reason I didn't think they should get married is, I was worried about Molly."

Oh God! You should have seen this coming. "How awful!"

"I told my parents but they didn't believe me. Mom got angry and said I should never talk about it."

"It wasn't your fault. You understand that, don't you?"

Julie nodded. "I've read a lot of books. I know I didn't do anything wrong. It's just...I don't like to think about it."

"Have you seen a therapist?"

She shook her head.

"Therapy really does help."

"Maybe someday."

Cassidy sat in silence, giving Julie some time. She saw that the young woman's tears had stopped and her breathing evened out. "Could you tell me exactly what he did to you?"

Julie looked down at her hands. "I've told you enough. I'm not going to say another word."

"I really appreciate that you were willing to talk about it." Cassidy lay her hand on the younger woman's arm. "I have to tell Claire, you know. We have to find out if he ever touched Molly."

Julie nodded.

As Cassidy drove toward the Eisenhower, she thought through this new information about Max. She had the impression that older brothers molesting younger sisters was not altogether uncommon. She also had the impression that some youthful offenders were budding pedophiles, while others never abused anyone except their sisters.

So there's some chance Max never molested outside his home. Two things, however, made him appear suspect: his volunteering to tutor children and his choosing a fiancée and a best friend who were both parents of young girls. *But you can't condemn him on that. Could be pure coincidence.*

Reaching the entrance to the Eisenhower, Cassidy joined the light flow of eastbound traffic. She dreaded telling Claire.

Look at all the unsavory things you've uncovered about Max. And now the worst—Julie's molestation. If you hadn't been so damned eager to investigate, Claire could have kept her illusions intact.

Which would have allowed her to continue idealizing Max the way she idealizes her father. Which is exactly the reason she ends up with narcissistic men. All of whom have big fat warts but she refuses to see.

Cassidy realized she was focusing on the woman who'd been her client instead of the child who might have been abused. *Molly's the one who needs attention here, not Claire.* The first step would be to find out whether or not the abuse had occurred, which meant that Molly would have to be evaluated. The best choice would be to take the child to a specialist, but the last time Cassidy had referred a client to such a person, the client had had to wait several weeks for an appointment.

You took that seminar. You could do it yourself. Six months earlier, Cassidy had learned the technique but she'd had no occasion to use it, which made her feel a little insecure.

You'll be fine. The evaluation is almost a cookbook approach.

Yeah, but Claire might prefer an expert. This is her decision to make, not yours.

NINETEEN

A BEARER OF BAD TIDINGS

A NOTE FROM Zach lay on the dining room table.

I'M OUT HITTING THE BARS. SHOULD BE HOME BY SIX.
LET'S TAKE THE SKETCH TO THE NAPERVILLE RESTAURANT
TONIGHT.

Cassidy knew that Zach's purpose in bar-hopping on a
Sunday afternoon was to show the compu-sketch to the
alcohol enthusiasts who appeared at their favorite watering
holes even on a bright, springy, church-going day. Kris
Kristofferson's froggy version of *Sunday Morning Comin'
Down* played in her head.

Stepping into her therapy office, she opened a drawer in
her metal file cabinet and withdrew the folder labeled
CHILD SEXUAL ABUSE INTERVIEWS. She read through
her notes, then took the anatomically correct drawings upstairs to her desk, where she called Claire. "I need to talk
to you. Would it be okay if I came to your place this afternoon?"

"Uh...sure," Claire said in the same listless tone Cassidy had heard from her since Max's death. "Does this
mean you've found something?"

"I have some information about Max." *Give her a warning.* "I'm afraid this isn't good news."

"Oh Lord. If it's another one of his screw-ups, I don't
want to know."

It's as if the sins of our lovers become our sins because we were stupid enough to choose them.

Cassidy moistened her upper lip. "This is something you have to hear."

"Tell me now."

"I can't do that either. Look, I can probably be there in half an hour."

Sliding the drawings into a large brown envelope, Cassidy stuck the envelope in her tote, then drove to her client's lakeview highrise.

Claire led Cassidy into the living room, where Molly sat in a striped easy chair playing with a Gameboy. The child didn't look up.

Kneeling beside her daughter, Claire said, "Would you mind going into your bedroom for a while? Cass and I need to talk."

Molly gazed up at Cassidy with thickly lashed, dark brown eyes that looked as if they'd been cloned from her mother's face, her expression appearing hostile.

"Are you gonna tell my mom more bad news?" Molly demanded.

"Unfortunately, I have to."

"She's sad enough already. You should just keep it to yourself."

Claire ran her fingers through the child's tousled curls. "Remember when we talked about that, honey? Sometimes you have to hear things you don't like."

Pulling away from her mother, Molly stared at Cassidy. "I don't want her getting more depressed!"

"You just go play in your room and don't worry about it," Claire said to the child.

Walking slowly down the hall, Molly turned to look at Cassidy one more time, then disappeared into a room on the right.

As Claire sank into the striped chair, Cassidy seated herself on a low-backed wine-colored sofa. Beside the sofa stood an end table holding silver-framed photos.

"I shouldn't have told her about your phone call," Claire said. "These things just make her worry."

Cassidy remembered listening to her mother's troubles as a child, probably the reason she'd become a therapist. "When you have a daughter as mature and sensitive as Molly, it's always tempting to confide in her. But it would be better if you could talk to a friend instead."

"I'll try." Claire hunched her shoulders, her slender body folding in on itself. "Just tell me the bad news and get it over with."

Cassidy felt heaviness settle over her. "Julie told me that Max molested her when she was eight."

"Oh no!" Covering her mouth with her hand, Claire turned away. "It can't be true. Max said Julie lies about things. She's been doing it ever since she first came to live with them. You can't just take her word on a thing like that."

Being the bearer of bad tidings isn't really so bad. Not any worse than being the person who throws the switch on the electric chair.

Cassidy asked, "Why do you think it couldn't be true that Max molested her?"

"I couldn't be that wrong about him. Couldn't have made such a terrible mistake. If the second man I picked turns out to be as bad as the first, only in a different way, I'll have to take a vow of chastity."

"Even if you think Julie's lying, we can't ignore what she said. We have to—"

"Omigod!" Claire's hand went to her mouth again. "You think he molested Molly?"

"Did Max spend any time alone with her?"

"He used to stay with her on Saturday afternoons so I could run errands."

"Then we have to check it out."

"Oh shit! If Max so much as touched her, I'll—oh God, I don't know what I'll do."

"If he did anything to Molly, we'll set her up with the

best child therapist we can find. But first we have to determine whether or not anything happened. There's a special interview technique used to evaluate children. I can give you the names of some people who've had a lot of experience doing this.'' She paused. ''I've also taken a class on the subject and could probably conduct the interview myself. But I've never done it before and I can't guarantee the results.''

''I can't wait, I just can't. I want you to do it.''

Cassidy stood, the tote in her hand, her chest feeling tight. ''You'll need to stay out here while I talk to Molly in her room.''

Cassidy knocked on Molly's door and the child yelled, ''Come in.'' Entering a sunny, blue and yellow bedroom, Cassidy sat on a twin bed covered with a puffy patchwork quilt.

Molly, who'd been playing solitaire on her computer, turned toward Cassidy and scowled. ''Did you make my mom feel bad?''

''I'm afraid I did, and I'm almost as sorry about it as you are.''

''I want her to be happy, the way she used to be.''

''I know, I want the same thing.'' Cassidy took the envelope out of her tote and laid it on her lap. ''Eventually she'll get through this awful time and her normal self will come back.''

Swiveling her small chair, the child returned to her game.

''Molly, I came in here because I need to talk to you.''

''What about?'' Molly asked, her eyes still on the monitor.

''I have some questions to ask. It's important. Your mom wants me to do it.''

Molly twisted around toward Cassidy again. ''Why?''

This kid's pretty assertive. Not a victim-type at all.

''I can't explain. I just need you to answer the questions.''

The child pushed her index finger up under her chin and regarded Cassidy silently for about three beats. "Okay."

Cassidy asked, "Do you know the difference between the truth and a lie?"

"Everybody knows that!"

"If I told you the sky was blue, would that be the truth or a lie?"

"The truth!"

Cassidy posed three more truth-or-lie questions, then showed Molly the face-up drawing of a naked girl. Giggling, the child pressed both hands to her round cheeks.

After asking the child to name several nonsexual body parts, Cassidy pointed to the girl's breasts. "What do you call those?"

"That's her boobies. When I get bigger, I'll have boobies like my mom."

Cassidy pointed to the drawing's vagina.

Molly giggled again. "Her pee pee."

Cassidy took out a face-down drawing and pointed to the buttocks.

"That's her butt."

Cassidy pointed to the breasts again. "Did anybody besides your mother ever touch you there?"

"When I spilled my Coke, Ginger took my shirt off and washed me all over." Cassidy knew that Ginger was the nanny.

"Did anybody else ever touch you there?"

"My dad did. And my grandma. But they weren't bad touches."

"So you've heard about good touches and bad touches. Has anybody ever given you a bad touch?"

"No!"

When Cassidy asked if anybody had touched Molly's vagina or buttocks, the answers were similar.

Cassidy asked another question, "Have you ever seen a man or boy without his pants on?"

Molly grimaced in embarrassment. "I saw Daddy once. Going into the shower."

"So you know what boys look like?"

"Kinda."

Taking out a drawing of a naked man, Cassidy pointed to the penis.

"What do you call that?"

"A boy's pee pee."

"Did anybody ever ask you to touch his pee pee?"

Molly closed her eyes and shook her head vigorously.

This does not sound like a kid who's been molested.

"These questions must seem pretty silly."

Molly went to sit in her computer chair again.

"You know, when I was your age my mother had a lot of problems, sort of like your mom does, and I'd worry about her and try to help."

Turning her back, Molly resumed her game.

This effort you're making is futile. A lump rose in Cassidy's throat as she contemplated how burdened Molly must feel. *There's no way you can talk a kid out of trying to rescue her mother.*

Cassidy plowed ahead anyway. "Then, when I grew up, I realized my mother never really needed my help and it would've been better if I'd just gone off to play with my friends."

Molly put a red seven on a black eight.

Cassidy patted the child's shoulder and returned to the living room, where Claire was sitting in the easy chair, her right hand rubbing her left arm.

"It's okay," Cassidy said. "I didn't see any sign of sexual abuse."

"Oh thank God!" Heaving a large sigh, Claire stood up. "I knew Max couldn't be a child molester, I just knew it. This has to be another of Julie's lies."

His not having molested Molly doesn't mean he never molested anybody. But it could mean he wasn't a pedophile and hadn't molested outside his home.

"I know Max had his problems with money," Claire continued, "but he was still a basically decent guy. He really cared about people. I've never known anyone who was kinder or more loyal than Max."

This is a woman who really doesn't want to hear the truth.

THE LIGHT WAS almost gone from the western sky when Zach came through the doorway and dropped into his desk chair. "I must've shown that sucker to more than fifty people, and all I got were blank stares. But I handed my card out everywhere, so maybe someone will call."

Swiveling to face him, Cassidy rested her elbows on the arms of her chair. "Was it just yesterday I was saying we should be able to run him down now that we have the sketch?"

"Oh, we'll find him eventually. Somebody who knows him will figure there's money to be made on the deal. Actually, a snitch is more likely to call later than tell me face to face, since he won't want anyone to know he's talking to me."

"Well, I've had quite a day." Cassidy brushed a loose strand of hair back from her face. "But I don't want to get started telling you about it till we're in the car driving toward a restaurant. All I've had to eat were a few peanut butter cups on the way to Julie's and some fruit after I got home."

"You want to have dinner at Cypress, don't you?"

"I'm sick of cuisine. I need comfort food. You know, macaroni and cheese, meatloaf, hamburgers."

Zach thought for a moment. "There's a place not far from Cypress. It doesn't have much in the way of atmosphere but the burgers are good. Or is Naperville too long a wait?"

Forty-five minutes. Oh, you can hold out that long. "That's okay. I can nibble a few more peanut butter cups in the car."

"You ready to leave now?"

She pictured Susan in her low-cut, short-skirted, electric blue dress. "Since we're going to Cypress afterward, I ought to wear something classier than jeans." Cassidy stared at the dresses hanging in her closet. *Considering that the woman's over fifty and carrying more than her share of avoirdupois, you ought to be able to hold your own with her.* But not one of Cassidy's outfits could compete with the dress Susan had worn. Not one was the least bit provocative or would make Cassidy stand out from the crowd. *If you and Susan were lined up side-by-side, no one would even notice you.* "I need new clothes," she yelled over her shoulder.

"You mean, you wish you had a little blue number that showed off your tits?"

She scowled at Zach. "Will you please stop reading my mind? I've already had to put up with astrology today."

Crossing the room, he drew her into a warm hug. "Susan's good to look at—albeit a little over the hill—but those brass balls of hers are enough to keep most men away."

"Well, I wouldn't want to scare men off, but I wouldn't mind just once in my life walking through a room and seeing every guy's jaw drop."

"You just need the right clothes."

She envisioned herself in a mini-skirted dress with a neckline so low her breasts were in danger of falling out. Feeling a rush of heat to her face, she said, "I think I'll have to content myself with you being the only man who ever gives me more than a passing glance."

Cassidy donned a simple wine-colored dress that she'd been perfectly happy with before she compared herself to Susan. As they drove west on the Eisenhower, Cassidy told Zach about Julie's molestation and the sexual abuse interview she'd conducted on Molly.

Zach said, "So you don't think there's any reason to doubt Julie's story."

"She was so reluctant to tell me—I can't imagine she was making it up."

"What about false memory syndrome?"

"Julie's memories were never repressed. She told her mother at the time it happened." Cassidy looked at Zach. "Why are you so skeptical?"

"It's just that Julie's such a flake. But if you believe her, I guess that's good enough for me."

They arrived at the restaurant and were seated in a round vinyl booth facing the bar. Above the bar sat three TV sets, the one on the right showing a golf game, the one on the left a Cubs game, the one in the middle a movie.

After they ordered, Zach said, "Even though Max didn't molest Molly, it's always possible he molested other kids. So what about Garrett's daughter?"

Cassidy pressed her knuckles into her cheek. "I've been trying not to think about that."

"I'm usually the avoider in the family, not you."

"I've already had to deliver upsetting news to one parent today. It's not something I'm eager to repeat." *What would the social work code of ethics have to say about this? Doesn't matter. Ashley may have been harmed so you have to tell Garrett.* She let out a sigh.

"You want me to do it?" Zach asked, folding his arms on the scarred wooden table.

"I should be the one to tell him. But there's no imminent danger so I don't have to do it tonight."

They sat in silence for a while, Cassidy's gaze fixed on the movie, a man and woman making love on a sun-drenched beach. *That's where you and Zach should be, off in the tropics, locked in each other's arms—with grains of sand working their way into your thong bikini.*

Zach pulled a napkin out of the chrome dispenser and placed his fork on top of it. "You didn't say a word about your astrology session. You holding out on me or what?"

As soon as his words were out, she realized there were some aspects of the session she would prefer not to share.

Are you obligated to tell Zach that the planets regard you as self-centered? Or that they predict a crisis dead ahead?

"You're taking too long. That means you *are* holding out."

"I'm just trying to remember. It's been a long day." She recounted many of the more neutral observations Julie had made, then said, "I figured out how she does it. It's so easy, I could be an astrologer."

"Well, good. If your therapy practice ever goes under, you'll have something to fall back on."

"My practice is going to double within the year," she boasted. "No, listen, this is how astrologers are able to nail down people's personality traits. They throw out random comments, and when they get a positive response, they say more, and when they get a negative response, they drop it like a hot potato and move on to something else. It's all a matter of reading cues. I do it all the time as a therapist."

He shook his head. "Julie may be flaky but she doesn't strike me as a con artist."

"She does it unconsciously. She thinks she's reading the chart but she's really reading the person."

Their hamburgers arrived and Cassidy devoted her complete attention to filling her stomach. After polishing off the last crumb, she began speaking again. "You know, I just now realized why I dislike astrology so much."

"I thought you just didn't take it seriously."

"No, I actively dislike it. As a therapist, I try to get people to take responsibility, to understand how they bring negative consequences on themselves. Astrology sends a totally different message. It removes accountability. It tells people the reason they failed is because they started in the void of the moon. Or the reason nobody likes them is because of the position of the planets at their birth. Astrology tells people that their fate is sealed, that they can't change things. It's the opposite of empowerment."

"Maybe that's why so many people like it."

TWENTY

MADONNA AND MIND READING

"WELL, CASSIDY AND ZACH," Garrett Hillard greeted them from the host's station at Cypress. "What can I do for you?"

Cassidy looked into his darkly handsome face. "Is Susan around? We'd like to talk to her."

"Can I ask what this is in regard to?"

Zach said, "We have a police sketch we'd like to show the staff."

Brows lifting in surprise, Hillard asked, "Why here?"

"There may be a connection between the guy in the sketch and Max."

Hillard kneaded the short beard framing his jawline. "I'll get Susan."

Crossing the brightly lit dining area, he went through a swinging door at the far end of the room. Cassidy was pleased to see that most of the tables were empty, which increased the odds that Susan would let them talk to her employees. While they waited, Cassidy's gaze settled on the whimsical mural with its drawings of planets and stars. *The heavenly bodies. Just can't escape them today.*

A moment later, Susan and Hillard stood in front of them, the restaurant owner wearing a clingy crochet dress that should have emphasized every bulge but somehow managed to look good on her.

Crossing her arms, she drew her brows together. "What's this I hear about a police sketch?"

"Let's sit down and I'll show it to you," Zach replied.

"Why not just show it to me here?"

His eyes flicked toward Hillard. "I'd rather speak to each person separately."

Susan pursed her bee-stung lips and appeared to think about it. "Oh hell, why not?" She looked at Zach, her mouth easing into a sly smile. "Besides, I want to find out what you're up to."

They sat at a table near the entrance, Susan leaning forward to provide Zach with a clear view down her scoop-necked dress. "So," she asked, "who's the guy in this sketch of yours?"

"I'd rather not say."

"You've got your nerve," Susan responded, her voice oozing with sexuality. "Why should I let you show it to my staff if you won't explain yourself?"

God, is she ever brazen. Flirting with my husband right in front of my face. Cassidy was torn between resenting Susan's predatory behavior and admiring her ballsiness.

"The reason to let us show the sketch is because you want the truth to come out about Max's murder."

"Why should I give a shit about that?"

"Because you're curious. You don't like leaving things unfinished. You want answers."

"You're good." Susan laughed raucously. "But not good enough. If you want permission from me, you'll have to spell everything out."

Zach told her about the parking lot guy.

One of the few times I've seen Zach cave to someone other than me. Cassidy felt an even greater admiration for Susan.

"So it was horseshit, what you said before about not trying to track down the killer."

"That's about right."

Susan's so locked into Zach, there's not much point in you even opening your mouth.

"Now the question is—what's in it for me?" Susan delicately touched the tip of her tongue to her upper lip.

This is Madonna when she turns fifty.

"You said you were fond of Max. You had a fling with him. Don't you want to see his killer pay?"

"It won't bring him back." A small sigh. "Well, hell, I guess I would like to see the killer get what's coming to him."

Zach placed the sketch in front of her.

Cassidy watched Susan's expression as she looked at the drawing. Something flickered in the older woman's face. *She has seen him.*

"Never laid eyes on the guy."

"So," Zach asked, "how shall we proceed with the rest of the staff?"

"You go have a drink at the bar, spend some money. I'll tell everybody you're coming."

Cassidy and Zach settled on barstools, and the bartender, a muscular young man with spiky hair, brought them drinks. Wanting to assert herself after feeling invisible during the discussion with Susan, Cassidy fished a bill out of her wallet and placed it on the bar. *However much drinks cost in a place like this, a twenty should cover it.* Although Zach usually paid, at times when Cassidy was feeling overshadowed, she sometimes laid money down faster than he could as a way of evening things out.

The bartender took the twenty and returned with a five and three ones. Cassidy hesitated over the tip.

"Two bucks," Zach whispered in her ear.

She was on the verge of asking the bartender to look at their sketch when he zipped off to serve a customer at the opposite end of the bar.

A short time later, Susan collected Cassidy and Zach and took them into the kitchen. He showed the sketch to the chef, while Cassidy listened. When Zach was done, she said, "Let me do the next one."

They talked to the kitchen crew, then returned to the dining area. Cassidy noticed that everyone on the staff was young, well built, and attractive. *Not a couch potato in the lot. If Susan's able to surround herself with all these beautiful people and not feel old and ugly, her self-confidence has to be way higher than yours.*

The fourth server they approached was a wholesome-looking waitress, her ginger hair pinned up in back. After she shook her head over the sketch, Cassidy handed her a business card. "We're looking for information regarding Max. If you know anything that might be connected to his murder, please give me a call."

"If someone had information, how much would it be worth?"

Cassidy hesitated, hoping Zach would step in. When he didn't, she said, "Well, I guess I could go as high as a hundred."

The waitress creased her brow. "But you could say it was something you already knew and refuse to pay."

"I wouldn't do that. Not if the tip was legitimate."

"Let me think about it." The young woman slipped the card into her pants pocket and walked away.

"She's going to call." Cassidy felt excitement bubble up in her chest.

"Probably. Unless she loses her nerve. But keep in mind, people sometimes try to sell you worthless information."

"When she asked about the money, I was complete thrown off. I've never done anything like this before." Cassidy paused, then said accusingly, "Why didn't *you* tell her how much?"

"Half the time you yell at me when I step in, the other half you yell at me when I don't. How am I supposed to know what you want? You just told me not to do mind reading."

She grimaced at her lack of consistency. "You're right,

I shouldn't expect you to know when I need rescuing. So, was a hundred anywhere near the right number?''

''I would've offered fifty, but I just make it up as I go along.''

''If someone sells you information, how do you know if it's valid?''

''You don't. You have to get corroboration elsewhere.''

When they finished in the dining room, Zach showed the sketch to the bartender.

''This is a black guy, right?'' He pointed to the lines shading the face.

''Yeah.''

''Scruffy-looking? More like a street person than a businessman?''

''Right again.''

''I might've seen him. This black guy came in, maybe a couple of weeks ago—some night when we were pretty crowded. I saw him standing near the entrance, then when I looked again he was gone. Only reason I noticed is, he wasn't anything like our usual customers.'' The bartender gazed at the face again. ''But all I got was a glance so I can't be sure.''

At last! Somebody who may have seen him. And you thought Susan recognized him as well.

The only person Cassidy and Zach had not yet shown the sketch to was Garrett Hillard. Leading the way toward his station, Zach said, ''Think I'll offer to buy him a drink. Make a friendly gesture. Grease the wheels in case we need to talk to him again.''

''It must be my turn,'' Hillard said, as they came to a halt in front of him. He looked at the sketch, then shook his head. ''Sorry, it doesn't ring any bells.''

Handing Hillard his card, Zach asked him to call if he thought of anything else.

How could he not have seen a scruffy-looking black guy standing near the door?

Could've been in the kitchen, the men's room, taking the

night off. You can't convict him on his not passing the face-recognition test.

Zach shoved the sketch back in his briefcase. "Will you let us buy you a drink before we take off?"

Hillard frowned, his intense blue eyes scrutinizing Zach's face.

Thinks we're up to something. Which, for once, we aren't.

"Well…business is slow…I guess I could sit down with you for a while."

Hillard found a waiter to take his place at the host's station, then they went to the bar, Zach sitting between Hillard and Cassidy. After drinks were served, she leaned her elbow on the smooth wooden surface and looked at Hillard. "So, how's your daughter?"

His expression brightening, he lit a cigarette, then launched into an account of how Ashley had won a certificate for reading more books than anybody else in her class.

Someday you're going to have to tell him his best friend may have been a child molester. But not tonight.

A brief silence, then Hillard started up again. "You asked me to let you know if anything else came to mind about Max. Well, I just remembered something." He lined up his cigarette pack, his ashtray, and his glass of scotch. "Several months ago, a lone woman started coming into the restaurant two, three nights a week. She always wanted a booth, preferably near the kitchen. Now these are big booths we have here, and we generally reserve them for parties of two or more, but she'd come in on an off-night and be pretty insistent, so I'd give her one. Then she'd scoot back into the corner and make herself as invisible as she could. A while back she stopped coming. Knowing what I know now, I figure she disappeared around the time Max and Claire announced their wedding plans. Well, I had no idea who she was until I ran into her again at the rehearsal dinner. I saw her, she saw me—I think we were both a little stunned. Then Claire introduced this woman as her sister.''

"What?'' Cassidy blinked in surprise. "Are you saying it was Erin? What on earth was she doing? Spying on Max?''

"That's what it looked like.''

Zach asked, "Did Max spend much time out in the dining room?''

"He was pretty gregarious. Whenever he had a break, he'd come out and talk to the customers. If anybody didn't like the food, he'd instantly comp them a meal, even when the complaint was minor.''

Remembering what Susan had said on their first visit, Cassidy asked, "Did he flirt with the female customers?''

Hillard thought about it. "I wouldn't call it flirting. Far as I could tell, he treated men and women the same. He just liked being with people.''

TWENTY-ONE

VITAL RECORDS AND EMBROIDERY

MONDAY MORNING Cassidy fed Roscoe in the den while Zach went downstairs to make coffee and provide breakfast for Starshine. The kitten, who had to be shut up at night because he made so much noise, was always in a state of happy delirium when Cassidy opened his door at the beginning of the day. He scarfed down a few bites, hopped into her lap, jumped to the floor and chased a ball, then spent another couple of seconds at his bowl.

When footsteps sounded at the bottom of the stairs, Roscoe raced off to greet Zach. Although the kitten was in a state of constant hunger, he was too excitable first thing in the morning to focus on anything, even food.

Cassidy, who didn't have any clients until ten, sat in bed and sipped coffee, her lap sadly empty, Starshine having stayed downstairs with Roscoe. *Never has time for me anymore. Not since the monster's been unleashed.*

When Zach returned from the shower, Cassidy watched him get dressed. Silver threads laced his black hair, and he was thicker in the waist than he used to be, but he looked even sexier to her now than when they'd first met.

We should make love more often. Go riding bikes together. Stop fighting over anything smaller than a house.

He donned a lightweight gray jacket. "We need to set up a meeting with Erin. Tonight if possible."

Cassidy frowned. "I suppose that means you want me to call."

"Do you mind?"

"I'm not looking forward to it. Not after we made her talk about trashing Hank's apartment and breaking her father's watch. If I were Erin, I wouldn't have anything more to do with us."

"You want me to do it?"

What excuse do you have for being on the investigation if you won't even make a simple phone call?

"No, that's all right. I'll take care of it."

After Zach left, she dialed Erin's number. When the machine came on, she didn't leave a message.

Cassidy showered and dressed, then went downstairs to check on the cats. Starshine lay on the sofa, her ears pricked forward, her eyes glued to Roscoe, who stared back at her from one of the armchairs. Neither cat acknowledged Cassidy's presence. *Doing surveillance on each other. Which evidently takes precedence over Starshine's morning nap. And that might be a good thing, since my little sleeping beauty tends to snooze her life away.*

Pretending to be invisible, Roscoe slid off the chair, flattened himself against the floor, and oozed across to the sofa, where he sat on his haunches and slapped Starshine's tail. She struck back, and he went running into the kitchen. *They've reached an accommodation. Starshine gets to be the boss, Roscoe gets to be the pesky kid brother, and both are having the time of their lives.*

Cassidy went back upstairs and logged on at the computer. Five messages in her mailbox, including one from Vitalrec.com. According to the report, Garrett Hillard had been born in Walnut Creek, California, thirty-seven years ago, and a search of state records revealed no marriage, divorce, or death certificates under the social security number she'd typed in.

Well, shit. I was hoping for a death certificate. Which'd

prove Garrett's using a stolen identity. This doesn't tell us anything.

She left a message on Zach's voicemail at work, then called Gran.

"I wanted to let you know about the report I just got from Vitalrec." She informed Gran about the lack of certificates.

"Does that mean Garrett Hillard is who he says he is? Or that he isn't?"

"I haven't figured it out yet."

"Well, there's always that other Website. The one that spies on people you might want to sleep with. So, how's Roscoe doing? Has he made friends with Starshine yet?"

"A better question would be, how's Lillybeth doing?"

"Lillybeth is still in the hospital but on the mend and planning to embroider you some dishtowels."

"Oh dear. So Lillybeth is an embroiderer, is she?"

"A rabid embroiderer. Half-blind but she doesn't let that stop her. She embroiders dishtowels, pillowcases, those thingies you put on the wall, and she doesn't have nearly enough people to hand them off to. It used to be a problem back when she was driving. She'd call to say she was coming to see me, and I'd have to run around hanging up homilies and dishtowels. But now that she doesn't come over anymore, the embroidery goes straight into the Goodwill bag."

"I always have a hard time getting rid of gifts I can't use."

"I used to feel bad about it too, but then I realized it was best for both of us. If I kept all her gifts, I might start avoiding her like some other people do."

"You know, Gran, you're right. I'll graciously accept whatever she wants to give me and follow suit with the Goodwill bags."

AT THREE P.M. Cassidy finished with her last client of the day. Climbing the stairs, she fantasized about her practice doubling. *That's the problem with predictions. They worm their way into your unconscious and can be as hard to eradicate as roaches.*

When Cassidy saw that Starshine was asleep on the bed, she closed the door to keep Roscoe out, then sat down and gathered the calico onto her lap. Starshine squinted up at her human and purred fervently, providing large dollops of the affection Cassidy had been missing.

A couple of minutes later, the calico's ears swiveled backward, indicating that she'd heard Roscoe coming up the stairs. Starshine abandoned Cassidy's lap and went to stand in front of the door, beneath which furry black feet began to protrude. The calico pounced on the paws, which instantly withdrew, then returned to be pounced on again. *Footsie under the door. There's no way you can compete with that.*

Sitting in her chair, Cassidy stared at the list of numbers Zach had left on her desk and tried to work herself up to call Erin. But the phone rang before she could pick it up.

"Um...last night you said you'd pay a hundred bucks for information about Max." The waitress from Cypress. Sounding as if she'd take flight at the least wrong move.

"You have something for us?"

A pause. "I guess I do."

"When would be a good time for you to meet with us?"

"I could probably do it tomorrow—sometime around one. Mom could take the kids then. Um...the Old Graue Mill is only a few minutes from my house. We could meet by the water wheel."

Cassidy said she would see her there at one.

Here's hoping I get more for my money from the waitress than I did from Vitalrec.

Cassidy picked up the phone again. *Maybe Erin didn't mind that you asked all those embarrassing questions.*

When the other woman answered, Cassidy said, "We've just received some new information we need to discuss with you."

"Once was enough." The phone clicked down.

Cassidy drew in a breath through clenched teeth, mad at herself more than anything. She hated pressuring people but in this instance could see no way out of it. She dialed again and the machine picked up. After two more tries, Erin answered.

"Wait, I have something important to say. We have information you would not want to see show up in the *Post*. If you can give us a satisfactory explanation, Zach may not use it. But if you refuse to meet with us, it's definitely going to be included in his story."

"You're threatening me."

As much as I don't like to do it, I am.

"No I'm not. I'm just giving you the opportunity to defend yourself."

"Bullshit!" A deep sigh. "When do I have to do this?"

"Six-thirty. We'll come by your place."

Cassidy realized that her hands were trembling and a small queasy feeling had started in her stomach. *You're turning into Zach. Cynical, amoral, the ends justify the means.*

He may believe that but you don't. You believe in respecting the rights of others. At all cost. No matter what.

That may be what you believe, but that's not how you act anymore.

SEATED AT the dining room table, beer in their glasses, pizza on their plates, Cassidy said to Zach, "It's my guess that our guy in Chicago stole the identity of the real Garrett Hillard, who never married and is still alive. That would explain the lack of certificates, and it also fits with my initial impression that our guy was lying."

"If two Garrett Hillards file income taxes under the same social security number, at some point the IRS will drag their asses in and demand an explanation."

"So maybe our guy stole a social security number from somebody he knew would never file. A friend who's left the country. A Downs Syndrome brother who's never going to work.''

"I suppose that's a possibility.'' Zach chewed on a bite of pizza and drank some beer. "But there are some other explanations that work just as well. One is that the search results are wrong. Everything that comes over the Internet is not sacrosanct, you know. Another is that Garrett married and divorced outside the state of California, which is the only place you searched.''

"I thought about doing the whole country but the cost seemed prohibitive. What do you think? Should we search nationwide?''

He shook his head. "Let's wait and see what we get from that dating-partners Website. And from the waitress tomorrow. I admit that Garrett's identity seems a little shaky, but there are a couple of suspects I like even better. Hank still has the best motive. And the other one who looks good to me is Erin.''

"Why Erin?''

"Because of her prior act of violence. And her convoluted relationship with Claire. She just seems so whacked out I can see her having her sister's fiancé killed—either because she's trying to protect Claire from the evil Max, or because she can't stand to see Claire getting married when she's not.''

"One of our biggest problems is, there's no way to rule anybody out. We have this group of people, some with obvious reasons to want Max dead, others with no reasons we're aware of. But any one of them could have a hidden motive, and they all have means and opportunity.''

TWENTY-TWO

UNDERCOVER ERIN

ERIN OPENED THE DOOR, an angry light in her large green eyes, her lips pressed so tightly together that puckers had formed in her square chin. Without a word, she pulled the door wide so they could pass through into the living room.

Cassidy said, "I'm sorry for the way I pressured you this afternoon." *Bullied would be more accurate.* "It's important that we talk, but I shouldn't have coerced you the way I did."

From Zach's expression, she could tell he thought she was nuts. *Has no idea why I apologized. From his point of view, forcing people to talk is normal.*

The fierceness in Erin's face abated a little. "Does that mean you'll go away and leave me alone?"

"Not at all," Zach replied. "I'm the one writing the story, and I have no intention of leaving until I get my questions answered."

Apologizing to Erin does not absolve you. You only did it to appease your conscience. You knew Zach would never let her off the hook.

Erin glared at them. "If you're determined to go ahead with your intimidation tactics, then let's get it over with."

Cassidy and Zach settled on the sofa draped with fringed shawls, while Erin sat in an armchair opposite them.

Zach said, "The manager at Cypress told us you used to

frequent the restaurant on a regular basis, and I'd like to know what you were doing there."

"Watching Max. I wanted to see what he was up to."

"What made you think he was up to something?" Cassidy asked.

Raising her eyes to Cassidy's face, Erin said, "When Max started working at the new restaurant, he told Claire she couldn't go there. Well, it seemed pretty obvious he had something to hide. I tried to convince Claire that there was something off, but she wouldn't listen. So I decided to see what I could see on my own."

"You didn't believe Max's story about his business partner having a crush on him?" *Why should she? You didn't believe it either.*

"Since Claire's never picked a normal guy in her life, it didn't seem possible that Max could be this perfect person she thought he was."

"You don't think that all of Claire's work in therapy might have done her some good?" *That's a stupid question. You know Max was a bad choice.*

"It's not that I don't believe in therapy. I've spent some time in it myself. It's just that there were too many warning signals." Erin caught Cassidy's gaze. "Tell me the truth. Didn't you think there was something wrong with him too?"

"I can't comment on that."

A small smile of vindication. "So you *did* think there was something wrong."

Zach asked, "What did you hope to accomplish by spying on Max?"

Gazing at her lap, Erin clenched her hands together. "I assumed he had a girlfriend at the restaurant. I thought I might catch him playing kissyface with a waitress. Or that business partner of his."

"Did you?"

"No, but that doesn't mean he didn't have some little chickie tucked away on the side. He probably kept Claire out of Cypress because he didn't want his workplace girl-friend to find out about his off-hours girlfriend.''

You know Susan accepted sexual favors from Max but you don't know if Susan and Claire overlapped. You should've nailed Susan down on exactly when she dumped him. You avoided the question because you didn't want any more bad news.

"Did you observe Max doing anything inappropriate?" Zach wanted to know.

"He was way too charismatic. Every man Claire's been involved with had that same overblown charm. Whenever I see a guy playing up to people the way Max did, I know he's a manipulator.''

She's right. Charming males like Max and my ex should be avoided.

"I presume you didn't tell Claire about your undercover work at Cypress," Cassidy said. "Weren't you afraid Max would blow the whistle?''

Erin stared at the wall behind them. "When I first started, the relationship was fairly new and I thought I'd be able to discover something that would get Claire to break off with him before anybody found out. But that didn't happen, and a few months later they announced their wedding date. When I heard about the marriage plans, I thought for sure Max would remember seeing me at the restaurant and tell Claire. I didn't mind so much about Claire finding out. I mean, I was only doing it for her own good and we fight all the time anyway. But I hated the idea that Max would think I was some kind of weirdo.''

You don't want people thinking you're a weirdo, you shouldn't act like one.

"Was the rehearsal dinner the first time you actually came face to face with Max?''

Erin nodded slowly. "It was awful. I knew I'd have to meet Max, but I wasn't expecting to run into the restaurant manager as well. When Claire introduced me to Max and Garrett, I could see in both their faces that they recognized me. All evening long I kept expecting that one or the other would make some wise ass remark, or that Claire would drag me into the bathroom and stage a major confrontation.'' A perplexed look came over Erin's face. ''But nothing happened. Not that night or any time afterward. I guess they both did the decent thing and kept it to themselves.''

''SO MAX WASN'T all bad,'' Zach said, driving toward Oak Park.

''I need to keep that in mind. I've been dwelling on his dark side so much I've kind of lost perspective.''

Zach changed lanes, pulling up behind a blue sedan with a red left rear fender and a dangling bumper. ''I told you earlier that I liked Erin for the murder, and after hearing what she had to say tonight, I like her even better.''

''Because she went to such lengths to break Claire and Max up?''

''Everybody appears to have liked Max except Luke, Hank, and Erin. And as far as we know, Erin was the only one who actively tried to make trouble for him, and what she did was pretty bizarre. How big a leap is it to go from spying on someone to hiring a hit man?''

''Pretty big, I think.'' Tilting her head, Cassidy mulled it over. ''But I can see Erin as the murderer. From the time she was young, her mission in life was to protect her sister from abusive men, starting with their father. And here Claire was, about to marry another charming man that Erin saw as an abuser in the making. When she couldn't talk Claire out of it, the only thing left was to kill him. Sort of like a mother tiger defending her young.''

''The only thing that doesn't add up is having Max killed at the wedding. If Erin wanted to protect Claire, why schedule the execution for Claire's big day?''

Pressing her fist up under her chin, Cassidy stared at the pedestrians on the sidewalk. ''Maybe because Erin has two competing parts. One is a nurturing, caretaker part, the other a punitive, slap-Claire-down part. Maybe the nurturing part wanted to protect Claire, and the punitive part wanted to cause Claire maximum pain.''

Zach smiled and shook his head. ''No matter how odd or contradictory the behavior, you're always able to concoct some kind of psychological explanation.''

Her brows drawing together, Cassidy looked away from him for the next three blocks, then let go of her irritation. ''The discouraging thing is that Erin, who says she's been in therapy, is a complete mess, and Claire, whom I've had as a client for nearly four years, picked another charming, manipulative man. It makes me wonder if therapy ever really does any good.''

Zach put his hand on her knee. ''You've told me before that there are some people who can't be fixed. Wouldn't you say Erin fits in that category?''

Distorted thinking, mood swings, a lot of rage. ''Yeah, she probably has a personality disorder.''

''And weren't you the one who finally got Claire to leave her husband?''

''What's this? A minute ago you accused me of concocting psychological explanations and now you're defending therapy?''

''I saw what you did with Bryce when he was suicidal. I know how good you are.''

ZACH HANDED CASSIDY her purple cat mug, then sat in his desk chair facing her. ''I got the appraisal back. The house is worth two-fifty.''

She stared at him over the rim of her mug, her eyes widening. Although she knew real estate prices had appreciated, she wasn't expecting to hear that her house was now worth three times what she'd paid for it. *Doesn't matter. You still don't want to sell.*

''You must be pleased,'' she said in her neutral, therapist voice.

''I called a reporter at the Oak Park paper and got referrals on three real estate agents. For about five minutes I was tempted to fall back into my old habit of doing things behind your back. Thought maybe I'd pick an agent on my own, then try to bully you into signing the contract. But remembering all the fights we've had over my lack of forthrightness, I decided I'd be better off telling you up front. Especially since there's no way I can sell this house without your participation.''

Cassidy's jaw tightened. "I commend you on making a good decision.''

Ignoring her sarcasm, he continued. "I think we should interview these agents together." He paused, giving her a chance to respond. When she didn't, he went on. "Since I don't know when you have clients, you should be the one to make the appointments." He looked her in the eye. "Will you do it?''

Avoiding his gaze, she stared at the leafy maple outside the north window. *He's backed you into a corner. Have to either make those calls or tell him you plan to chain yourself to the door. Which would set off a major battle. A battle you're not ready to have because there's still some part of you hoping you'll find a way to talk yourself into doing what he wants.*

"Okay, I'll call the agents.''

He ripped a page out of his notepad and put it on her desk. "When?''

Gritting her teeth, she said, "Today.''

"Good." Removing the newspaper from its plastic wrap, he laid it out on his desk. "Since we're driving to Oak Brook this afternoon, I think I'll work from home.''

CASSIDY HAD JUST slipped a bright, springy, lavender and green dress over her head when the phone rang. Struggling to pull the dress down over her hips, she hurried across the room to pick up the handset. She said her name, tugging at the skirt to straighten it, but no one answered back.

She was on the verge of hanging up when a child's voice said, "This is Molly.''

"Well, Molly...what a surprise. Is there something I can do for you?"

"It's about my dad."

"There's something you want me to do that involves your father?"

"He's started coming over and I don't want him to. I thought you could tell Mom not to let him do it."

Oh shit! It was just last night Zach gave me credit for getting Claire to leave him.

"You sound a little upset. Did your dad do something that bothered you?"

"He stayed over last night. He never does anything to me, but he says mean things to my mom."

"Did he say something mean last night?"

"I guess not. Mom seemed happy this morning. Sometimes he's nice but he always gets mean after a while."

"And you want me to talk to your mom about it?"

"Uh huh."

"Did you tell her how you feel?"

"I said I didn't want him here but she didn't listen."

"I'll talk to her, Molly, but I'm not sure she'll listen to me either."

"She always says you're the one that got her to leave Daddy before."

Cassidy sighed inwardly. *And here she is, back with him again.* "Is it okay if I tell her you called? She'll be more likely to take it seriously if she knows how worried you are."

"Um...I guess so."

TWENTY-THREE

SECRET ENGAGEMENT

STANDING AT THE west window, Cassidy gazed down at a group of teens playing football in the middle of Hazel. A knot formed in her stomach—anger at Claire for creating so much chaos in her daughter's life.

Now stop that, her therapist part demanded. *If you're pissed at Claire, you won't be able to help her. The woman's been under incredible stress, and you know perfectly well that stress can lead to backsliding. You saw it happen to Zach when he was working undercover at that club, and you experienced it yourself when you had that flare-up of jealousy last fall. You need to understand Claire, not judge her.*

Cassidy pictured Claire at the wedding, her dress soaked with blood. She thought about Claire's fragility, and the fact that her client had only recently overcome a lifelong dependency on abusive men. She called to mind how common it was for abuse victims to go back to their abusers.

Having worked herself into a more empathic frame of mind, Cassidy left messages for Claire on her office voice mail and with her nanny at home. Crossing into the computer room, she sat next to Zach at the long built-in table and told him about Molly's call.

"You must want to smack Claire upside the head. What do you think? Will you be able to bring her to her senses?"

"It won't be easy. Claire's probably feeling desperate to

have some man to lean on, and I'm sure Hank's putting on his best sensitive-guy performance."

Cassidy expelled a long breath, then forced herself to focus on the tasks at hand. She had clients to see, agents to call, and a waitress to bribe. *But first, check your email.*

She asked Zach if she could use the computer, logged on, and found the compu-dating report sitting in her mailbox.

Printing out two copies, she handed one to Zach and studied the other herself. The report informed them that Garrett Hillard had no criminal record; it contained four previous addresses; it indicated that he had left his most recent address two years earlier; it showed no record of his having lived with anyone; and it listed his occupation as bartender.

Cassidy threw up her hands. "I have no idea what to make of this." She reread it more slowly. "Well, at least it corroborates the no marriage, divorce, or death certificate information from the first report. In fact, it doesn't appear that this Garrett ever lived with anybody."

Zach creased his brow. "But it does say he worked as a bartender and left California two years ago, both of which fit with what the Chicago Garrett told us."

"Except the Chicago Garrett has a kid, and the California Garrett lived alone." Cassidy shivered. "Jesus, I hope he isn't one of those monsters who steal children and keep them as sex slaves."

Zach put a reassuring hand on her arm. "Actually, I believe he could've been living with his daughter in California and it wouldn't register on this report. They cross-reference mailing lists to find other people living at the same address, and kids' names usually don't show up on those lists."

"So what are the possibilities?" Cassidy tilted her head one way, then the other. "I still think the most likely scenario is that the Chicago Garrett is wanted somewhere, and this Garrett—" she held up the printout "—is the person whose identity he stole."

"Then where did the California Garrett disappear to a couple of years ago?"

"He was an alcoholic, lost his job, joined the ranks of the homeless. And our Garrett snapped up his social security number, abducted Ashley from her mother, and took off for Chicago where his old roomy Max could help him get settled."

"Well, that works." Zach stared into space. "But how about this? Garrett and some woman he didn't live with had a child together. Later on, the mother got bored with raising a kid and handed Ashley over to Garrett. Or he abducted her. Either way, he brought his daughter to Chicago, then invented a marriage so his kid wouldn't grow up thinking she was illegitimate."

"You know," Cassidy said, jiggling a pen between her fingers, "the real issue isn't Garrett, it's Ashley. What we need to find out is whether or not he has legal custody. And if he doesn't, we need to get that kid back where she belongs." Cassidy drummed the pen against the table.

"Too bad we can't submit Garrett's fingerprints to AFIS. If the guy's ever been arrested, the feds would have his name and social security number on file."

"AFIS—is that the national fingerprint database?"

Zach nodded. "Most people who've ever been booked are in it, plus the latents found at crime scenes."

"We don't have any reason to think Garrett's been arrested."

Zach cocked his head. "You might be surprised at how many of us have a youthful indiscretion or two on our records."

Cassidy remembered that Zach had been falsely charged with assault and battery when he was in his twenties. "So your fingerprints are in AFIS?"

"Yep."

"I suppose it's true that a lot of males have been arrested

at least once—a DUI, reckless driving, something. So, if Garrett's ever been charged with a crime and we could break into AFIS, we could get his real name?''

"Yeah, but law enforcement types are the only people who can submit prints."

Propping her elbow on the table, Cassidy pressed her forehead against her upraised fingertips. ''I can't stand thinking that Ashley may've been taken from her mother. Or that the mother may be going crazy because she doesn't know where her daughter is. I had a client once whose child was abducted. This woman was a wonderful mother. Then all of a sudden her child was gone and she was devastated.''

"I just can't see any way we could get Hillard's prints into AFIS."

"What about Emily? She could do it, couldn't she?'' Emily was the Chicago police detective Zach had dated before he met Cassidy, back in the days when he took flight any time his sensors picked up that the woman was thinking commitment. Emily had helped Zach with cases before, but that was when she still had some hope of getting back together with him.

"She'd be in seriously deep shit if she got caught. And besides, what possible reason could she have for wanting to do me any more favors?''

Usually totally brash about requesting help from anybody. But how can he ask Emily to put herself at risk? Then again, how can he not ask if she's our only hope?

"Well, but she's a detective, isn't she? Wouldn't she want to see an abductor brought to justice? Or is she too jaded after working for the CPD all these years?''

"Emily's an honest, hard-working cop. Actually, she's a lot like me. She bends the rules, but only for a good cause.''

"Let's lay the situation out for her then. Tell her about our suspicion that Ashley's been abducted. Maybe Emily will feel the same way I do.''

Zach reread the report, gazed out the window, then said,

"How shall we set this up? That time I went behind your back and saw Emily by myself was a disaster." Zach had arranged to meet Emily at a bar they'd frequented while dating. His purpose was to get information about a police case, but she'd assumed he wanted to start seeing her again.

"Let's invite her to have a drink with the two of us. It's been so long since you and Emily were involved, I doubt that she'd have a problem with my being there."

"I never know what women are going to have a problem with." Zach went to his desk in the bedroom and looked up Emily's number in his Palm Pilot.

Going to sit at her desk also, Cassidy asked, "Would it be okay if I listened in?" *I want to hear how she sounds, if she's friendly or not.*

"I suppose."

"You don't want me to?"

"It's a little awkward, calling my ex-girlfriend with my wife on the phone."

Let it go. You don't have to win every little skirmish.

"I'll keep my mouth zipped. She won't even know I'm on the line."

Giving Cassidy a curt nod, Zach dialed on the cordless while she picked up her desk phone.

"Yeah," Emily said.

"This is Zach."

"Well…what a surprise." Her voice guarded.

Can't tell if she means a good surprise or a bad surprise. Probably some of both.

"Remember that wedding-day murder?" Zach asked. "Well, I've been investigating—actually Cass and I are working on it together—and I've uncovered some interesting possibilities. The trouble is, I don't have the resources to nail anything down."

"You want me to do something that could get me busted, right?"

Heading in the direction of unfriendly.

"At this point all I want is for you to let Cass and me

buy you a drink. I'd like to explain the problem we've run into, then you can decide whether or not you want to help. If you say no, that'll be the end of it.''

"How can you even imagine that I'd put myself on the line for you again?"

"I can't," Zach said, sounding less cocky than usual. "I've wracked my brain trying to conceive of some kind of argument to get you to do this, and I've come up blank.''

A long silence. "Shit! You've done it to me again. Made me just curious enough that I can't quite say no. At least I can't at the moment. But after I've heard your pitch, I'm sure I'll have no trouble turning you down.''

They made arrangements to meet at nine that night at a bar near the building where Emily worked.

As Zach hung up, Cassidy said, "You're amazing. You have such a knack for presenting yourself in exactly the right light with each different person. If you'd come across in your usual self-confident way, it would've been easy for Emily to dismiss you. But instead, you took a one-down stance, and that disarmed her enough that she wasn't able to say no.''

He offered a sardonic smile. "The only person I'm not able to work my persuasive miracles on is you.''

A FEW MINUTES before one, Cassidy and Zach emerged from the Subaru in the parking lot across the street from the Old Graue Mill. The heat instantly zapped her, an anti-energy pill, making her feel as wilted as yesterday's salad. They started along the brick path, bordered by wooden fences, toward the three-story mill building, which appeared in amazingly good condition for its hundred-and-fifty-year-old age.

Zach took her hand. "You want me to sit on the sidelines? Or step in if you start to look unsure of yourself?''

It's good to do things on your own. Tell him to stay out of it.

Yeah, but Zach has tons of experience at this sort of

*thing, and you have zilch. Why take the chance of screw-
ing up?*

"I want you to read my mind and respond accordingly."
She raised both hands, palms out. "Just kidding. I'd like
to try this on my own"—*bribing people for information is
such valuable experience, after all*—"but if I stand there
with my mouth gaping for more than thirty seconds, feel
free to speak up."

When they reached the glistening black water wheel—
clearly not the original model—the path was empty. *Hope
she hasn't changed her mind.* To their left was a roaring
sluice channeled off from Salt Creek, the water slapping
the underside of the wheel. To their right, the river itself,
white froth churning from a small dam upstream.

Fifteen minutes later the ginger-haired waitress came
dashing up to them. Resting an outspread hand on her
throat, she gasped out a "Sorry to be late." When Cassidy
had seen the woman at Cypress, she'd looked like a well-
groomed young beauty. Today, in a frayed tee with a large
pink stain on the front, she looked like a harried mother.

"My two-year-old swallowed a cigarette butt and I had
to take him to the ER. I was planning to change—this shirt
went into the wash along with a red crayon—but after I
dropped the kids off at Mom's, there wasn't time to go
back home."

*Motherhood—probably more harrowing than any mur-
der investigation.*

"So," Cassidy said, "you have something to tell us."
Zach pulled out his notepad.

The waitress cast an uneasy glance at Zach, then blinked
several times in rapid succession, her brown eyes displaying a spark of anxiety. "I've never done anything like this
before, and I wouldn't be doing it now if that asshole ex-
husband of mine would just pay the damn child support.
Susan would kill me if she knew I overheard her. She'd
especially kill me if she knew I was talking to reporters. I

shouldn't be doing this. She's always been nice to me. Blabbing her secrets is such a betrayal."

I better find some way to stop her before she talks herself out of completing her mission. Although—if I were in her shoes—I might back out myself. Cassidy took out a hundred dollar bill and held it in her hands.

"I can understand why you feel bad about this. But you have to put your kids first, and it sounds like right now you need a little extra."

"It's the phone bill. Ameritech's going to turn it off if I don't pay. And then it'll cost a small fortune to get it hooked back up again."

Cassidy had been broke herself before Zach added his income to hers. *If it's just you, you can live on bread and water. But you can't do that with kids.* She felt a small urge to simply give the waitress the money, but knowing what Zach would think of that idea, she quickly squelched it.

The waitress looked at Cassidy. "Okay, I'll do it. But you have to promise not to let Susan know that I told you. In fact, you shouldn't even let her know that you know. And you definitely can't use my name."

Don't even know her name. "No one will find out that you talked to us. But we'll probably need to run your story by Susan."

"She'll be so humiliated." The waitress blinked several times again. "You can't use this in the paper—you absolutely can't."

Oh shit. What would Zach say? Cassidy glanced at her husband but his eyes were fixed on the waitress. *Told you you couldn't use the information unless you get corroboration elsewhere.*

"We can do this off the record," Cassidy said. "But if we hear the same thing from someone else, it may show up in the paper."

Shifting her weight, the waitress folded her arms beneath her breasts. "This is something I overheard a couple of days after Max made his wedding announcement. The restaurant was closed, but I had this one table left—a lovey dovey couple who sat around staring into each other's eye and wouldn't fucking leave. I hate seeing people who make such a big show of being in love. Sometimes I just wan to shake the woman and say, 'What do you think it'll be like ten years from now when you're raising your kids or your own?'"

She paused, then went on in a calmer voice. "Anyway after the couple finally took off, my car wouldn't start. I was past midnight and I didn't want to wake my mother so I called my ex. Well, get this—he was playing poker and said he couldn't leave for another hour." She pushed a strand of ginger hair back from her eyes. "You can imagine how pissed I was, but there was nothing I could do about it, so I planted my butt in one of the booths, leaned against the wall, and put my feet up.

"A few minutes later Susan and her friend Vincent came into the dining room and plunked down at a table not far from where I was sitting. They couldn't see me but I could hear every word."

The pink-stained tee shirt rose and fell in a deep sigh. "Susan was telling Vincent about the thing Max had done to her. She said Max'd pretended to be in love with her— even given her a ring and told her they were engaged— and that she'd completely fallen for it. No one else knew about this secret engagement of theirs, but Susan still felt like he'd made a total fool of her."

"You mean they'd kept the relationship a secret from the staff?" Cassidy asked. "Why would Susan do that?"

"She's Jewish and Max's mother is Catholic. He told Susan his mom was being treated for cancer and he didn't want to tell her—or anybody else—about the engagement until she finished her chemo. Susan was so gaga she took him at his word. Gave him the partnership and everything else he wanted. Then one day Max walks into the restaurant and announces he's marrying someone else."

"My God!" Cassidy said. "Talk about having the rug yanked out from under you."

"Susan was a real mess that night I heard her talking to Vincent. I started at the Chicago Cypress over six years ago, and most of the time Susan acts like she's hard as nails. But that night she was actually sobbing." The waitress rubbed her fingers against her forehead. "It broke my heart to hear her cry like that. She said she felt like the world's worst idiot for getting taken in by Max. But I can see how it could happen. All the women at Cypress thought he was such a prize."

Cassidy hooked her thumbs into her jeans waistband. "Susan told us she was too independent to get married."

"She says that to cover up the fact that she feels like such a failure with men. She's usually pretty much okay with her life, but every now and then she goes through a blue spell and talks about how she's missed out by never getting married."

So Susan isn't this invulnerable, I-Am-Woman person she pretends to be.

Zach edged in closer to the waitress. "Her friend Vincent. What did he have to say?"

The woman looked away from them. "Nothing."

"That's not true, is it? Vincent did say something and we need to know what it was."

"He asked Susan if she wanted him to take care of it."

"How did Susan respond?" Cassidy pressed.

"She said she wasn't sure. She'd let him know."

Zach asked, "And did this Vincent have an Italian surname?"

"Santori," the waitress said in a whisper. She took in a breath through her mouth. "That's all there is. I've told you everything. Now will you please just give me the fucking money and let me go?"

"I appreciate your help." Cassidy handed over the bill.

"I'm glad you're happy, 'cause I just screwed somebody who's always been decent to me." The woman turned on her heel and started hiking back toward the parking lot.

TWENTY-FOUR

NO REASON TO BE SCARED

CASSIDY STARED AFTER the waitress, a hollow feeling in her rib cage.

"What's wrong?" Zach asked.

"I don't like myself very much right now."

"You shouldn't be doing this kind of thing," Zach said, his eyes troubled. "It's your job to be empathic. You can't keep playing bad cop like this without blunting your sense of compassion."

"How do you do it?"

"I detach myself. I know you detach somewhat as a therapist, but I take it way further than you do. I started at an early age so it comes naturally to me, but it's all wrong for you."

You know he's right. So why don't you just bow out and leave the investigating to him?

Because you can't stand feeling like Zach's the tough, strong husband and you're the sensitive little wife. Because deep down inside, there's some part of you that wants to be as ballsy and invulnerable as the façade Susan puts up.

ZACH WENT INTO the waiting room, Cassidy coming behind him. A cat lay in each of the two fan-backed chairs in front of the window, a svelte Egyptian-princess calico in one, a fluffy black kitten in the other.

Scratching Starshine's chin, Cassidy addressed the cat,

"Well, does the fact that you and Roscoe are in client chairs mean you've decided you need a little therapy to work out your differences?"

Starshine bounced to the floor and trotted toward her bowl. Darting after her, Roscoe pounced at her tail, then ran off when she turned to smack him.

As Zach fed Starshine, Cassidy crossed the kitchen, stepping over the curling seam in the mottled gray linoleum. Most of the time, she was able to cast a blind eye on the house's defects, but every now and then, the shabbiness and disrepair came into sharp focus. Today she couldn't stop herself from noticing that the varnish had long since worn off her wooden cabinets, that the once green linoleum countertop had been rubbed down to a cloudy gray color, and that the window above the sink had a small crack in the corner.

The creeping rot is so bad you ought to be jumping for joy at the opportunity to leave it behind.

I don't care if it's a mess! This house has been a haven for me for a lot of years and I don't want to let it go.

She leaned against the counter to talk to Zach as he washed out Starshine's bowl. The cat had eaten only a few bites, then disappeared from the kitchen, probably in search of her playmate.

"I think the waitress must've been telling the truth," Cassidy said. "She seemed genuinely fond of Susan. If she was inclined to invent a story just to get the money, there'd be no reason to make her boss look so guilty."

"All that fondness could've been an act. Maybe she hates her boss and wants to stick it to her. Like I said before, any information you pay for needs corroboration. Which means, I have to try to get Susan to talk."

Cassidy wiped up the little crumbs of cat food Starshine had left on the counter. "I doubt that Susan will admit anything."

"You never know. It's amazing what people will tell

reporters—things they absolutely shouldn't say to any-body."

He's right. People have such a need to justify themselves.

"This business about Max being engaged to two women at once is really sleazy. Claire's going to be crushed when I have to tell her all the things he's been up to."

Zach prowled through the refrigerator, emerging with a Pepsi. "So why do it? Sounds to me like she'd be better off not knowing."

"The way Claire gets herself in trouble is by idealizing charming men. I'm hoping that if she hears all this slimy stuff about Max, it'll help her see that the kind of guy she's drawn to almost always has a fatal flaw." Cassidy expelled a heavy breath. "But I still dread telling her."

"It's my opinion that if she goes back to Hank, she's too stupid to live and you shouldn't waste time on her."

Crossing her arms, Cassidy scowled at him.

"Look, I'm a reporter. I don't have to be sensitive."

"This is only a relapse," Cassidy retorted. "Sooner or later Molly and I will get Claire back on track."

Taking a swig of Pepsi, Zach went into the dining room, Cassidy at his heels. "First I want to set up a meeting with Susan," he said, "then I have to interview some people about an honor roll student killed in a drive-by. The sad thing is, I've covered so many of these shootings, I could do it in my sleep."

As they settled into their desk chairs, Cassidy said, "We should interview Susan at her house. So she can't just walk away when we ask hard questions."

Zach gave her an approving nod. "You're getting to be almost as good at this as I am. But if you try to go for your P.I.'s license, I'll do everything in my power to stop you."

He punched up Susan's number on the cordless, while Cassidy listened in on her desk phone.

"I've received some new information about your rela-tionship with Max," he told the restaurant owner. "I could just run with it, but I thought you'd want an opportunity to comment."

"Somebody's bullshitting you. There isn't any new information." Susan paused. "Reporters are the scum of the earth, you know that?"

"You better believe it." Zach scrawled Susan's name on the yellow pad in front of him. "Is there some time today Cass and I could come by your house?"

"I'll be at the Chicago restaurant later tonight. You can hook up with me there."

Zach tapped his pen against the pad, leaving a small circle of dots. "Look, I've got an important story here with a source that's willing to be named. I'm doing you a favor by letting you have some input. You either schedule a meeting with us at your house today, or I'll submit the story as is."

"And you'll submit it where? Unless you give me a chance to respond, your story'll be so unbalanced the *Post* wouldn't touch it."

"I *am* giving you a chance. You can agree to let Cass and me come by your house, or I'll take your refusal as a 'no comment'."

The bell rings, and the scum-of-the-earth reporter wins round two against the oversexed Susan, who took round one by making him explain his sketch.

"Shit!" Susan paused again. "If I have to, I suppose I could squeeze you in at seven."

Zach wrote down the address, then left to cover the shooting.

With a therapy session coming up soon, Cassidy went to her desk and began searching for her calendar. Rummaging through piles of paper, she came across a library book that was due the next day. *You better return it this afternoon, or before you know it, you'll have accumulated a week's worth of fines.*

HER KEYS AND the book in one hand, Cassidy stepped out into the soft, early evening light. She halted on the stoop, as she always did now, and scrutinized the part of Briar she could see from that vantage. Several cars were parked on the street, but none had a ball-capped driver sitting behind the wheel. *You knew you wouldn't see him. Wherever it is he watches you from, it isn't here.*

As she was backing out of the garage, she remembered that she'd left her cell on its charger. She stopped in the driveway and considered whether or not to return for her phone. *You're going to the library, five minutes away, in the heart of Oak Park. Almost zero opportunity for your personal shadow to harass you.*

She trundled off toward the new library building on Lake Street. Sliding her novel into the book drop next to the double glass doors, she climbed back into her Toyota and headed for home. Turned east on Briar, cruised for a block, then checked her rearview mirror. The battered sedan was a car-length behind her.

Her breath caught and a low buzz started in her brain. *Just wants to scare you,* her no-nonsense voice stated firmly. Sucking in air, she managed to dispel the staticky noise in her head. She passed through the Hazel-Briar intersection, then drew up to the curb between a minivan and a Beetle that were sitting about twenty feet apart. The sedan stopped beside her Toyota.

The parking lot guy, ball cap turned to the side, yelled at her through their open windows. "Din't I tell you, bitch, I was gonna get you if you din't stop askin' questions?"

She rolled up her window, then made sure her doors were locked. *Oh shit! If only you'd gone back for your phone.*

This time he's going to hurt you, a voice shrilled inside her head.

He wouldn't dare. Not out here in front of all the neighbors.

Peering up and down the block, she tried to find someone she could call to for help, but the only person in sight was the man who glared at her from the other car. She leaned on her horn for a full minute, sweat popping out on her forehead, but not a single door opened. Wiping her brow, she turned on the air conditioning.

She squeezed her eyes shut, propped her elbow on the steering wheel, and rested her cheek against her hand. *Zach'll be home soon. You can wait it out.* She stole a glance at the other driver. He was still gazing straight at her. Her stomach twitched and the buzz in her brain revved louder. The idea of staying in her car until Zach returned seemed like more than she could bear. She contemplated making a run for her house. She thought she would be able to get to the door before he did, but then she'd have to stop and unlock it, and he would catch up with her.

Twisting her head, she estimated the distance between her Toyota and the minivan to be about eight feet—enough space to back out behind the sedan. That would enable her to read his rear license plate, then speed past him on the left, turn right onto Austin, and drive to the police station. She put the car in reverse and stomped on the accelerator. She was just starting to turn the rear end of her car out toward the street when the sedan rolled backward, boxing her in.

She jammed the car into drive and tried to pull out in front of him, but he moved along with her.

A cold shiver ran down her arms. *You're trapped. There's nothing you can do.* She gripped the wheel and stared straight ahead. Five minutes later, the sedan backed up to the Hazel-Briar intersection, turned south, and drove away.

Cassidy went inside and collapsed on the sofa, taking deep breaths and rubbing her arms to warm them. A while later she heard Zach come in the back door. Hurrying into the kitchen, she wrapped her arms tightly around him and leaned her head against his chest.

He gathered her into a close embrace. "This is way more of a greeting than I usually get."

Stepping back, she told him about her encounter with the

parking lot guy. "It's ridiculous to let this thing get to me.
I was locked safely away in my car. There was no reason
to be so scared."

"Scared is exactly what you should be."

TWENTY-FIVE

A HYPOTHETICAL WOMAN

SUSAN, IN A LACY black dress with a deep frontal slit, admitted Cassidy and Zach to her highrise condo.

"Since being strong-armed is one of my least favorite things, I fortified myself with a martini." Susan waved toward a triangular glass on a table next to a leopard-spotted chaise lounge. "That means you have to drink too. To level the playing field."

"I'll take a beer. Cass'll have red wine."

"C'mon Zach, why don't you belly up and have a real drink?"

"Not tonight."

Susan went to the wet bar across the room, returning with a Moosehead for Zach and wine for Cassidy. "I hate getting lubricated all by myself," she said, pouting.

Cassidy and Zach sat in side-by-side armchairs while Susan arranged her Rubenesque body on the lounge in a pose that fell just short of being centerfold material.

Where do women learn how to do that? Do they practice in front of a mirror? Or is it some gene I missed out on?

"Okay, Tiger," Susan said to Zach, "Let's hear what you've got."

He told her what he'd learned about her engagement to Max, including Vincent Santori's offer to take care of the problem.

While Zach talked, Cassidy studied Susan. Her expression remained unreadable, but the color drained from her face. Although she didn't change position, she seemed to withdraw from them, her eyes not making contact, her body sinking into lethargy.

Susan emptied her glass, then shook her shoulders and pulled herself into a more upright position, the sensuality she had previously radiated completely disappearing.

"What an awful shock that must've been," Cassidy said in a soft voice.

Susan's darkly outlined eyes threw Cassidy a venomous look.

Boy, did you ever take a wrong turn there. What you intended as empathy must've come across as pure condescension.

To Zach, Susan said, "Who told you that cock-and-bull story?"

"I'm not at liberty to name my source. I just need a comment from you."

"Not a word of truth to it. Your source is obviously some creep who's got a hair up his ass about me. Or maybe it's a her. The lady friend of some guy I fucked. Some chick who's jealous because I had access to Max's stud services and she didn't."

Susan returned to the bar and mixed herself a second martini, then took out another Moosehead. Placing her glass on the end table, she carried the beer over to Zach, who had not finished his first, and put it in his hand, deliberately touching her leg against his.

Resents people who are married. Wants to stir up trouble between them. Now that Cassidy understood where Susan's outrageous behavior was coming from, she was less upset by it, especially since she could remember a time when she'd found it difficult to be around happily married couples herself.

Assuming another provocative pose on the lounge, Susan directed her gaze at Cassidy. "So the reason you follow Zach around is, you're afraid that if you let him off his leash, he'll go stick his nose up some other chickie's crotch.''

Susan stirred her drink with her finger.

"You can't be too careful, you know," Cassidy agreed cheerfully.

"So you're standing by your original story—that you never were serious about Max," Zach said. "But if some hypothetical woman who was planning to marry him got dumped for somebody else, what do you suppose she'd do?"

Susan stared at the windowed wall so long Cassidy thought she wouldn't answer. But then she turned her eyes on Zach and said, "Well, if you're talking about some *hypothetical* woman, my guess is she'd start off being so pissed she couldn't see straight. She might even want to kill him, but she wouldn't do it because civilized women don't go knocking people off every time somebody puts one over on them. At first she wouldn't want anything to do with the jerk, but if he kept explaining himself and explaining himself, she might come to see that when he first started pursuing her, it wasn't just because he wanted a partnership. That he initially had a crush on her, that he felt privileged to be invited into her bed. But as time wore on, he started to feel uncomfortable with the age difference, and then—" her voice turned snide—"he met this sweet young thing who bowled him over with her niceness." Susan spat out the word as if it were an obscenity.

Thought for sure she'd stonewall us. But can't resist telling her side of the story. And also doesn't want us considering her so naïve as to be taken in by Max.

Cassidy asked, "But why would Max wait until the wedding was only a month off to 'fess up about his other fiancée?"

"He always wanted to be the good guy. Couldn't stand admitting he'd done anything wrong. In fact, Max was such a liability, this hypothetical woman might have eventually come to realize he was more trouble than he was worth.''

"So I take it Max was pretty much of a bad boy," Cassidy said. "Probably into bed-hopping. He could enjoy the favors of both women and—since he worked late on weekends—not even have to worry about who got Saturday night."

A desolate look came over Susan's face. She gazed out the windowed wall for several seconds. "He said he was depressed. About his mother's cancer. And that was why he couldn't do it."

Cassidy blinked in surprise. *Well, what do you know. That's twice now we've caught Max out doing the decent thing.*

"Even though he was a liability, he evidently wasn't all bad," Cassidy said, curling her fingers beneath her chin. "There obviously was some goodness to him, which is probably why the hypothetical woman liked him so much."

Her eyes softening slightly, Susan took a long pull at her drink.

Zach asked, "Is there anything you'd like to say for the record?"

Susan touched her tongue to her upper lip, then suggested to Cassidy, "Why don't you leave stud muffin here with me for a couple of hours, pick him up later?" She laughed raucously.

Zach tucked his pad away and stood up. "Thanks for your time."

WITH MORE THAN an hour to kill before their nine o'clock meeting with Emily, they decided to head for Andersonville, a neighborhood crammed with various ethnic restaurants, and find some interesting hole-in-the-wall place to eat.

As they cruised west on Belmont, Cassidy asked, "This place Emily picked—is it a cop bar?"

"It's some anonymous watering hole I never heard of. Emily wouldn't want to meet us at a cop bar because someone would be sure to remember that she and I used to date, and then they'd all razz her about being part of a three-some."

They drove a while without talking, then Cassidy inquired, "What did you think of Susan's hypothetical woman story?"

"I'd guess that Max made up his I-really-did-love-you spin to mollify Susan, and she latched onto it to salvage her pride."

"You're always so cynical."

"So what do you think?"

"One part I absolutely believe is that Max stopped sleeping with Susan about the time he became intimate with Claire."

"Susan has such a dominatrix personality it'd be easy to get tired of her."

"Well, but it's possible Max was genuinely attracted at the beginning. I bet a lot of guys get turned on by her out-there sexuality."

Zach gave Cassidy a bemused smile. "Max wanted to believe that his reason for courting Susan wasn't purely mercenary. Susan wanted to believe that she hadn't been made a complete fool of. And you want to believe that after all the work you've put into Claire, she wasn't entirely nuts in choosing Max."

CASSIDY AND ZACH sat in small roller-footed armchairs in the brightly lit interior of Katie's Place, a yuppie drinking establishment on Chicago's north side. The place was half-filled, the other occupants all younger, buffer, and more stylishly dressed than either Cassidy or Zach. No one was smoking, and the air smelled as clean and fresh as a newly opened bottle of Evian water.

The polished wood door swung inward and a graceful woman in a softly tailored jacket and skirt approached their table. Cassidy and Zach rose to greet her.

"Emily," Zach said with warmth in his voice, "it's good to see you."

*He'd acted so friendly two years ago, you'd be breathing
fire and brimstone. What a relief to have your jealousy
demons finally put to rest.*

She nodded toward Zach and said "Hey" to Cassidy,
and they all sat down.

Emily and Zach chatted about people they knew while
Cassidy sat back and watched. The detective, with her
honey-colored hair and amber-flecked eyes, looked much
the same as when Cassidy had seen her last, nearly two
years before. Early on in Cassidy's relationship with Zach,
she'd wondered why he'd picked her over the pretty detective, but now she had a better understanding of why he was
drawn to her.

From time to time, Emily's gaze snicked toward Cassidy.
She probably wonders why he picked me too.

After drinks were set in front of them, Zach said, "I
guess I better explain why I called." He told Emily about
their investigation and why they suspected Garrett Hillard
of using a false identity. "Our main concern is his daughter," Zach concluded. "If Hillard abducted her, we want
to get her back where she belongs."

Tapping her nails on the tabletop, Emily regarded Zach
curiously. "I don't get it. Why are you and Cass working
this case together?"

"Because I wouldn't stay out of it," Cassidy interjected.
"Because it was my friend who asked for help. Because I
like answers and I don't want the killer to get away with
what he did to Claire." *Except it was the killer who saved
her from marrying slimy Max.*

Leaning forward, Emily asked Zach, "So, who do you
like for the murderer?"

"I'd say either the bride's sister or the victim's business
partner." He turned to Cassidy. "What do you think?"

"If I had to pick, I guess it would be Garrett Hillard and
the blackmail angle. Given how desperate Max was for
money, I can just see him telling Garrett he'd turn him in

for child abduction if Garrett didn't start making hefty payments."

Emily said, "Do you know what would happen to me if I got caught processing fingerprints for a reporter?"

"You'd get busted down to patrol?"

"Worse. And in addition to what the department would do, if Hillard found out about it, he could sue you, me, the Chicago PD, and the *Post*."

"True."

She shook her head. "You still haven't given me a single reason to go out of my way to help you, much less do something as risky as this."

"Because of the child." Cassidy hunched forward and crossed her arms on the table. "Children who are taken from their mothers often suffer severe emotional damage. When the maternal bond is broken, the child frequently finds it impossible to ever form a normal attachment. They spend the rest of their lives adrift."

"But what if the mother was unfit?"

"Even with unfit mothers, children need regular contact."

"Well, maybe." Emily stared toward the bar, then narrowed her eyes at Zach. "But only if I get some answers."

Zach's brow creased, a remote look coming over his face. "I don't know what you mean, but all right."

Emily sent him a bright, slightly false smile. Turning toward Cassidy, she said, "I intend to have a little talk with Zach. If this makes you uncomfortable, we can move to the bar."

"Oh no, I'm perfectly okay with it." *If Emily's willing to expose herself to all the things a former lover might say, she's a far braver woman than I. Except she knows Zach would never trash her.*

To Zach, Emily said, "I want to make it clear—even if you weren't married—I'd have no interest in seeing you again. The only reason I'm asking these questions is, I want to make sense out of what happened."

"I'll do what I can."

"Well, then…." She took in a breath. "It always seemed to me that we were pretty good together."

"We were."

"We knew the same people, had the same interests. We could almost finish each other's sentences."

"Yeah, I remember that."

"Then—just about the time I started thinking we were going somewhere—you told me that long term commitments weren't part of your plan."

His skin turning a shade darker, Zach broke off eye contact with Emily.

"And then a year later you moved in with Cass, and before I knew it, you were married."

Can see why this would seem so strange to her, especially since cops and reporters usually don't have much use for social workers.

"So what happened?" Emily prompted. "Was there something wrong between us I wasn't aware of? Was that business about not wanting commitments just a line?"

Zach shifted in his chair, looked away, then brought his gaze back to Emily. "I meant everything I said at the time I said it. Back then, I was convinced I'd never marry and I didn't want to string you along."

"So what changed?"

"I reached a point where I didn't want to keep running any longer."

"What was it? Some cliché like a midlife crisis? You hit forty and developed a sudden yearning for a house in the suburbs?"

Zach could say "yes" and make it easy on both of them. Cassidy waited to see what he would do.

"No, that wasn't it." He gazed into space for a moment. "It was Cass. The way she hammered at me with her questions. She made me tell her all the things I never wanted to tell anybody. And then, once all the shit was out, I didn't need to run any longer."

Emily gave him a hard, cop-like stare. "That's it?"

"That's it." He took a long swallow of bourbon. "You know, I'm glad we had this talk. I always felt bad about not explaining anything."

Cassidy felt a sudden rush of warmth toward her husband. *Zach's great at lying, but he's also good at the truth.*

"Well," Emily wrapped her hands around the base of her glass, "I guess I got what I was looking for." After a moment she added, "Okay, I'll get your guy's fingerprints into AFIS."

TWENTY-SIX

A PERSONALITY TRANSPLANT

THERE WAS NO return call from Claire on the machine when Cassidy and Zach got home that night, and no one picked up the phone when she made a second round of calls Wednesday morning.

Her purple mug in hand, Cassidy sat next to Zach in the computer room, where he was reading his email. "Claire's avoiding me."

"It's been less than twenty-four hours since you started leaving messages."

"Yeah, but I'm pretty sure she would have called if she was going to. On one hand, Claire isn't my official client any more, so breaking down her door and forcing her to talk might not be the most ethical thing to do. But on the other hand, Molly needs a responsible person to step in, and I can't just ignore the fact that she asked for my help."

"So you're going to break down Claire's door?"

"Actually, I thought I'd drive to her building tonight and lean on her buzzer. It should be harder to refuse to let me in than to not return phone calls." Cassidy thought it through. "I'll wait till nine. She's sure to be home from work by then."

Signing off, Zach turned to look at Cassidy. "What if Hank's there?"

"Then she probably won't answer the buzzer."

Heading back toward the bedroom, Cassidy saw Starshine walk into the den and go straight for Roscoe's not-quite-empty bowl, which he'd abandoned to play downstairs.

The remnants of the kitten's breakfast looked dry and unappetizing, the sort of leftovers Starshine would disdain entirely if she encountered them in her own bowl. She sniffed at the crumbs, started to walk away, then returned to devour every last bite, licking the container until it was shiny and clean.

"You didn't even like it, did you? You just couldn't resist the thrill of taking something away from Roscoe. And for all you know, he may be down in the kitchen right this minute polishing off your food."

Zach left for work, and Cassidy, with seven clients to see before dinner, started to get dressed. She'd just finished buttoning her magenta blouse when the phone rang.

"This is Irene, Max's mother." The voice flat and unfriendly.

"Well, Irene, what can I do for you?" Cassidy drew a sour-looking cartoon face on the back of an envelope.

"I have something to say to you and your husband, and I want both of you to come to my house and hear it."

"Could you give me some idea what this is about?"

"I'm not saying one word till I have the two of you here in front of me."

A feeling of resistance welled up in Cassidy, but she knew she couldn't refuse Irene's request, even though it had sounded more like a demand. Gazing through the west window at a torrent of rain pouring out of a smoke-colored sky, she asked, "When would you like us to come?"

"I'm going to be out all day Thursday, so let's make it eight o'clock Friday morning."

I'll listen to what she has to say, but I'll be damned if I'm getting up at dawn to do it. "We'll be there at ten."

AT DINNER that night, her mouth filled with the Thai car-ryout Zach had brought home, Cassidy gazed at rain streaking down the dining room window.

"You still planning to drive to Claire's tonight?" Zach asked, scooping up the last forkful of orange noodles from his plate.

She nodded.

"It's really lousy weather out there."

"I'll leave early to make up for the traffic."

Refolding his unused napkin, Zach laid his silverware on the edge of his plate. "I'd feel a lot better if you'd let me drive. I could drop you off at the door, then wait in the car. That way you won't have to walk in the rain."

He thinks I'm going to melt?

He's worried. Afraid the parking lot thug will get you. Or remembering that friend of his who drove away in a rainstorm and never returned.

"A ride would be nice."

Now that wasn't so hard, was it?

JUMPING OUT OF the Subaru, Cassidy waited under the canopy while the uniformed attendant opened the door for her. Inside the marble entryway, she pushed the button next to Claire's name.

"Who is it?" Claire's voice through the intercom.

"It's Cassidy. I have to talk to you."

"You're here? In the building?"

"I couldn't reach you by phone."

"I was going to call."

Cassidy pounded her fist lightly against the orange-veined wall. "Just buzz me up."

"I'm a little busy right now."

"I came all the way down here to talk to you and I'm not going home till I do."

A three beat silence, then Claire agreed to let her come upstairs.

"If you'd just given me a little more time," Claire said,

following Cassidy into the living room, "I would have gotten back to you. It's just...I've been putting in so many hours...I hardly have a minute to myself."

"That's all right." Cassidy parked herself in the striped easy chair. "It's better for us to talk face to face anyway." She marveled at how rested her client appeared. *First you've seen her without bags under her eyes since the shooting. Too bad it's all based on false hope.*

Claire sank down on the burgundy sofa next to a pile of clothing Cassidy thought was probably unfolded laundry. A few books and toys lay on the Oriental carpet.

"Sorry the place is such a mess," Claire apologized, her shoulders hunched, her gaze fixed on the floor.

"Molly called me. She wants me to convince you to stop seeing Hank. She's afraid he'll start mistreating you again."

"Poor Molly, I've put her through so much." Claire darted a glance at Cassidy, her brown eyes filling. "It's going to take some time for her to realize that her father's a different person now."

"Oh? And when did this personality transplant occur?"

"He's learned his lesson," Claire said defensively. "He understands now that I won't put up with any of his bullshit."

Oh right. And cats learn not to chase mice.

"I'm sure Hank's treating you like gold right now. But how is that different from the way he acted when he first met you?"

"You can't imagine how wonderful Hank's being," Claire insisted. "Whenever I need to talk, he puts everything else aside and listens to me. Yesterday he had flowers delivered to my office. Every night he brings food in so I don't have to cook. He'd be here now except he has a meeting."

"But didn't he do similar things before you were married?"

Delicate lines etched themselves across Claire's forehead. "He's just different, okay?"

What's it going to take to yank her out of her fantasy world? "Do you remember the thing Hank did that finally got you to leave?"

Sending Cassidy a vague look, Claire shook her head.

"Molly had just turned four. You had to work late that night so you picked up a pizza for dinner."

Claire's face went pale.

"What did Hank do?"

"He ripped pizza slices out of the box and started throwing them around the kitchen."

"What was he so angry about?"

"He said it was because I didn't make home-cooked meals. That we were living on junk food. That if I really loved him, I'd stay home and take care of the family."

"Had Hank ever exploded over pizza before?"

"We'd both picked up pizza plenty of times and it never bothered him. I had no idea he'd go crazy like that."

"What happened next?"

Claire raised her shoulders as if warding off blows. "He started yelling. He called me a filthy name."

"What name was that?"

Turning away, Claire refused to say it.

"Didn't he call you a 'stupid cunt'?" Cassidy said in a soft voice.

Claire made a slight ducking motion with her head.

"And what did you do after he called you that?"

"I was crying really hard. I curled up on the bed and covered my ears. Then Molly came in and kind of laid on top of me—trying to protect me, I guess." Claire's chest heaved in a large sigh. "Hank grabbed Molly and threw her off the bed. He told her I was a lazy bitch and she should stay away from me."

"How did you feel when that happened?"

"I wanted to die."

They sat in silence for a moment, then Cassidy said, "You need to let go of that memory and come back into the present."

Claire blinked and looked at Cassidy. "Why'd you do that to me?"

"Can you understand now why Molly's so scared?"

"But Hank would never do anything like that again." Claire rubbed her right hand up and down her left arm.

Cassidy didn't reply.

"Why can't you believe me when I tell you he's changed?"

"Do you remember how we used to talk about Hank's core personality? How I told you he was a narcissist and then you began to identify narcissistic traits in him yourself? And how we talked about the fact that narcissists can make you feel really special at the beginning, but in the long run the abusiveness always returns?"

Her voice faltering, Claire said, "So you think I should stop seeing him?"

I believe that's the message I've been drumming in for the past half hour. "What does Molly need from you?"

"Oh God, I've been such a terrible mother." Tears started streaming down Claire's face. She pressed both hands to her cheeks, her fingertips touching the folds of skin beneath her eyes. Crossing to sit beside her, Cassidy wrapped her arms around her client's shoulders. Claire leaned against Cassidy and wept.

After Claire had cried herself out, Cassidy slid to the opposite end of the sofa.

"So, what are you going to do about Hank?"

"I have to stop seeing him. I have to make myself remember what he's really like. I have to do it for Molly."

"I want you to imagine yourself calling Hank and telling him it's over."

Claire stared into space for several seconds, then looked at Cassidy and nodded.

"You think you can do that?"

Her voice steadier now, Claire said, "I have to."

"Okay," Cassidy got to her feet, "I guess I'm finished here."

Following her to the door, Claire gave her a big hug. "All I ever do is give you grief. I don't know why you put up with me."

"Because someday you're going to get it all together, and then you'll be awesome."

TWENTY-SEVEN

FEELING LIKE A CHUMP

THE STORM WAS STILL raging when Cassidy left Claire's building. Shivering, she climbed into the car and Zach pulled out into traffic. The windshield-wipers swished. In the distance, a flash of jagged light, the sound of muffled bowling balls.

"Mission accomplished," she announced, going on to fill in the details.

When she finished, Zach said, "While I was waiting, I got a call from this guy I work with who lives in Oak Park. He knows I'm looking to move, so when his neighbor told him she was putting her house on the market, he got in touch with me right away. This place is on LeMoyne— west of Oak Park Avenue—and he says it's in A-one condition. I think we should get in to see it before the owner signs with an agent."

Cassidy pressed her lips together. A silence ensued.

"You're not even willing to look at it, are you?"

That fight you've been trying to avoid is careening toward you like an avalanche. "Could we not talk about this tonight?"

"I'm not putting it off any longer."

What a turnaround—Zach forcing you to talk. Huddling in on herself, she stared out the side window. Neither spoke again until they were home.

In the kitchen, Zach said in the polite tone he used with

other people, "I'm going to have a bourbon and soda. You want one?"

You should say no. Booze is to fights what gasoline is to fires.

"Um… Okay."

They went upstairs, Zach sitting in his desk chair, Cassidy on the bed. His face grim, he gulped down a portion of his drink. "I want you to agree to move. I want you to do it willingly. Even if it's not your first choice. I want you to give in to me because we're a team and I've given in to you plenty of times in the past. I want you to do it just because it's important to me."

If only I could.

Her eyes were gritty, her mouth dry. She took a sip of bourbon. "I can't do it. I've tried and tried to talk myself into it, but I can't."

He looked at her coldly. "You can't? Do you know how ridiculous that sounds? Come on, Cass, you can do better than that."

"But that's what it feels like. When I try to think about moving, I run into this huge wall of resistance. I can't even force my mind to go there."

"You don't have to," he said in a soft voice. Leaning forward, he rested his arms on his legs. "You can let me take care of it. You won't have to do anything except sign the contracts. When moving day comes, I'll just put you in the car and take you to the new house."

You could do that, couldn't you? Just pretend you're going out for the afternoon and never come back?

You made a commitment to yourself to stay here.

She shook her head miserably.

Pulling himself up straight, he said, "What is so fucking important about this house?"

"It isn't just the house. At first I thought it was. I thought I was afraid to let go of the house because it was such an anchor during my divorce. But now I realize there's more to it than that."

"More to it?" he said, biting off the words. "Like what?"

She pressed her hand against her forehead. "I know I'm not making much sense, but please try to understand."

"Go on."

"When I was a kid, the whole idea of Oak Park taking on this mission to become integrated really captured my imagination. Gran took me on some marches and protests and it was the most thrilling thing I'd ever done. I loved being part of a community that was doing something important. Back in the beginning, the thing the leaders used to beat the drum about most was preventing white flight. The key to keeping the village integrated has always been getting white people to live along the eastern border."

"Yeah, I know all that stuff."

"Kevin didn't want to buy this house. He wanted to play it safe and invest in some area that wasn't at risk. But I was earning most of the money and I insisted that we live here. Owning this house was really significant to me. It made me feel like I was part of the mission. Like I was participating in something I believed in."

Zach rattled his ice cubes. "It's too bad you're not religious. You would've made a great fanatic."

"Don't make fun of me."

"Then stop sounding so preachy."

"But I thought you believed in Oak Park as much as I do."

"Oak Park's too self-righteous for my taste and sometimes you are too."

Feeling a prickle of irritation at the back of her neck, she took in a breath and let it out slowly. "So what I'm trying to tell you is, when I bought this house I made a commitment to stay planted right here. To not let myself get scared off by racial change or high crime or even a mugging." She paused, then continued in a lower voice. "Lately I've been pushing people around, pressuring them, behaving in ways I'm not too proud of. But the one thing I always feel good about is living on this block.''

"The *one* thing?" His eyes darkened. "What about our marriage?"

"I didn't think I had to tell you." *You sound just like those inarticulate guys you see in therapy.*

"You mean I'm supposed to know how much you love me even though you're acting like you don't?"

Bunching up the neckline of her shirt, she said, "Oh God, Zach, you have to realize you're the most important person in the world to me."

"You know, those words sound a little empty right now." He finished his drink and set the glass on his desk. "You know something else? I'm beginning to feel like a chump."

She stared at him in amazement. Zach always appeared so tough and strong and in control. She couldn't imagine that anything would make him feel like a chump.

He stood. "I've had enough. I need to get out of here."

Cassidy watched as he left the bedroom, then followed him out into the hall and watched as he went downstairs. His leaving was not a surprise.

Whenever they fought, Zach walked away, usually in the direction of one of the bars he used to frequent. She knew that sometime in the early dawn he would return, and that he wouldn't be entirely sober.

She even knew that Zach was right to walk away. *What you always tell couples. Go to your separate corners. Don't say another word until you've cooled off.*

She understood that Zach's leaving was for the best, but understanding didn't ward off the panic. The same panic she felt whenever anyone she loved left her. The panic that had started in her childhood when her father walked out of their house.

Even though she knew Zach wouldn't abandon her, she couldn't stop herself from breathing in short rapid gasps, couldn't stop the jolts of anxiety from surging in her stomach.

Turning off the overhead light, she swiveled her chair toward the window, propped her feet on the radiator, and stared at the tops of enormous trees billowing in the wind.

Worst of it is, he'll be drinking and driving. It was something Cassidy hated. Years ago a friend had died because she got behind the wheel with too much alcohol in her system.

Zach's usually so good about turning over his keys. The only time he isn't is when he's pissed at you. She flashed an image of the Subaru piling into a semi.

Now stop that! There's nothing you can do so don't think about it.

She replayed the argument, ending at the point where Zach told her he was beginning to feel like a chump. *You are so wrong in not agreeing to move. He's the center of your life, he's done so much for you—why can't you do this one thing for him?*

Her backbone turned rigid. No matter how much she thought she ought to agree, she knew she wouldn't.

TWENTY-EIGHT

FINGERPRINTS

SHE WAS SITTING ON the bed, Starshine and Roscoe curled up beside her, an old movie playing on the television, when the calico pricked her ears, then trotted off downstairs with Roscoe behind her. *Thank God he's home.*

Clicking off the movie, Cassidy looked at the clock. Three-thirty. The windows had not yet started to lighten. Drawing her knees up to her chest, she wrapped her arms around her legs and waited for Zach.

A moment later he came into the room, switched on the light, and sat down heavily in his chair. "Okay, I admit I'm a little drunk,"—she heard the mushiness in his voice—"but I've got some things I need to say and I don't want you brushing them off on the grounds that I'm wasted."

"I won't." She got a lump in her throat, realizing how relieved she was that he'd made it home, driving through the rain, after drinking as much as he had.

His eyes had a glazed look to them. He creased his brow as if struggling to hold onto his thoughts. "Do you know why I never wanted to fall in love?"

A wave of guilt washed over her. "Because you didn't want anyone to have the kind of power over you that I have?"

"I never thought I'd let anybody tell me I had to stop hanging out in bars. Or cut back on my drinking. Or live in-a house that wasn't my choice.''

"Zach—I never told you you had to do anything.''

"No, of course not. If you'd *told* me, I could've ignored you. But I knew my drinking made you unhappy, and I couldn't stand seeing that anxious look on your face. However, you seem to have a higher tolerance for my unhappiness than I do for yours.''

Oh, God, am I that insensitive?

"I realize you've made a lot of changes to keep the peace between us. And I can't tell you how much I appreciate it. But I never got the sense you were unhappy. If you were, you kept it pretty much to yourself.''

He squeezed the back of his neck. "Okay, maybe I could see you were right about the drinking. But insisting I include you in the investigation, demanding that we keep going when that thug threatened you, refusing to move— that's just you never giving in on anything.''

"I know I've been selfish.'' *Julie even told you. She said you were headed for a crisis, and here you are, right smack in the middle of one.*

"When I walked out of here tonight, there was a part of me that wanted to just keep going. I started telling myself that I'd be fine without you. That if I went back to my old life, I could do whatever I pleased.''

Pain flared in her chest.

"I considered getting a hotel room, but when it came right down to it, I couldn't do it. So maybe I do understand what you mean when you say you can't leave this house.'' He ran a hand over his face. "I'm not ready to call it quits tonight. I may not be ready for a long time. But if you keep ignoring my wishes, the day will come when I won't want to be here any more.''

Exactly what will happen. No matter how much we love each other, this marriage won't survive unless I mend my bossy ways.

"I feel just terrible about what I've done to you."

His bleary eyes settled on hers, his gaze gradually growing warmer.

"Come over here."

Standing in front of him, she wrapped her arms around his shoulders and drew his head up against her breasts. Zach let out a small sound, almost a sob, as she bent to kiss his hair. He held her for a while, then told her he was ready to collapse. They went to bed, Cassidy sprawling half on top of him. He fell asleep right away. She lay awake for a long time, her head on his chest, listening to him breathe.

"HOW YOU DOING?" Cassidy asked as she came into the bedroom carrying two mugs of coffee. Zach had pulled a pillow over his head when the alarm went off a few minutes earlier, but now he was wrapped in his blue robe, sitting in his chair, his hair sticking up in back.

"I just sloshed down a handful of aspirin, so I'll be okay."

"So, um, are we still on speaking terms?" Cassidy settled into her place on the bed.

"You've obviously made your decision. Since I hate to fight, staying mad doesn't buy me anything."

A feeling of tenderness washed over her. *Zach's a better loser than you've ever been.*

"You know," he continued, "one of the things I admire about you is your ability to take a stand. I wouldn't want you to be any different from the way you are." He smiled wryly. "But at the same time, I'd like you to be more docile and accommodating when it comes to me."

He loves you even though you are a little tyrant. But that doesn't mean you can get out of practicing your psych 101 lessons on the art of compromise.

Later, when he'd finished his shower and returned to the bedroom, Cassidy asked, "You still want to go to Cypress tonight and steal Garrett's glass?"

He pulled on a pair of black jeans. "Liquor holds no appeal at the moment. But by the time tonight rolls around, I'm sure I'll have recovered my taste for booze."

"I suppose prints don't stick very well on a cold glass." She laid a finger across her lips. "Let's see—what did Garrett have before? I think it was scotch."

Zach sat down to put on his black Reeboks. "The best choice would be a warm drink—brandy or red wine. A wineglass would be good. Garrett would probably touch the bowl, and then I could pick it up by the stem." Zach tied his shoes, then straightened and looked over at her. "Getting a clear print is harder than most people realize. They watch cop shows and think that anything a person touches is going to have prints on it. But when evidence techs dust a crime scene, they usually come up empty."

"So our efforts may be in vain?"

"We'll get prints. We just have to plan ahead and do it right."

GARRETT HILLARD, seated behind the counter at the host's station, rose as Cassidy and Zach approached.

"Susan isn't here."

Zach rested his hands on his belt. "You're the one we want to talk to tonight." It was after nine, and the place was half empty.

Hillard's expression tightened into resistant lines. "I've already told you everything I know."

"We're not here to ask questions," Cassidy said. "We've uncovered an unsettling piece of information. Something you need to know." Seeing that Hillard's body language hadn't softened, she added, "It's about Ashley."

Alarm flashed briefly on Hillard's face, then his countenance smoothed into its professional maitre de look. "I doubt that there's anything you could tell me about my daughter I don't already know."

"Just hear us out," Zach pressed. "Let's go get a drink and then Cass'll tell you what she's got."

Hillard kneaded the short beard that framed his jaw. "Well...all right. But I have to find someone to fill in for me first."

"We'll meet you at the bar." Zach laid his hand on Cassidy's shoulder, guiding her in that direction.

Cassidy and Zach seated themselves on barstools, leaving an empty place between them. When the muscular, spiky-haired bartender appeared to take their order, Zach requested a bottle of Shiraz and three glasses. By the time Hillard arrived, a half-full bubble glass awaited him in front of the empty stool.

"You ordered for me?"

"I wanted you to try this Shiraz," Zach replied. "It's from Australia. One of the best reds I've come across. We drink it all the time."

Since Hillard was facing Zach, Cassidy allowed herself to grimace at the patronizing attitude her husband had adopted. *But guys talk that way all the time, so Garrett won't think twice about it.*

"I've tasted every wine we serve here, and personally I favor the Sirrah." Hillard swiveled in Cassidy's direction. "Now what's this information you say you have about Ashley?"

"Did Max ever spend time alone with her?"

"I'm not sure." A muscle pulsed at Hillard's temple. He tapped out a cigarette and lit it. "I think there may've been a couple of times he offered to watch her while I ran errands." Hillard stared hard at Cassidy. "What are you trying to tell me?"

"Julie said her brother molested her when she was eight."

"You think Max might've done something like that to Ashley?" Hillard's face registering shock, he took a long drag on his cigarette.

Cassidy was relieved to see that he held his glass by the bowl. *If he only touched the stem, our effort here would be as big a waste as casting a Democratic vote in Florida.*

She replied to the restaurant manager, "All I'm saying is, it's a possibility. The only way to find out for sure is to have your daughter interviewed by a child sexual abuse expert." Cassidy fished a list of names out of her purse and handed it to him.

"I can just ask her. She'd tell me the truth—I know she would."

Placing a hand on his arm, Cassidy said, "It's really important that you not say a word about this to Ashley. If you raise the subject, she'll figure out that you have a high stake in hearing her tell you that Max never touched her. Kids who are honest about everything else will lie about sex abuse. The only way to get a reliable assessment is to take her to an expert."

"Max would never have abused my daughter." Hillard asserted. "He was a nice, normal guy—one of the best friends I've ever had. There's no way he could've been a pervert."

There Garrett goes, straight into denial. Even though we see nice-guy deviants on the news all the time, no one ever wants to believe that any of their own nice-guy friends could be one.

"I'm sorry if I've upset you."

"I'm not upset," he said emphatically.

"Well, I'm glad to hear it," Zach interjected. "Cass was afraid you might take this pretty hard."

"I'm fine." Hillard turned toward Zach, his glass in hand.

Now I'm the enemy and he's happy to have me out of his line of sight. Which is a good thing, since we need him to be facing Zach.

"Well, changing the topic," Zach said, "I'd be curious to know how long it takes a new restaurant like this to start showing a profit."

From where she sat Cassidy couldn't see Zach's glass, but she knew he would be keeping his wine at the same level as Hillard's. While Zach engaged the other man in a discussion of the restaurant business, Cassidy kept her gaze fastened on her husband's face.

Less than a minute later, Zach made eye contact, telegraphing her that Hillard had set his glass on the bar and removed his hand from it. She dribbled out a small quantity of wine next to his elbow.

"Oh shit! Garrett, I spilled wine on your sleeve."

He swiveled toward Cassidy and began patting at the red stain with his cocktail napkin, giving Zach the opportunity he needed to exchange glasses. Cassidy soaked up the puddle with her napkin and babbled apologies. Hillard talked over her, insisting there was no harm done. The bartender handed Hillard a towel.

"God, I hope the stain comes out," Cassidy said. "You be sure and send me the cleaning bill, okay?"

"We have something in the kitchen that'll take care of the problem in no time. You just enjoy that Shiraz. I'll be right back." Folding his jacket over his arm, Hillard set off toward the swinging doors at the rear of the dining room.

Zach emptied Hillard's glass and slid it down the bar to Cassidy, who now had her purse open on her lap. She dropped the fragile piece of stemware into a plastic bag, sealed the bag, and zipped it inside her purse.

Zach moved over to Hillard's stool. "We still have some wine left in the bottle, but you know what? I don't even feel like drinking it."

"Then let's get out of here."

In the car Zach called and set up a meeting with Emily later that night to give her the glass. Turning to Cassidy, he said, "I can either take you with me or drop you off at the house."

"Just drop me off."

He gave her a probing look. "You mean, you aren't going to play Siamese twin?"

She yawned. "I can't even remember why I used to think I needed to do that."

TWENTY-NINE

MOTHER AND DAUGHTER

"I'LL BE PICKING Lillybeth up from the hospital some time tomorrow," Gran's voice said from the answering machine. "And I'm sure she'll be eager to see that little dickens Roscoe. If you don't have time to bring him over, I can always come get him. I bet you'll be glad to have him outta your hair."

So Roscoe's going home. Cassidy looked down at the kitten, who'd followed her into the bedroom and was now stalking a piece of twine he'd found in the computer room several days earlier. Starshine, sitting erect on the waterbed, also watched him.

"What do you think?" Cassidy asked the calico. "Should we tell Lillybeth that possession is nine-tenths of the law and refuse to give him back?"

Mwat.

"So you don't approve of stealing kittens from little old ladies? Well, I guess I'm not ready to sink that low either."

Cassidy picked up Roscoe, who climbed onto her shoulder and nibbled her chin. "How will we ever get along without you?"

IRENE O'CONNELL, a tense angry expression on her face, ushered Cassidy and Zach into her living room. A dull light filtered through the lace-covered windows, and stiff uncomfortable-looking furniture stood in a boxy seating arrangement.

The air was stuffy and overheated, making Cassidy regret that she'd worn pantyhose in an effort to live up to Irene's standard of formality. *Pantyhose are irrelevant. When my last pair goes, I'll delete them from my wardrobe—send them to the recycle bin along with girdles and heels.*

Julie, her body stiff, her face defiant, occupied a wingback chair across from the sofa.

Think I know what this is about.

Cassidy said "Hey" to the astrologer, then she and Zach sat on the sofa, while Irene lowered herself onto a matching wingback chair.

"Claire called me," Irene announced to Cassidy. "She wanted to know if what you told her was true. If Max really did molest his sister."

"Don't blame Julie," Cassidy responded. "I pressured her into telling me."

"I'll blame whomever I choose. And in fact, I think all three of you have gone way too far in your attempts to destroy Max's reputation." She looked Zach in the eye. "You told me your story would consist of quotes from the people who loved him, but what you've really been doing is digging up every little lie and rumor you could find. From what Claire tells me, I have to assume your real purpose is to exploit his murder in print."

Cassidy suddenly understood how betrayed Irene must feel. *The woman's got to be desperate to protect her son's good name.*

"I'm sorry you see it that way," Zach said, his detached expression firmly in place.

"And you," Irene said to Cassidy, "you manipulated my daughter into telling you her story about a molestation that never took place."

"Yes it did!" Julie stood as if to leave.

"Sit down," Irene instructed in a steely voice.

Julie wavered for a moment, then sank back into her chair.

Irene jabbed her finger at her daughter. "Now you tell these people what really happened."

Tugging at a strand of strawberry-blond hair, Julie glared back. "What Max did was nasty and I don't want to talk about it."

"If you won't tell them, I'll do it myself."

"No! You won't tell it right. You always take Max's side. He'd tease me and tickle me and sometimes he'd even hit me and you never stopped him."

Irene squared her narrow shoulders. "I didn't believe in interfering. I thought children should work things out for themselves."

"Max was your favorite," Julie shot back at her mother. "That's why you never punished him. You protected him and gave him money behind Dad's back. You're the reason he was so materialistic, the reason he got himself in so much debt. Poor Max—he never was able to evolve beyond the most primitive level."

"You didn't really love your bother, did you?" Irene jabbed her finger again. "You were always jealous of him."

"I adored him." Julie's red-brown eyes grew shiny with emotion. "And I miss him so much."

Leaning forward, Irene said in a softer tone, "Of course you miss him. We both do." She pulled herself up straight. "But you said something to Cassidy that wasn't true. Now you have to tell her what really happened so it won't come out in the paper that Max was some kind of monster."

"But Mama, he did do what I said."

"The psychologist told us it was normal. That lots of boys do what he did."

"I hated that psychologist. He asked all kinds of embarrassing questions. And he was on Max's side, just like you are."

"Tell these people what Max did."

Julie's skin turned a delicate shade of pink. Pressing both palms against her cheeks, she let out a heavy sigh, then dropped her hands into her lap and began speaking. "He took off all his clothes and showed me his penis. It was standing almost straight up. He danced around the room and kept yelling at me that I had to look at it. He even wanted me to touch it, but I wouldn't."

Irene clasped her blue-veined hands tightly together. "Did he force you to do anything?"

"No, he didn't force me." Julie took in a breath through her mouth. "The next day I told a friend and she said what Max did was bad. I was afraid if I told Mama she'd say it was my fault. Then he did it again and I was so scared I had to tell."

There may be times when Julie lies but this isn't one of them. This is Julie hanging on to her belief that her brother molested her—regardless of what anybody else has to say. A belief that may serve as a metaphor for what her life in this family was like—even though a ten-year-old showing off his erection doesn't qualify as sex abuse.

Irene said, "Your father and I called a child psychologist and he saw both of you kids several times. Then he gave us his evaluation. He said—"

Julie put her hands over her ears. "I don't want to hear it!"

"He said that Max's behavior fell within the normal range but that you felt a need to draw attention to yourself because you were adopted."

A stricken look came over Julie's face. She stood abruptly, walked out of the room, and started up the staircase in the hall. Irene sat frozen, her gaze fixed on some object at the far end of the room.

Cassidy said to Zach, "I have to go after her."

Inside Julie's room, Cassidy found the young woman standing at a window across from the door. "It must've been pretty hard to grow up with a mother who favored your brother and didn't take you seriously."

Turning to face Cassidy, Julie curled a strand of hair around her finger.

"Mama always said she couldn't tell whether I was lying or not."

Talk about your self-fulfilling prophecy.

"When you were a kid, your mother hurt your feelings by saying things like that. Now you're the only one she has left." Cassidy moved a couple of steps closer. "You deserve a lot of credit for keeping your mother's flowers alive during this time of mourning. Right now, she's so dead inside she can't give anything to anyone. I just hope the day will come when she'll be able to appreciate all that you're doing for her."

Hugging the astrologer, Cassidy concluded, "I have to go now. But don't give up. Things always get better eventually."

As Cassidy and Zach were heading home, she called Hillard and Claire and told them she'd been wrong about Max molesting his sister.

WHEN THE PHONE RANG at four that afternoon, Cassidy lifted the handset off the kitchen wall.

Gran said, "Lillybeth's home now and she'd like to have Roscoe back anytime you're willing to let him go."

Heaviness settled on Cassidy's shoulders. "Do I have a choice?"

"I thought Starshine was ready to give him the boot ever since the day he first arrived. And that you weren't exactly thrilled with him, either."

"We've changed our minds."

"Does that mean I have to run out and find another kitten that looks exactly like Roscoe to keep Lillybeth happy?"

Cassidy laughed. "Look, I've got clients scheduled for five, six, and seven. Do you suppose Lillybeth could bear to wait until sometime after eight?"

"I could come get him."

"Oh, let me do it." Cassidy leaned against the doorjamb.

"I want to tell Lillybeth about all the cute little things Roscoe's been doing at our house."

"Now remember, when she hands you this big pile of embroidery, don't overdo the 'thank you's' or she'll turn around and give you more."

As Cassidy hung up, she wondered how Zach would react to her plan to drive to Lillybeth's by herself. Even though the parking lot guy appeared to be harmless, Zach, who had a meeting to cover, was still not crazy about her driving alone at night. She wasn't worried about any actual danger, but she was concerned about irritating her husband again. *Of course I'm bound to piss him off sometimes, but I'd rather not do it right on the heels of our last fight.*

Gritting her teeth, she called Zach and told him about her plan to return Roscoe.

"Okay," he said in a resigned voice.

THIRTY

TAKING ROSCOE HOME

AFTER HER LAST client left, Cassidy went searching for Roscoe. She found him asleep on the sofa next to Starshine, the two cats curled like commas, their heads nearly touching. Cassidy wondered if Roscoe would miss them. She'd heard that cats were more attached to places than people, but she didn't believe it.

Carrying the kitten, with Starshine trotting at her heels, Cassidy went up to the den, where she discovered that Roscoe had invented some new ways to entertain himself. He'd shredded half a roll of paper towels, knocked an ivy off an end table, and disgorged chewed leaves in three different places on the rug.

"A little something to remember you by," Cassidy said, dropping the kitten to the floor. He leapt joyfully at the paper-towel roll again, but she snatched it away.

After putting the den to rights, Cassidy hauled Roscoe's pet carrier out of the closet. Starshine, who'd made several trips to the vet inside a carrier, flew downstairs, with Roscoe streaking after her.

Oh shit. Hope the basement door's closed.

It wasn't. Cassidy went down the cracked concrete steps into a subterranean level overflowing with junk. She called "kitty, kitty," which usually brought Roscoe running, but this time it didn't. She got out a flashlight and probed beneath an upside down wheelbarrow, behind a broken lawn mower, in back of a row of metal shelves. After considerable searching, she shone her light into a small box pushed under the stairs. Two feline faces stared back at her, Starshine on the bottom, the kitten curled up on top of her.

Later, when Cassidy set the pet carrier down next to the back door, Starshine touched the kitten's nose through the wire mesh, then wandered away. Cassidy remembered how the calico had reacted when her offspring left home. She'd done everything in her power to prevent the new owners from taking the kittens away, and then, as soon as they were out of sight, she appeared to forget that they'd ever existed. *Not a sentimental bone in your little sweetheart's body. But plenty of those kind of bones in yours.*

CASSIDY PARKED on a residential street in front of Lillybeth's building, a yellow brick structure with a manicured lawn, a waist-high hedge around the front of the building, and a well-lit entrance. Before getting out of the car, she looked around. A woman was power walking past the Toyota; three kids chased each other in the middle of the street. As Cassidy approached the ground-level door, earsplitting rap assaulted her from a window to her right. *Hopefully Lillybeth's too deaf to notice.*

Half an hour later Cassidy left the building, a shopping bag full of pillowcases and dishtowels over her arm. She stepped out onto the concrete apron, then glanced up at the window that was still spewing noise.

A strong hand grabbed the back of her neck. Another hand circled her right arm. The attacker pushed her forward, tripping her over his leg, then jerked her sideways. Suddenly she was flat on her back in the dirt, a prickly hedge on one side, a brick wall on the other. The thug's body pressing down on hers. His mahogany face glaring at her. A blade against her throat.

Omigod! Omigod!

"Whassa matter, bitch? You din't do what I tole you." His raspy voice merged with the music. She could feel tiny drops of spittle land on her face, could smell his rancid breath.

Cassidy's arms and legs were immobilized. Her wrist ached where he'd twisted it. She couldn't gather enough breath to scream.

"You din't make your old man stop with his questions so now I gotta cut you."

Her heart pounded. Blood pulsed in her ears. She was aware of the knife slicing across her throat but felt no pain.

"Hey, what's going on?" A voice from somewhere near the door.

Her assailant jumped up and started running away from her along the path between the hedge and the building.

A thirtyish man peered down at her, his skin pale, a stunned look on his face. "Are you all right?"

"I think so."

He reached over and helped her to her feet. She put her left hand on the wall to hold herself up, while her right hand covered the warm sticky wound on her throat. Stumbling out from behind the hedge, she propped herself against the door. Her hair was clogged with dirt; twigs and leaves clung to her clothing.

"We have to call 911," her rescuer said.

She thought he was probably right but couldn't stand the idea of being hauled down to the station. She begged him not to make the call. After collecting her purse and shopping bag, he assisted her to her Toyota and she drove home.

As CASSIDY REACHED the top of the stairs, Zach, sitting in front of his computer, swiveled to greet her. "My God!" He was instantly out of his chair and standing in front of her.

"I was so wrong when I said the parking-lot guy wouldn't do anything." Hugging herself, she went on to tell Zach what had happened.

"Shit! When you called this afternoon, I should've forbidden you to leave the house. Since you're trying to keep me happy right now, you might even have done what I said."

"Oh, I don't think I'd've gone that far."

He inspected the cut on her throat. "This looks pretty superficial but I still have to take you to the ER."

She moaned. "Half the night sitting in West Sub's waiting room."

"That's what you get for not letting me drop the investigation."

"Same thing the stalker said."

Several hours later they were seated in bed, Cassidy leaning against Zach's bent knees, his hand massaging the back of her neck. Having taken the pills the nurse handed her, Cassidy was no longer experiencing any pain. Although Zach had handled everything in his usual stoic manner, she could tell he'd been hit pretty hard by this new attack against her. *It's happened so often, you'd think he'd be used to it by now.* She hoped the drink on his nightstand would do for him what the pills had done for her.

Zach stretched the neckline of her lavender tee and kissed her on the shoulder. "You know you have to report this to the police tomorrow, don't you?"

"I do?" She squinted in thought. "You mean so the cops'll have something serious to charge this guy with if they ever catch him?"

"The Oak Park police aren't likely to find him because he keeps disappearing into Chicago. But I intend to track the asshole down and send them to him."

THE NEXT DAY, Saturday, Cassidy and Zach talked to the police, then came home and tackled their yard, neglected far too long during prime weed-growing season. After working for several hours, they went to sit on the concrete stoop, Zach taking the step above Cassidy's.

"As long as we're planning to stay," he said, "I think I'll put in a garden next spring. Grow some vegetables."

She smiled to herself. *When you first met him, you told*

*yourself to stay away from bed-hopping reporters, look for
a backyard tomato-grower instead.*

Leaning against his knees, she asked, "Do you really
hate living here?"

"It's not so much that I hate the house as that I hate not
having a choice. I wanted us to start over in a place that
was really ours. A place with a modern kitchen and no
cracks in the ceiling."

That night they ordered carryout from Gepetto's, a local
restaurant that served portions so large Cassidy could make
three meals out of a single spaghetti dinner. She concentrated on twisting noodles around her fork and lifting them
to her mouth. Each time she made the attempt, most of the
noodles slipped away. Watching Zach, whose spaghetti
seemed to magically adhere to his utensil, she wondered
what his secret was.

"So what's the plan for tonight?"

"I'll leave the house around nine, nine-thirty. Since our
black street thug undoubtedly works for one of our white
suspects, I'll start with the Chicago Cypress, move on to
that bar where the girl disappeared, then radiate out from
there."

"Don't forget—the bartender at the Naperville restaurant
thought he'd seen our guy." *And you had a gut feeling
Susan had seen him as well.*

"Yeah, but I don't know of any place in Naperville
where this guy'd be likely to hang. He sounds more like a
Chicago type to me."

"I suppose you'll be out pretty late."

"You definitely don't want to wait up."

She ran her fingers along the bandage on her throat.
"You won't be having a drink at each of these bars, will
you?"

"You still upset because I got behind the wheel when I
was loaded?"

She nodded in confirmation.

Gazing at the window, he said, "I was thinking about

that. The fact that I was pissed isn't much of an excuse for doing something flagrantly stupid. It even occurred to me to wonder if I was getting back at you. You know—you refused to take precautions so I did something to put myself at risk.'' He shook his head. ''God, I'm starting to talk psychobabble just like you.''

''I do not. I make every effort to avoid jargon.''

He narrowed his eyes at her. ''If you bring this up the next time I'm ready to walk out, I'll deny I ever said it.''

''IS ZACH THERE?'' Emily's voice asked.

It was almost noon on Sunday, and Cassidy had picked up in the kitchen because Zach, after staying out most of the night, was still in bed. ''He isn't available. Did you find a match on the fingerprints?''

A short pause. ''I was planning to leave a message and have Zach call back if he wasn't there. But I have to get over pretending you don't exist.''

''I know you're not interested in Zach anymore, but that doesn't mean you have to be gracious to your replacement.''

Emily laughed. ''Is there any time when you don't sound like a therapist?''

Leaning against the doorjamb, Cassidy gazed out the kitchen window at a pot of red geraniums hanging from her neighbor's porch. ''You seeing anybody now?''

''Not at the moment.''

Maybe you could fix her up with Manny. Cassidy pictured the Oak Park cop with his carved features, warm brown eyes, and expensive Italian suits. Manny Perez had once flirted with Cassidy. At times when Zach was behaving badly, she sometimes regretted that she hadn't accepted Manny's invitation to lunch.

''I know an Oak Park detective who seems like a pretty decent guy. If he's still available, I could introduce you.'' *That is, if Manny's over being pissed at me for interfering in his case.*

"A fix-up? How embarrassing. I never imagined I'd be going through the ordeal of a fix-up at this age in life."

"So, is that a yes?"

"I'll think about it. Anyway, the reason I called is to tell you that nothing popped out on the prints."

"Does that mean Hillard isn't wanted anywhere?" Cassidy creased her brow, trying to make sense of it. "No, all it means is that he's never been printed in connection with a crime."

"Right. He could've abducted his daughter and been long gone before the warrant was issued."

Damn you, Garrett, why couldn't you have made just one little slip? A small previous arrest—that's all I'm asking for. Why isn't there anything about you that's clear-cut and unambiguous?

THIRTY-ONE

A KINDLY, SOFT-SPOKEN PIT BULL

CASSIDY WAS MAKING lunch on Monday when Zach, who'd left for work a few hours earlier, came in the back door.

"What are you doing home?" Leaning against the sink, she noticed signs of tension on her husband's normally calm face.

"There's been a new development. I didn't want to tell you over the phone."

"How bad is it?"

"Let's sit down."

He took the chair at the end of the dining room table and she sat at a right angle from him, her arms folded beneath her breasts.

"Garrett was killed last night in a hit-and-run."

"Garrett?" Pressing an outspread hand against her chest, Cassidy gaped at her husband. A heavy lump formed in her stomach as she pictured the dark-haired man kneeling beside his daughter. "Oh Lord, how could this happen? And what about Ashley? Did DCFS take her?"

"I talked to one of the detectives. They found Ashley at Hillard's apartment with her babysitter. When the cops couldn't locate any family, they called DCFS and a social worker came and got her."

"Oh that poor child. Nobody knows where her mother is and now she's lost her father." Cassidy's throat constricted. "How did you find out? I wouldn't imagine a hit-and-run would be much of a story in Chicago."

"We have this cop-house reporter. He's a lousy writer but he's made friends with half the cops on the force and they fill him in on just about everything that goes down on the police beat. So he takes all these story ideas around to other reporters in search of somebody who'll write them up and share their byline. This morning he dangled five different incidents in front of me, one of which was the hit-and-run."

Cassidy laid her hand on Zach's arm. "It was nice of you to come all the way home to tell me."

"Actually, the main reason I'm here is that I thought we could put our heads together and try to come up with some theory as to who might've wanted Garrett dead."

"You don't think it was an accident?"

"Doesn't it seem a little strange that a groom was killed at his wedding and then a few weeks later his best man dies in a hit-and-run that has all the earmarks of a murder?"

"What earmarks?"

"Sunday was Garrett's day off. He called the babysitter in the middle of the afternoon and asked if she'd be willing to put in a couple of extra hours that night. Garrett went out around nine and appeared to be walking back toward his apartment at the time he was hit. It's my guess that the killer invited Garrett out for a drink, then ran him down afterward."

"So you think the same person killed both Max and Garrett. Maybe because Garrett knew something he shouldn't."

"The first person who leaps to mind is Susan." Zach took out his pad, turned to a fresh page, and wrote down her name. "Garrett worked for her, and she had an excellent motive to want Max dead—he jilted her."

"Even worse, he made a fool of her. Susan's not the kind of woman to let any guy get away with that."

"And having Max killed at the wedding would've served

a double purpose—revenge on Max and Claire at the same time."

"This is too good. It makes too much sense." Cassidy rubbed the back of her thumb across her chin. "The bartender recognizing the sketch. Garrett being her manager. It all fits together too well. Nothing in real life is ever this neat."

"Well, then, let's take a look at Nicky Andrews." Zach wrote his name beneath Susan's. "Both Max and Garrett worked for him, although it's been a while since they quit. Max got a large cash advance out of Nicky, then left him in the lurch. According to Luke, they even came to blows over it. Nicky could've pretended to forgive and forget but really been biding his time for a chance to get even."

"But then we're back to the why-do-it-at-a-wedding question."

"You objected to Susan on the grounds that she was a perfect fit. Now you're objecting to Nicky because he isn't."

"Okay, Susan and Nicky are both contenders." Cassidy tilted her head.

"What about Luke? He knew both men and apparently he's the only guy who managed to resist Max's charm and stay mad at him. He's also the only person who wouldn't tell us anything about himself."

"You made a connection with Luke the last time we were at Kincaid's. You think you could use Garrett's death as leverage to get Luke to open up?"

"Leverage?" She lowered her brow at Zach. "Do you realize how callous that sounds?"

"Is it just now coming to you that I have to be pretty thick-skinned to do my job?"

"Don't you feel anything about Garrett? Or Ashley?"

He slanted his face away from her. "I have to jump on Garrett's death and use it to further the investigation. I can't afford to have feelings."

You know exactly what he means. When clients tell you

horror stories, you have to turn off your feelings just like he does, or you'd drown along with them.

"I'm sorry if I sounded like I was judging you."

"Hey—no big deal. I'm used to it."

She clenched her teeth to keep defensive words from coming out. *But you know you do get judgmental.* After taking a couple of breaths, she said, "Okay, back to Luke. I'd like to take a shot at getting him to talk. Maybe we can chase him down when we're finished here."

"So—let's see—who else?" Zach stared into space. "If Garrett really was Max's roommate, Irene would've known him from way back. I think we ought to lean on her, see what else we can get her to tell us."

"Both Julie and Claire were close to Max and knew Garrett by association, but neither of them had any motive to kill Max."

"Actually, if Claire found out about Susan, she might've had a motive, but she wouldn't have had him killed at the wedding and she certainly wouldn't have called us in to investigate."

"That leaves Hank and Erin," Cassidy said. "And as far as we know, Hank never crossed paths with Garrett."

"Erin." Zach's eyes took on a speculative look. "Erin wanted to stop Claire from marrying Max, which gave her a reason to kill him. She also was jealous of Claire and might've wanted to punish her sister by having Max shot at the wedding. And Erin had some contact with Garrett during her spy missions at Cypress."

"Yeah, but that doesn't give her a motive to kill him."

"She's such a nutcase, maybe she had some delusional belief he was on to her. Hell—we don't know everything. Maybe he *was* on to her." Zach wrote Erin's name on his list. "When's your next session?"

"I'm done for the day."

"Good. We won't have any problem fitting in Luke and Irene."

IRENE WASN'T HOME but Nicky Andrews agreed to call Luke and ask him to call Cassidy. Luke did and she was able to persuade him to meet her in an hour. Zach dropped her off at a café in Evanston with tables on the sidewalk. "I'll wait over there in that tow zone," he said, tilting his chin at a stretch of empty curb on the opposite side of the street.

The air was hot and sticky, the temperature in the nineties. Cassidy purchased a diet Coke, then seated herself in a patch of shade at an outdoor table. The humidity sapped her energy and dampened her armpits, despite the heavy layer of antiperspirant she'd applied that morning. Her wound itched. She reached behind the scarf around her neck and tried to scratch it.

She saw Luke, slender, blond-headed, his stride as graceful as a cat's, coming toward her. He gave her a wave, then veered off into the café, reappearing with a can of soda in his hand. Flopping down across from her, he pulled the tab and said, "I shouldn't have let you talk me into this. What happened between Max and me is ancient history. It couldn't have had anything to do with his murder."

"I'm sure you're right," Cassidy concurred. "I'm sure there's no connection between your fight with Max and his shooting. But there's been another death. Garrett Hillard was killed in a hit-and-run that looks more like a murder than an accident."

"Garrett's dead?" Luke stared at her in surprise. "He was a really good guy. And he had that little girl. Oh God—that's awful!"

"Max's death and Garrett's—there's got to be a connection."

"I don't understand why you're so involved in this. Shouldn't you just let the cops do their job?"

"The state police are investigating Max's shooting. The Chicago police are looking into the hit-and-run. The Oak Park police are trying to find the guy who attacked me." Cassidy pulled her scarf away from her neck so he could see the bandage. *This may or may not be true but it sounds good.*

"You were attacked?"

"Remember the sketch Zach was showing at the restaurant? The guy in the sketch cut my throat as a warning to stop asking questions."

"Jesus!" Luke thrust his face forward. "Then you *should* stop. Why are you putting yourself in danger like this?"

"Because I'm not about to let some street thug push me around." She paused. "Please tell me your story, Luke. Even if it has nothing to do with the murders, it'll help us identify the underlying pattern in Max's behavior. It's always possible that whatever Max did to you is the same thing he did to the murderer."

"No." Luke shook his head emphatically. "It couldn't have been the same." He let out a long breath. "This is very difficult. I've never told anyone before."

"When you have a secret and never talk about it, it turns into this big monster in the closet. Telling someone you trust can cut the monster down to size."

So why would he trust you, considering you're working with Zach on a news story?

Because you have this way about you that makes everybody trust you whether you deserve it or not.

Luke said, "I suppose you've already guessed that I'm gay."

"I kind of had a hunch."

"I'm not out to my family or anything. I'm a little afraid of what my dad might do if he found out. Actually, I had a hard time admitting it to myself. Before Max started hanging out with me, I was still thinking I just needed to find the right girl." He rolled the soda can across his brow. "Max was the most popular guy on the staff—everybody loved him. Me, I was always off in a corner by myself. Then one day he invited me to lunch. Well, you could've knocked me over with a feather. I didn't think he even knew I existed.''

''You must've felt honored.''

''To put it mildly. So anyway, we met for lunch and Max told me he admired my taste in clothes. He said he loved to shop but had trouble finding anyone to go with him. I suppose he must've guessed I was gay and that's why he thought I'd be interested in doing something like that.''

''And that's what you did? You went shopping?''

''We must've put in a hundred hours at Water Tower Place and Bloomies and all the great stores on Michigan Avenue. Max bought a lot of stuff, but he was always complaining that he couldn't afford the kind of clothes he really wanted.''

''What about you? Could you afford all that shopping?''

''I have pretty low credit limits so I couldn't buy much.'' Luke ran his thumbnail along the seam in the can. ''Well, as you can imagine, I developed this huge crush on Max, and I was just waiting for him to make some kind of move. Then I got into this crazy thinking. I started telling myself that I had to pass some kind of test—I had to prove I could give Max what he wanted—before he'd move the relationship to the next level. So I did this thing.'' Propping his elbow on the table, Luke rested his forehead on his hand. ''I stole my father's credit card and spent ten thousand dollars buying clothes for Max.''

''It's not unusual for people to go to extreme lengths to win the love of someone they're hooked on.''

''I'd never done anything like that before. When I finally came to my senses, I felt just terrible.''

''Don't you think you should be allowed at least one huge screw-up in your life? I don't know anybody who's reached the age of thirty without doing a few massively dumb things.'' *I married Kevin—which turned out to be far worse than a mere felony.*

Luke frowned. ''I can't just let myself off. My family's

always believed in me.'' He ran a delicate long-fingered hand through his hair. ''I can't even explain to them why I did it.''

She asked softly, ''So what happened next?''

''After I started buying things for Max, I was sure he'd get physical. I fantasized about it all the time. But he never did.'' Luke paused. ''So one night I got a little polluted and tried to initiate something myself.'' He glanced at her, then looked away. ''And Max told me he was straight. He was nice about it, but I've never been so humiliated in my life. I decided he'd been scamming me from the beginning—leading me on so I'd buy him things. From then on I barely spoke to him.''

''That must've been pretty awful.'' *Same stunt Max pulled with a lot of people. Turned on the charm so they'd give him money or clothes or a partnership.*

''But the thing that surprised me the most was, he kept trying to make friends again afterward. For weeks he'd come around and try to chat me up, even though I didn't encourage him at all.''

''He really took advantage of you, didn't he?''

''That was how I saw it for a long time. I convinced myself that Max was this incredible con-meister and I'd just been one of the suckers who'd fallen for his tricks. But then, after he was killed, I started to rethink it.'' Luke gazed at some point off in the distance. ''There were two things that floated Max's boat—shopping and making people happy. I think he noticed how shy I was and felt an urge to befriend me. He also recognized that I was gay and saw me as a potential shopping companion. Then later, when I offered to buy things for him, he probably realized I was getting in over my head but he couldn't resist taking all that stuff. I know he had this huge weakness for shopping, but apart from that, I think he was basically good hearted.''

The age-old tradition of idealizing the dead. Couldn't stand him when he was alive, but now that he's not around to bother me anymore, he was a great guy.

"I don't know," Cassidy responded. "From what you said, I certainly get the impression he was stringing you along."

Luke shook his head. "Doesn't make sense. He knew I was broke from the beginning. If he wanted to lead someone on, he could've flirted with one of those rich gay guys that come around the restaurant all the time."

Is it possible you've been wrong about Max? Given all the people he hurt and ripped off, it doesn't seem likely.

"Well," Cassidy said, "I appreciate your telling me what happened. Now that your secret's finally out, how bad was it?"

He smiled shyly. "No worse than being mauled by a pit bull."

She blinked in surprise. "A pit bull? Is that how I strike you?"

"A kindly, soft-spoken pit bull."

And you thought you put everyone at ease.

THIRTY-TWO

THE IDENTITY BUSINESS

"WE'RE DRIVING TO Hinsdale," Zach said as Cassidy climbed into the Subaru. "You need to pee or anything before we start?"

She consulted her bladder and decided she could easily handle the hour-plus trip. "You got hold of Irene?"

"About ten minutes ago. I didn't give her any choice— just told her we were coming."

They were driving west on the Eisenhower when Cassidy's cell went off.

"Well," Claire said, "I did it. I told Hank I wasn't going to see him anymore. At first he begged me to change my mind, then he cursed me out. It wasn't fun listening to him call me names, but it did serve as a reminder of what he's really like."

"So, how you doing?"

"You know, it's funny. Standing up to Hank made me feel stronger. For the first time since Max's death, I really believe I'm going to make it on my own—without having to find some man to take care of me."

Cassidy smiled. "Of course you are."

"I'm so thankful for all you've done. I want to take you and Zach out to the best restaurant in Chicago—at least the best restaurant I can get last minute reservations for."

"We've talked about this before. I can't socialize with clients. Not even former clients."

"Well, then, we won't call it socializing—we'll call it an informational meeting. You can update me on the investigation. How about tonight? Now don't try to wiggle out of it—I won't take no for an answer."

That same sharp tone she used on Julie. Trying to assert herself after showing all that weakness with Hank.

Cassidy said in a mild voice, "I understand that you really want us to meet you for dinner, but it's not okay to be so demanding."

"Was I demanding? I'm sorry, I didn't even realize I was doing it. It's just that there are times when something comes over me and I feel like I have to have what I want."

Well, and Claire's not the only one who has that tendency, is she?

"Okay, I could do a dinner meeting but let me check with Zach."

Holding her hand over the mouthpiece, she asked if he wanted to have dinner with Claire.

"I need to catch up at the office. I could drop you off at Claire's condo, pick you up when you're done."

"Since Claire's feeling so feisty, this might be a good time to add a little tarnish to that golden-glow image she has of Max." *But what are you going to tell her? You're not even sure yourself what you think of him.*

Cassidy told her client that she would meet her at her condo at seven.

HATE HAVING TO DO this—just hate it. Death notifications are not a part of social worker training and you shouldn't have to do them.

Yeah, but the only other option is to dump this into Zach's lap, and he shouldn't have to do it either.

A heaviness settling over her, Cassidy moved a hair's breadth closer to her husband, the two of them standing side-by-side in front of Irene.

"I have some bad news," Cassidy told the other woman. "You might want to sit down."

"I'm not so old that I need anyone telling me when to sit down," Irene retorted.

"Garrett Hillard was the victim of a hit-and-run accident last night."

Irene rubbed her upper arms as if to warm them. "What happened? Is he in the hospital?"

"I'm afraid he didn't survive."

Curling her hands into fists, Irene pressed them against chest. "Oh no! Oh no! This can't be true!"

Zach went off toward the kitchen.

"Would you like me to call anybody?" Cassidy asked. "Is there anything I can get you?"

A dazed look coming over her face, Irene inched backward until her calves hit a chair and she collapsed into it. Zach returned and squatted next to her, offering a glass of water. She clutched the glass and gulped down half its contents.

"Garrett was like a son to me," Irene said, her voice trembling. "He's been calling almost every day since I lost Max. He even came out to the house and took down the storm windows for me. I don't know how I'll get along without him."

Cassidy and Zach sat on the sofa facing Irene. "When did you first meet Garrett?" Cassidy wanted to know.

"When Max went off to…." Her eyes becoming more focused, Irene put a hand over her mouth. She paused a moment, then asked, "But what about Ashley? Who's going to take care of her?"

"DCFS has temporary custody. But you started to tell us about Garrett—how he and Max were roommates at Notre Dame. It's important that we find out what Garrett's real name was."

Crossing her arms beneath her breasts, Irene refused to speak.

"Do you know what'll happen to Ashley if DCFS is unable to locate her mother or some other family member? She'll get dumped into the foster care system. *In Chicago*," Cassidy added, hoping to take advantage of the fears many suburbanites had about the city. "Do you realize how awful that would be?"

Irene's narrow face paled. "I watch television. Of course I do." She gazed down at the oriental carpet, then raised her eyes to Cassidy's. "I suppose I could take her. I'm sure that's what Max would want me to do."

"I'm afraid you wouldn't be eligible." *Actually, she might, but she doesn't need to know that.* "The best choice would be for Ashley to go back to her mother."

Deep lines formed in Irene's brow. "Oh, I don't think that would be a good idea. Her mother's an alcoholic, you know. That's the reason Ashley's wearing that brace. She was in the car when her mother crashed into a building. Her mother was drunk, of course, but she refused to take the sobriety test and her attorney got her off."

"What a tough thing for a kid to go through."

"It certainly was. Ashley's mother went on binges, you know. Garrett said she just got crazy when she drank. I don't understand how a woman could get drunk in front of her daughter. When my children were young, being a good mother was my top priority. Max always said I was the best, but Julie never gave me credit for anything."

"Well, I can certainly see why Garrett thought he had to take Ashley away from her mother. But we can't let Ashley go into foster care, now can we? After losing her father, to have to live with strangers would be so hard on her. Right now she needs to be in a familiar place with a familiar person, even if her mother is impaired."

Cassidy could see the struggle on Irene's face. The older woman said, "I promised Max I wouldn't tell."

Zach took out his pad. "But everything's different now. Besides, you've already said enough to implicate yourself. At this point, you have only two choices. You can tell us everything and I can pass it on to the detective on the case without revealing my source, or I can tell the detective you know who Garrett is and he'll haul you in for questioning."

"It's nobody's business," Irene muttered.

Cassidy and Zach waited.

"Oh, all right," Irene said angrily. "You can find Ashley's mother in Cleveland—her name's Meg Blanding. And Garrett is Tom Blanding."

Zach said, "And Tom Blanding was somehow able to take on Garrett Hillard's identity."

"After the car crash, Tom was just desperate to get Ashley away from her mother. He used to cry on Max's shoulder about it all the time, and then eventually Max came up with a solution. I love Tom, I really do, but I have to say he was always a little unsure of himself. Always needed someone else to show him the way. Not a leader like Max." Irene paused to sip some water. "Max had these friends who arrange new identities. At first Tom was afraid to do it, but Max finally convinced him."

"So Max hooked Tom up with some mob guys."

Irene sent Zach a withering look. "My son did not consort with criminals. These men were running a business."

Could Irene really be this naïve? No, of course not. She's just maintaining her illusions—something we all try to do.

"These people gave Tom the name and social security number of a man who'd recently died out in San Francisco," Irene added. "There wasn't any harm to it."

Zach said, "This guy who died. There should've been a death certificate on file. How did Max's friends get rid of it?"

Irene turned her face away. "They paid off a clerk. These men have similar arrangements in a lot of cities. But I don't know who the men were. Max never mentioned any names."

That's all there is to it? Here you and Zach've been driving yourselves crazy over an identity change with no death certificate, and it all comes down to a civil servant on the take.

"What else do you know about this identity-changing business?" Zach inquired.

"Nothing. I can't give you a single other piece of information." Irene looked down at her hands. "I suppose it was bound to come out eventually."

"Yeah," Zach said, "and this way you don't have to g[o]
through a police interrogation."

Cassidy fished her phone out of her purse. "Could you giv[e]
me Julie's cell number?"

After Irene recited it, Cassidy called Julie to tell her wh[at]
had happened.

Snapping the phone shut, Cassidy bent forward, getting a[s]
close to Irene as she could. "Julie's coming home so yo[u]
won't have to be alone. You know, she tries so hard to pleas[e]
you."

"No she doesn't," Irene said in a bitter voice. "She won'[t]
even go to church with me. It was Max and Tom who reall[y]
cared."

As Cassidy and Zach started toward the Eisenhower, h[e]
glanced over at her. "What you said about foster care—th[at]
it'd be worse for Ashley than being returned to her alcoholi[c]
mother—did you mean that?"

Cassidy heaved a large sigh. "Everybody talks about th[e]
best interest of the child, but half the time nobody knows wh[at]
that is. Most experts agree that children are better off stayin[g]
with a parent whenever possible, but I don't have any cryst[al]
ball, and there's no way I can guarantee that Ashley will b[e]
safe with her mother."

"OH MY GOD!" Claire, seated across from Cassidy, her el[-]
bows propped on the rose-colored tablecloth, held her head i[n]
her outspread fingers. "I just can't believe it. I can't believ[e]
Max could have done all those things. I mean, after I saw a[ll]
those credit card statements I knew something was wrong, b[ut]
to find out he cheated Nicky Andrews out of money…and h[e]
was engaged to Susan…." Her voice trailed off. Leaning bac[k]
in her chair, Claire raised her eyes to the ceiling. "I feel as [if]
my heart just died."

"I'm so sorry," Cassidy said, guilt oozing up inside he[r.]
*Why couldn't you keep your damn mouth shut? Zach told yo[u]
Claire'd be better off not knowing.*

A tuxedoed waitress, moving so quietly she was almost in[-]

visible, slipped between the two women and refilled their wineglasses.

Claire took off her ring and laid it in her left palm. "Why the hell give me this expensive diamond? What was he trying to prove?" Clenching her right fist, she pounded it lightly on the table. "I feel like tossing this damn ring down the sewer."

Cassidy laid her hand on Claire's wrist. "Don't do anything right away. Give yourself some time."

"He was in such a big hurry to get married. I suppose he couldn't wait to get his hands on my money. All those people who thought he was the best friend they ever had—he was just using them, wasn't he? Just stringing everybody along until he found some way to fleece them the way he did with Nicky, Susan, and me." The shadows beneath her brown eyes deepened. "Maybe the three of us should get together and form a Stay-Away-From-Players club."

Is that what you believe about Max? That he was nothing but a player? Something clicked in Cassidy's head and she suddenly realized that all the people who saw Max in a kindly light were probably not wrong.

Taking a sip of wine, Cassidy gazed into Claire's distraught face. "I think you're making Max out to be worse than he was."

"How can you say that?" Claire snapped. "After what you just told me."

"Max wasn't a villain—he was an addict. A spendaholic. A person who got the same kind of rush out of buying things that a doper gets from drugs. Addicts are so driven, they almost always do terrible things to the people around them. They'll rip off anybody just to get their next fix. But as screwed-up as Max was, I think he sincerely loved you. He just wasn't able to do any better than he did."

Claire's eyes moistened. "He couldn't have loved me. He was cheating with Susan all the time he was with me."

"He stopped sleeping with Susan when he started sleeping with you. Why would he do that if he were total slime? You used to idealize Max. You thought he was this perfect person.

Now you've flipped to the opposite extreme and see him a
the world's worst jerk. But the truth is, he *did* care abou
people. He was certainly flawed—he certainly caused a lot o
pain—but he wasn't all bad.''

Claire pulled a tissue out of her purse and wiped her eyes
"Is this supposed to make me feel better?"

"I was hoping it might."

"So what am I supposed to *do?*" Claire asked fiercely
"Feel sorry for him? I have all these feelings churning inside
me and I don't know what to do with any of them."

"You need to tell your story. Find people who can liste
and tell it over and over."

Tears streamed down Claire's face. She mopped her cheeks
gasped for air, made a small hiccupping sound. When the cry
ing subsided and she was able to breathe normally, she said
"I need you to be my therapist again. I like Maggie—she'
wonderful—but she doesn't know me the way you do."

Cassidy thought of Zach's relentless search for her attacker
Once we find him, the police should be able to snag the killer
"Soon. I'll be able to start seeing you again soon."

As she buckled herself into the Subaru, Zach asked, "So
what did you tell Claire?"

Cassidy filled him in.

"That's excellent. You told her the basic facts, then sugar
coated them so he didn't seem so bad. Much better than clob
bering her with the truth."

Scowling, Cassidy replied, "I believe that is the truth."

Zach awarded her with his are-you-nuts look. "You actually
think Max could've been a decent guy?"

"I wouldn't have said it if I didn't believe it."

Shaking his head, Zach said, "Given how much we're both
exposed to the dark side of human nature, your capacity fo
denial amazes me."

THIRTY-THREE

AN ANONYMOUS CALL AND A DOORBELL

As CASSIDY AND Zach walked toward the back door, vivid streaks of magenta and cornflower blue were smeared across the western sky. Upstairs, Zach went to sit in front of his computer while Cassidy headed into the bedroom, her gaze drawn to the blinking red light on the answering machine.

A guttural voice said, "Hey, dude, I can tell you where to find that guy you been lookin' for." He reeled off a number and hung up.

By the time the message ended, Zach was standing in the doorway. "Well, here's hoping this is it." He sat in his chair and picked up the cordless.

"Listen in?" Cassidy asked.

"Sure, why not."

She held the desk phone receiver to her ear.

"Yeah," the man answered.

"Zach Moran here."

"How much you gonna gimme for that information you want?"

"Twenty bucks."

The line went dead.

"Twenty?" Cassidy said in surprise. "That's nothing. I paid the waitress a hundred."

"Snitches expect an initial lowball offer. If I'd said fifty, he'd hold me up for twice that much."

You really ought to stop venturing opinions on things you know nothing about.

Zach pushed redial. "Thirty."

After a period of dickering, they agreed on fifty. The guttural voice named a bar at Howard and Clark Street. "Meet me there at nine-thirty." The line went dead.

"Are you going?"

"Of course I am. This is exactly what I've been waiting for."

Cassidy felt a prickle of unease. "But it could be a trap. That dude on the phone could be the parking lot dude himself."

"Yeah, but I can't not go. Besides, I'm not as easy a target as you are. We'll be in a public place, and if this guy tries anything, I should be able to handle it."

Cassidy stared at her not-quite-six-foot husband who didn't work out. "What on earth makes you think that?"

He grinned. "An adolescent sense of immortality?"

"Zach, this could be dangerous. I don't like it at all."

An intractable look came over his face. "I've shown that sketch to hundreds of people and this is the first time I've gotten so much as a nibble. You're not talking me out of meeting this guy."

"Could you get backup from the cops?"

"The cops don't encourage civilian investigations, remember?"

"Then how 'bout I follow you in the Toyota? I could watch to make sure you get safely inside."

"I don't want my wife following me around."

"But what harm could it do?"

Rising from his desk, he said, "Don't make me fight you on this."

There's no reason you shouldn't be able to follow him. He's just taking advantage of the fact that you're a little nervous about standing up to him right now. You should make him let you do it.

Are you crazy? A few days ago he nearly moved out because of the things you make him do.

She stood and looped her arms around his neck. "Okay, you do whatever you want."

"Where's my wife? And who put this Stepford woman in her place?" He landed a kiss on her mouth.

She picked up a book from her nightstand. "And just to make sure the wrong words don't come leaping out of my mouth, I'm going to shut myself in the den until after you're gone."

CASSIDY WAS SEATED on the bed, the air conditioner cranking away in the background. Starshine sat tall on the nightstand, her eyes focused on the dark window, her ringed tail pointing in Cassidy's direction.

"I wish you'd turn around. I'm in the mood for conversation and it's supremely unfulfilling to talk to your backside."

Cassidy was aware of a peaceful feeling that had settled over her after receiving word from Zach that he was in the bar and no menacing hulks lurked in any of the corners. *Peaceful. How strange. Not a feeling you've spent much time with.*

She had never quite believed there was anything—aside from managed care and a few recalcitrant clients—she couldn't change. As a child Cassidy had usually succeeded in arguing her mother down. Then she'd married Kevin, who had agreed with her to her face and cheated behind her back. And after that, Zach, who could be tough-minded and unyielding with everyone else but had difficulty denying his wife anything her little heart desired. *You are clearly a person who needs more "no" in your life.*

Starshine turned around, walked daintily across Cassidy's lap into the middle of the waterbed, stared at the closet door as if entranced, then returned and curled up in Cassidy's lap.

"The problem will be backsliding," Cassidy told the calico. "Right now it's clear that more accommodation on my part would keep Zach happier, improve my marriage, and even bring a little tranquility into my existence. But as soon as these life lessons fade from my consciousness, I know that bossy little part of me is going to try to take over again."

Starshine looked her in the eye and said *mwat*.

"Well, of course you'd like me to be more submissive. You're an even greater control freak than I am."

The phone rang. Cassidy went to Zach's desk and reached for the cordless.

"Got what I wanted," Zach announced. "The parking lot dude is Clem Williams. I have his home address and the names of his favorite haunts. Nailing the bastard should be a piece of cake. Unless, of course, the informant was bullshitting me for the money."

She sat back down on the bed. "And you're in the car now with the doors locked?"

"Turning the key in the ignition. I'll see you in an hour."

As Cassidy laid the phone on her nightstand, she looked at the clock. *Only ten P.M. We'll be tucked away before midnight and maybe I'll even sleep soundly tonight.* She picked up a Barbara D'Amato mystery from her to-be-read stack. Now that Zach had checked in, she would be able to concentrate on the story.

Minutes later the front doorbell rang. Pricking her ears, Starshine growled low in her throat, then went slinking down the stairs. Cassidy's stomach started to twitch. *No legitimate reason for anybody to appear at your door at this time of night.*

She followed the calico downstairs and turned on the porch light. Starshine, pressing her body against the front door, emitted a yowl, the sound she made when she wanted to go out.

"I'm not opening this door until I know what's up," Cassidy responded.

Peering through the oblong window, she saw a low-sided cardboard box about three feet from the door. Inside the box lay a tiny orange kitten, so wobbly it couldn't have been more than a couple of weeks old. *Oh my goodness! Why would anybody leave a kitten here?* She turned off the lights and looked through the picture window, surveying the porch, then the yard and street beyond. Nobody in sight.

Howling again, Starshine laid her ears back and fixed Cassidy with a baleful gaze, clearly angry at her human for failing to obey. With a flick of her tail, she marched off toward the kitchen. Cassidy ran after her and locked the cat-flap so she couldn't get out. *Don't need Starshine sniffing out that kitten before you do.*

Cassidy returned to the front door and gazed down into the box, her hand automatically reaching for the doorknob. *Stop! You can't be sure it's safe.* There was a space of about seven feet between the right-hand edge of the door and the left-hand edge of the picture window. *If someone were out there flattened against the wall, you might not see them.* Cassidy leaned her left cheek against the oblong window and scrutinized the outer wall. She went to the picture window and looked from the opposite angle. She didn't see anybody but couldn't be positive that the entire seven feet fell within her viewing range. *No reason to open the door now. You can wait for Zach.*

She went upstairs, Starshine trotting beside her, and picked up the book, but she couldn't get the image of the tiny creature out of her head. She assumed that the person who'd left the box on her porch was someone who knew about her fondness for felines, a neighbor or a client. As she pondered further, it seemed likely that the mother cat was dead. Otherwise there would be no good reason to remove a kitten from its spigot. Thoughts of the motherless kitten and the fatherless Ashley weighed on her.

Now stop being so sappy. You should definitely not open that door. Especially since Zach's anonymous call could've been a ploy to get him away from the house.

That's just paranoid, the sappy part responded. *The killer couldn't possibly know you have such a weakness for cats.* Her fingers itched to pick up the kitten and hold it. *If you don't go rescue that kitten, you'll be letting your fears control you.*

She started down the stairs again, Starshine thumping behind her. She gazed at the kitten, then pressed her cheek against the oblong window one more time. *This is about as paranoid as you've ever been.* She turned the lock and started to open the door.

A hand reached out from behind the porch wall, pushing the door wider. Starshine streaked out. Cassidy pivoted toward the staircase. A blood-curdling cat scream and a loud "Shit!" came from the porch.

Heart hammering, Cassidy flew upward. As she neared the top, panting and out of breath, she heard heavy footsteps behind her. She ran into the bathroom, locked the door, and yanked the window open. Pressing her face against the screen, she scanned her surroundings. No people on the street but lights in the houses across Briar. *If their windows are open, they might hear you.*

The doorknob rattled.

Cassidy jammed her fist through the screen, the ancient mesh crumbling like tissue paper. Sticking her head out, she yelled, "Help! Help! Someone's trying to kill me!"

A body crashed against the bathroom door.

She yelled louder, "Fire! Help! Fire! Call the police!"

The bathroom door broke open and banged against the counter. A man pulled her away from the window and stuffed a washcloth in her mouth, holding it in place with a large hand that blocked her nostrils. She glimpsed a white ponytail. *Oh, God—Nicky Andrews.*

THIRTY-FOUR

THE GIRL FROM LE BARRE

KEEPING ONE HAND over the cloth in her mouth, he used the other to twist her arm behind her back. He raised the arm higher, triggering a sharp pain in her shoulder.

"Now you just walk on into the bedroom." He jerked her around to face the doorway, pressed his wide-chested body against hers, and forced her to move. She tried to stiffen her back and dig in her toes, but he kept lifting her arm until the pain was so great she had to do what he wanted.

He pushed her up against the side of the waterbed. "I'm taking this rag out, but if you start screaming, it's going right back in." He threw the washcloth on the bed and Cassidy sucked air.

Nicky shoved her forward, knocking her face-down onto the bed, and straddled her hips. Pulling both arms behind her back, he tied her wrists with something that felt like pantyhose. One of his large hands dug down beneath her body and squeezed her breast. She clenched her teeth to keep from screaming. As he removed his hand, he shifted his weight, crushing her thigh against the wooden bed frame. She yelped in pain.

"Shut up."

Climbing off her, he swung her legs onto the bed and tied them at the ankles. As he stepped back, she started flopping around, getting herself into an upright position with her back against the headboard. She darted a look at the clock. Ten-twenty.

"At least half an hour before Zach gets here," Nicky said in a gloating voice.

Cassidy stared up at him. His dark eyes burned feverishly and his full-lipped mouth split into a rapacious grin. He was dressed all in black, a small gun tucked into his waistband.

"You wanna know how I found out when Zach's due?" He began punching his right fist into his left hand. "I tapped your phone. Got me this clever little gizmo that clamps onto the outside wire. Heard him tell you myself he'd be home in an hour. Didn't wanna come inside 'til after he called. There was too big a chance he'd notify the cops if he couldn't reach you."

Nicky puffed himself up, his chest swelling with pride, his whole body seeming to gain in height and girth. *Arrogant as a big loud-mouthed rooster lording it over a hen.*

"Gotta run downstairs," he added. "Can't leave that front door hanging open. Somebody might notice."

The pieces started falling into place. Julie telling them that Max had faked an alibi for one of his friends in high school. Nicky talking about the girl from Le Barre. Luke thinking it odd that Nicky had continued speaking to Max after Max ripped him off.

Nicky returned, rolled Cassidy's chair closer to the bed, and propped his Gucci loafers on the comforter. "We got a little time to kill. If there's anything you want to know, just put it out there."

You should ask what he's going to do to you. She started sucking in air through her mouth.

What? You're not scared enough already? You want more fear-chemicals sloshing around in your bloodstream?

Pushing these thoughts aside, she focused on getting the story straight. "You killed that girl at Le Barre, didn't you? Then you called Max for an alibi. Maybe he even went so far as to help you dispose of the body. And then, at some later point, he started blackmailing you.''

"You got some of it right, but you're off on a lot of the details.'' Frowning, he turned his face toward the window. "I never meant to kill her. I'd used roofies on a lot of other girls and none of them died.''

Roofies—that's a date-rape drug.

"Sex is better for you if the woman's unconscious?''

"I don't give them enough to knock them out. Just enough to make them more agreeable. Sorta like the old days when chicks did what they were told.''

Can't get it up unless the woman's totally passive?

"So what happened to the woman from Le Barre?''

He shrugged his broad shoulders. "All I know is, I put the drug in her drink, she started to get a little woozy, and I told her she should go throw water on her face. So she went into the john, and when she came out, I took her through the rear entrance and put her in my car. I started to drive to my condo, but a few minutes later she collapsed, and the next thing you know, she's dead.''

"And you called Max.''

Nicky's face clouded. "First I called Juiceboy. He's the guy that's been chasing after you. If only I'd been able to get hold of Juiceboy, none of this would've happened. But I couldn't reach him and I had to have an alibi, so I called Max. Max was somebody you could always count on, and since he'd been sucking up to me ever since that fight we had, I figured he'd do just about anything to get back in my good graces.''

"Did he take the body off your hands?''

"Nah. He freaked when he saw the girl was dead. I wanted him to help me bury her in Graceland cemetery, but he wouldn't have anything to do with it.''

"In a cemetery?''

"Yeah, sure. I found a fresh grave, dug it up, and put the girl's body on top of the coffin. Who'd ever think of looking there?''

Nobody. The jerk didn't need an alibi. If he'd just buried the body and left Max out of it, the whole thing would've gone away.

Nicky's voice turned irritated. "Max was so freaked he didn't even listen when I said I didn't kill her. But he did agree to tell the police he'd picked me up from the bar about the time the girl disappeared."

"Then he started blackmailing you?" Cassidy prompted.

"He borrowed money for the ring and the tickets—which we both knew he'd never pay back. In the past he'd ask for fifty here, a hundred there, and all I'd ever give him were advances on his salary. But now I owed him big time." Nicky's face darkened. "I didn't like that. Not one bit. But there he was with his hand out, wanting big bucks, and I knew it wasn't going to end with the honeymoon cruise."

"But isn't that the same as blackmail? You gave him money so he wouldn't turn you in?"

"Nah—he never would've gone to the police. The cops would've jumped him for giving a false alibi. The reason I had to kill him is two things. It started with not liking that sense I had that I owed him. But the worst of it was, I couldn't trust him to keep a secret. He swore to Garrett he wouldn't tell anybody about Garrett's taking the kid and then he let it slip to me. I kept thinking that someday for sure he'd blab about the girl. Then he told me about Claire's ex threatening her—the perfect opportunity. I knew if I had him killed at the wedding, everybody'd think the ex did it."

Oh. That makes perfect sense. And we never thought of it.

Cassidy reflected back over their dealings with Nicky. "The first time we came to your restaurant, you asked Zach what the police thought had happened to the girl. Why would you even bring it up?"

"'Cause I didn't know where the cops were with it. And with Max dead, I figured I was completely in the clear."

Nicky glanced at the clock. Ten-thirty. He stood and looked out the front window, then the side window. After that, he went into the den. Cassidy assumed he was surveying the back yard and garage, visible from the windows at the rear of the house.

As soon as he left the room, Cassidy began searching for something she could use to cut her bonds. Her eyes skimmed the nightstand, then returned to focus on the cordless phone, nearly hidden by the stack of books sitting next to it. She turned sideways so she could reach toward the phone with her hands. Stretching her fingers, she felt a polished wood surface, the spine of a hardcover book. She stared through the doorway, freezing when she saw Nicky leave the den. He came into the hall, then veered off into the computer room. Letting out the breath she was holding, she inched backward until her fingers brushed the surface of the phone. She jiggled it closer, then finally was able to scoop it up and hide it behind her back. *He'll be here any second. Can't dial till he leaves again.* Squirming around, she attempted to put herself back into the position she'd been in before.

When Nicky came into the bedroom, she said in a croaky voice, "My mouth's dry. Do you think you could possibly get me some water?"

"Nah—I'm not getting you anything."

"Please—I'm so dry. Just a little water—that's all I need."

"What do you think I am, your servant?" He stood near the bed, hands on hips. "If there's anything I hate, it's a whiny woman. I'm in charge here and don't your forget it." He punched his right fist into his left hand. "Yeah baby!"

"I won't bother you again."

Sitting in her chair, Nicky spread both hands in an expansive gesture. "Anything else you wanna know?"

"Since nobody could trace Max's murder to you, why send Juiceboy out to threaten me?"

"I didn't. It was that stupid fuck Garrett. He shoulda kept his cool. But not him. Always was a nervous Nelly. After Max died, he just seemed to fall apart."

"Why did Garrett think he needed to threaten us?"

"You asked Max's mother if Max and Garrett were roommates, and then she told Garrett you were on to him. Plus she told him about that guy mugging you. So Garrett thought he'd scare you off with Juiceboy. But Garrett never did get anything right."

Cassidy tried to recall how it had all transpired. She'd told Claire about the mugging in the alley and Claire had passed the story on to Irene.

"Okay, I think I get it," Cassidy said. "Except the part about Garrett's murder. What reason did you have to kill him?"

"That was just bad luck. Stupid, fucking bad luck. When I called Max to come give me an alibi, he was at Cypress having a drink with Garrett. So Garrett knew Max couldn't have been with me when he said he was. Then, when that story came out about the girl, I was afraid Garrett might put two and two together. But since he was hiding out from the cops himself, I knew he'd never turn me in. That is, until you and Zach got so suspicious of him. He knew you took that glass from the bar and he'd been printed once for a job, so he thought for sure you'd find out he was wanted for child abduction."

Didn't know we couldn't match against job-check fingerprints. Garrett was killed because he didn't do his AFIS homework.

"So you thought Garrett would get arrested and then he'd roll on you."

"I wasn't certain he'd figured out about the girl, but I couldn't take any chances. I mean, if he knew I'd killed her, he could maybe even buy himself immunity."

Sucking in her lip, Cassidy thought it through. "There's one other thing. How'd you know I'd open the door for a kitten?"

"Juiceboy saw how mushy you got over that cat when
t came running out to meet you."

"Oh. Of course." She paused. "Did Juiceboy kill
Max?"

"You think Juiceboy could hit a target at a thousand
eet?" Nicky barked out a laugh. "That was a job for a
professional. Fortunately I had the connections to get somebody good."

*Somebody who knows how to vanish completely and will
probably never be caught.*

"And now—because your fucking husband won't back
off on Juiceboy—I have to dispose of the two of you."
Puffing himself up again, he stood over her. "You want to
hear my brilliant plan?"

No you don't. You definitely don't want to know.

She nodded.

He pulled a syringe from his pants pocket and held it in
front of her. "First I'm gonna drug you. I got this nifty
potion here that'll knock you and Zach on your asses for a
good long time. After you're unconscious, I'll take your
clothes off and lay you both under the covers." The wolfish
grin reappeared. His gaze roamed slowly over her body.

Omigod! He's going to rape you! A long convulsive
shudder went through her.

She cringed as he ran the back of his hand along the side
of her face. "After I get the two of you tucked away, I go
burn newspapers in the kitchen. With newspapers there's
no evidence of arson. And then—soon as I get a rip-roaring
fire going—I'm outta here. Yeah baby!" He took a quick
look through each window, then returned to the side of the
bed. "I need to put you out of commission before Zach
gets here. I've already cut it a little close."

Cassidy glanced at the clock. Ten-forty-five. *Almost an
hour. Zach could be here any minute.* Raising her head, she
stared intently at the doorway, mimicking the way Starshine
reacted when Zach came in the house.

Nicky followed her gaze.

Cassidy screamed, "Don't come upstairs. There's a kill up here."

Nicky slapped her face so hard it made her teeth ratt! She squeezed her eyes closed, opening them again as soo as she heard his footsteps on the stairs. Unburying tl phone, she turned her body as far as she could to the le in the direction of the nightstand, and succeeded in layin the instrument face-up on the bed. Turning to the right, sl memorized the placement of the buttons. She turned bac toward the nightstand, held the phone in her left hand, an ran her right index finger over the touch pad. Locating tl on button, she pushed it and heard a satisfying little bee *Now the hard part.* She fumbled over the touch pad agai pushing what she hoped was 9-1-1. The cordless was siler She tried again and was rewarded with the sound of ringin

Twisting to the right, she laid the phone on the nigl stand, then twisted back around, getting herself in positic to speak. By the time a female voice answered, she wa leaning over the mouthpiece.

"There's a man in my house," Cassidy said quietl "Holding me hostage." She gave her address, then stuffe the phone under the covers. For a moment she could hea an indistinct voice, then the line went silent.

Oh please, oh please, don't let Nicky come back. Don let him touch me again.

His footsteps sounded on the stairs, then he was standir by the bed. "You little bitch! What do you mean pretendir Zach's here? You play games with me, you're gonna pa for it." He slapped her again.

When she opened her eyes this time, he was taking tl cap off the syringe. Pulling in air, she steadied hersel "Don't do that. The cops are on their way."

He laughed, his eyes glinting down at her as if she wei one of the gourmet dishes on his menu he couldn't wait t taste. He clamped his large hand around her upper arm.

She uncovered the phone, then twisted sideways to sho him she had it. Grabbing it out of her hands, he stared a e red light. His stubby finger touched the button to turn off.

"Don't think this is going to save you." He threw the one into a wastebasket, took hold of her arm, and pre-red to inject her.

"What if you need to use me as a hostage? Wouldn't it e a little awkward carrying me out over your shoulder?"

He stared at her a long time, went to look out the win-ow, returned to stare at her again, then replaced the cap the syringe and put it back in his pocket.

About three beats later she heard a car pull up in front the house. Nicky gazed down at the street. More cars llowed. Throwing open the window, he held up his gun. Don't come near the house. I got this woman here—Cas-dy McCabe. Anybody even steps on the lawn, this chick's ot a bullet in her brain."

Cassidy's hands began to tremble.

Slamming the window closed, Nicky stuck the gun back his waistband. The cordless and the phone on her desk ng in unison. He picked up the desk phone and bellowed, Go to hell!" As soon as he hung up, the two phones rang gain. He ripped one out of the wall and threw the other t the window.

He prowled restlessly from one room to another, his fin-ers clenching and unclenching in small jerky movements. isappearing into the den, he stayed away for a full minute. Vhile he was gone, Cassidy listened to the sounds from utside: tires squealing, more cars arriving, male voices elling at each other.

Nicky came back, sat on the waterbed, and began unty-g the pantyhose around her ankles. "I'm going to put you front of me and walk out of here."

She swallowed the lump in her throat. "They'll follow ou with helicopters. Like they did OJ."

"Goddamn you!" His teeth clenched and his eyes turned ery. "Why don't you just shut the fuck up?"

For the next hour Nicky circled the second floor, spend-

ing a few moments at each window. His mood swung ra
ically, from cursing her at one extreme to seeking her sy
pathy at the other. His skin took on a yellowish cast. H
shoulders drooped and his feet shuffled.

Cassidy thought about Zach standing outside with t
police. She knew that his face would be rigid and sto
that he would not allow his terror to show. *Please, Go
help him get through this if I die.*

After another prolonged period in the den, Nicky stepp
up to the side of the bed. She realized with surprise t
his carriage had straightened and his face appeared cal
Oh shit—this is not a good sign. She tried to pull hers
upright.

He held his gun in both hands and pointed it at her fac

Her emotions disconnected; her mind cleared. Meeti
his gaze, she said, ''I don't think you're a bad person.''

He looked at her as if she were speaking a foreign la
guage.

''You didn't kill that girl. It was an accident.''

''That's what I told Max but he freaked anyway.''

''The only reason you killed Max is because he g
greedy. He practically forced you into it. And Garrett—y
couldn't take the chance that he'd inform on you.''

''You're wasting your breath.''

''If you kill me, there won't be anybody to tell your si
of it. To explain about the girl and Max.''

''What do I care?''

If he didn't care, you'd be dead already.

''Don't you want the truth to come out?''

''You're not going to tell my side.''

She caught his eyes and held them.

''Shit.'' Dropping his arms, he left the bedroom, we
into the bathroom, and closed the door.

A shot rang out.

THIRTY-FIVE

KITTEN IN A BOX

THE TIME Cassidy and Zach left the police station and
led up next to their back gate, a glowing orange ball
ng above the roofline in the east. Standing on the side-
lk, she gazed up at the bathroom window, dark now that
e evidence technician had gone.

Zach had persuaded the police to let him poke his head
side the bathroom, but Cassidy had steadfastly averted
r eyes when taken out of the bedroom. Looking at the
ndow now, picturing what was on its other side, she shiv-
d.

Zach drew his arm tightly around her shoulders. "I'll get
mebody to clean up the mess later today. And we can
y at Gran's as long as you like."

"I have to get back on the horse," she muttered, the
me response she'd had to the mugging.

Starshine came running out to roll on the sidewalk in
nt of them.

At the sight of her cat, some of the darkness inside of
ssidy began to lift. "Thank goodness Nicky's big feet
dn't crush her."

They fed the calico, then shut her in the house while
ey went out on the porch to decide what to do with the
tten.

Squatting beside the box, Cassidy started to pick the tiny
imal up, but Zach stopped her.

"If there's any chance of getting this kitten back to mother, we shouldn't handle it."

"We don't have any idea where the mother is."

"She could be one of those restaurant cats. You kno the kind that lives in the alley and gets fed by the staff.

"Oh. I just sort of thought we'd keep it."

"We'd have to feed it around the clock."

"I know."

Zach's gaze enveloped her, his blue-gray eyes deepeni with emotion. "I suppose, if you really want to, we could

Zach's so concerned about what you just went throug he'd probably agree to adopt a rhino. You can't take a vantage of his kindness. And you also can't keep this kitt from its mother.

Cassidy cocked her head. "If the mother's a restaura cat, Luke might know where to find her."

Luke did and was glad to help.

WHEN CASSIDY PICKED UP the kitchen phone a week late Zach's voice said, "We got him. Wharton just now slapp on the cuffs."

"I bet the good detective is pissed at you for finding th offender before he did."

Immediately after Nicky's suicide, Zach had turned in story about the murders, then begun an obsessive campaig to track down Juiceboy. Zach had started by doing su veillance at the place where he'd met the phony informa On the third night the snitch returned to the bar and Zac had taken to following him around the city. After sever more days, the informant hooked up with Juiceboy, ar now Zach had finally run Cassidy's attacker to ground.

"Wharton just sighed and shook his head," Zach r sponded. "So—now that everything's wrapped up—wh say we open a bottle of champagne after dinner to cel brate?"

Cassidy smiled. "The last time we had champagne wa the night you asked me to marry you."

"And even though you already knew what an insensitive
[j]k I was, you went ahead and said yes."

A rosy twilight was gradually deepening into cobalt as
[th]ey sipped champagne on the porch a few hours later.
[W]ind chimes jangled overhead, children of various colors
[pl]ayed in the street, and Starshine kept watch from her open
[ba]sement window. *Another peaceful moment. Maybe you'll
[ge]t the hang of this yet.*

"There was something in my horoscope I didn't tell
[yo]u," she informed Zach. "Julie said I was self-centered.
[A]nd that a crisis was looming. And both things proved to
[be] true. It almost makes me wonder."

"You're not going to turn into a true believer, are you?"

She shook her head. "When I put things in perspective,
[I] can see that sometimes I'm self-centered, but a lot of
[ti]mes I'm not. And that everybody goes through an occa-
[si]onal crisis. Now I may exceed the national average, but
[th]at's because I keep getting myself into risky situations."

Zach leaned his chin against the side of her head.
["]Sounds right to me."

They sat in silence for a while.

"So," Cassidy said, snuggling closer beneath the crook
[o]f Zach's arm, "why don't you want another cat?"

"I thought you were going to leave me alone on that
[o]ne."

"It's been almost a week since I mentioned it. Don't I
[g]et points for waiting this long?"

"Such amazing self control." He pulled slightly away
[f]rom her. "I don't know why I don't want another cat. You
[k]eep pushing me to explain things when I don't have any
[r]easons."

*People always have reasons—it's just that sometimes it's
[h]ard to dig them out.*

After several seconds, Zach started to speak. "Before I
met you, there was no one in my life I cared very much
about. I didn't need to concern myself with anyone's safety
but my own. Now I have you and Starshine and Bryce.

Starshine refuses to stay in the house, you ignore all sensible precautions, and Bryce won't do a damned thing say.'' Zach paused to take a sip from his champagne flute. ''Having to worry about an unruly wife, cat, and son make me feel vulnerable. So I guess that's why I'm not eager to take on any additional responsibilities.''

''You're not responsible for me,'' Cassidy protested. *But of course he feels like he is.* She kissed him lightly on the mouth. ''Okay, I won't give you a hard time about a second cat.''

Zach topped off their glasses, then draped his arm along the rim of the couch behind her. ''You still having anxiety attacks about using the upstairs bathroom?''

''Not attacks, just anxiety. Since I have to go in there fairly often, it's disappearing pretty fast.''

Taking another swig of champagne, Zach stared at the street for a moment. ''Well, I've got something to discuss with you.''

Oh dear. Last time it was relocation.

''As long as we're going to stay here,'' he said, ''I propose we take out a second mortgage and rehab the house. I don't mean we do any of the work ourselves. It's way too much for us. I mean we pay big bucks to have tradesmen come in and rip everything up so we can start from scratch. It'll be a major aggravation, but the place is in such bad shape I don't see any way out of it.''

She sighed at the thought of dirt and noise and strangers in her house. *Rehabbing is probably a bigger cause of divorce than affairs.*

She said, ''You're right. That's what we need to do.''

''You're not even going to argue about it?''

''There's a part of me that would like to be balky and difficult and try to talk you out of it, but I'm going to sit on that part and just be nice.''

Niceness. How insipid. Nothing you'd ever aspire to.

Zach brought his hand down to trace a design on her breast. ''Have I told you yet today how much I love you?''

Niceness may be boring, but it's not all bad.

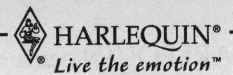

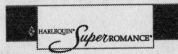

HARLEQUIN®
INTRIGUE®

WE'LL LEAVE YOU BREATHLESS!

If you've been looking for thrilling tales of contemporary passion and sensuous love stories with taut, edge-of-the-seat suspense—then you'll love Harlequin Intrigue!

Every month, you'll meet six new heroes who are guaranteed to make your spine tingle and your pulse pound. With them you'll enter into the exciting world of Harlequin Intrigue— where your life is on the line and so is your heart!

THAT'S INTRIGUE—
ROMANTIC SUSPENSE
AT ITS BEST!

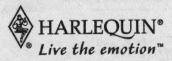

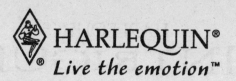

HARLEQUIN®
Live the emotion™

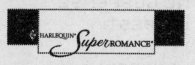